THE VAMPIRE AND THE CASE OF THE HELLACIOUS HAG

HEATHER G. HARRIS & JILLEEN DOLBEARE

PUBLISHED BY HELLHOUND PRESS LIMITED

Copyright © 2025 by Heather G. Harris and Jilleen Dolbeare.

All rights reserved.

No portion of this book may be reproduced in any form without written permission from the publisher or author, except as permitted by U.S. copyright law.

Published by Hellhound Press Limited.

Cover Design by Christian Bentulan.

AI: We will never use generative AI to write our books. Our books are written by beautiful flawed humans who love living in magical lands. If you accuse us of writing our books with AI, do know that Heather is a former lawyer and she is litigious as fuck. Defamation is a thing, kids. You'd better believe she'll come for you harder than an innocent human woman who was cruelly kidnapped by a sexy dark fae ruler. Wait ... plot bunny!

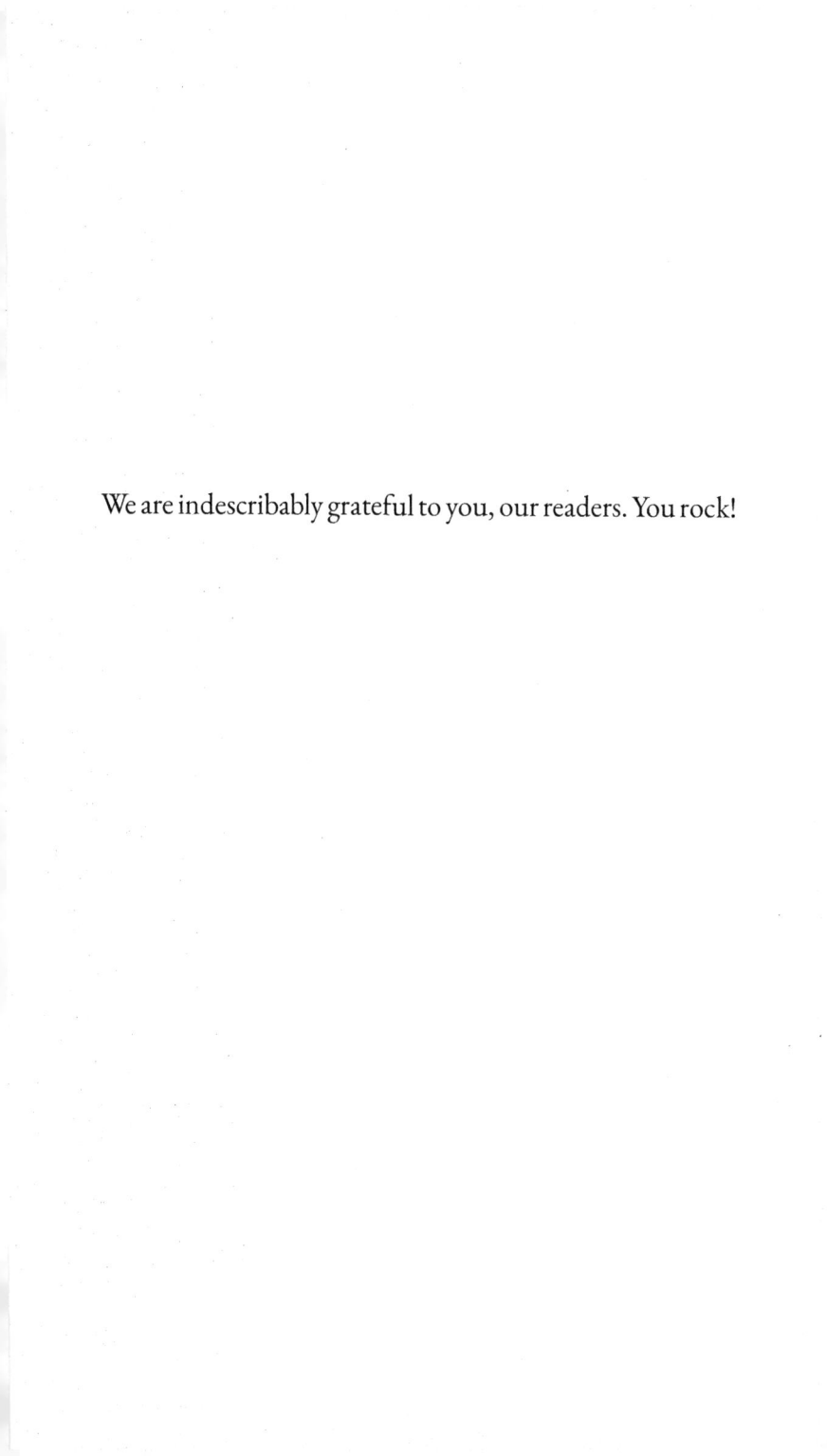

We are indescribably grateful to you, our readers. You rock!

Chapter 1

Gunnar and I stood over the cold corpse in the morgue. It was the body of a middle-aged man; despite his age, he lacked the usual rotund tummy and had a full head of chestnut-brown hair. He was handsome, too; if he hadn't been lying dead on a metal table, I'd have said he'd been lucky in life.

Helmud Henderson had apparently died in the Chrome Mine during a routine inspection. The miners were in an uproar, insisting that he'd been murdered by the hag that supposedly resided there. I knew a little about hags from my time at the academy: they were earth elementals – and they had metal claws instead of fingernails.

What was notable about the body was that it had no marks of any kind, no vicious claw marks, no slashes across the stomach, nothing. From what we could see, there was no sign that he'd been murdered. When he'd been found, his eyes had been wide, pupils blown in the darkness, his expression shocked. He looked like he'd just

KO'd, surprised by a heart attack he hadn't seen coming. It happens.

Gunnar turned to me. 'Well, Officer Barrington, do you have any thoughts?'

I had plenty, but none of them were particularly helpful. 'Heart attack?' I said. It was pure conjecture on my part because I had nothing. I'd looked over the body thoroughly and seen nothing except a little excess body hair and that his generous penis had been circumcised. Yep, he'd been a *lucky* man in life. Not so much in death.

Gunnar grunted agreement. 'We'll know more after the autopsy, but I thought you'd want to see the body before it got carved up.'

'Absolutely.' I took one last look. Using a gloved finger, I lifted up an eyelid that had frozen at half-mast and peered in to see if there was anything unusual. The pupils were dilated in death but there was no extra redness or anything that looked unusual. Everything pointed to a natural death – only this was Portlock and there was always the possibility that magic was the culprit. I turned to face my boss. 'Can we see where he died?'

Gunnar grinned. 'Great minds think alike.'

'And fools seldom differ,' I shot back with a smirk.

He laughed. 'I've already got a trip to the mines approved. We have an appointment there in—' he checked the time on his phone '—an hour and forty-five minutes.' He eyed my clothes dubiously. 'You'll need to dress warm. The mines can be cold as hell.'

'Isn't hell warm?' I sassed.

He gave me a flat look. 'You know what I meant, Bunny Rabbit.'

'Dress warm.' I sent him a mock salute. 'Layers. You got it, boss.'

We filled out the paperwork for the autopsy, left the hospital basement and drove back to the office in the Nomo SUV. It was a cold day, though to be fair it always felt like it was a cold day. Today it was cold *and* snowy, but I was grateful that it was only light for six hours a day this close to the winter solstice. Vampire heaven. Darkness ruled supreme and all the vampires in town were delighted and strutting around like peacocks.

Following Gunnar's orders to dress warmly, I slid home – I'd forgotten my cleats again. Luckily there weren't too many witnesses around to see my comedic foot-slipping routine. When I opened the front door, Shadow and Fluffy were waiting impatiently for me. I gave them each a fuss and checked their water and food bowls.

My German Shepherd dog, Fluffy, was actually a werewolf shifter called Reggie. He had been cursed to become a dog by my mum, and though the local shamans had broken the curse it was fair to say that Reggie was struggling to acclimatise to being human. Given a choice, he always chose to be a dog. I feared that if I didn't act soon his humanity would slip away forever and he would be left as nothing more than my furry best friend.

I loved him as Fluffy but I valued him as Reggie, and I wanted him to strive for more. I couldn't force him into anything, though; I could only be there for him the way he was there for me. Feeling wistful, I gave him an extra-long cuddle as I looked into his warm eyes. Happy to see me, he tapped his tail.

Home was delightfully cosy after the cold outside. I had to keep the house warm for my animal companions; it wouldn't do to leave my lynx kitten Shadow shivering. Cats loved their warm spots.

I needed something to heat me from the inside so I microwaved a cup of blood and made a glorious cup of tea to savour with a couple of yummy buttery biscuits, the type Mum wouldn't have approved of because of the high fat content. That was why I had two.

By the time I'd finished my tea, found my coat and switched to my insulated boots complete with cleats, Gunnar was waiting for me outside in the SUV. Fluffy whined at the door and looked at me hopefully. He wanted to go with us and I knew his nose could be very useful.

'Wait here, I'll run out and ask,' I told him. I jogged to the vehicle. 'Gunnar, I think we should bring Fluffy. Will they allow him inside the mine?'

'Thomas is meeting us and taking us down. The other miners can be – touchy.' Just as I thought he was going to say no, he flashed a mischievous grin. 'So let's bring him. You never know what he'll pick up.' He paused. 'But Shadow stays home this time.'

He didn't need to tell me that my cat could be a liability sometimes with his wild and wilful nature – and that reminded me that Gunnar still didn't know the half of it. I nodded. 'Yeah, good call. Shadow has been ... stranger than usual. I'll tell you about it in the car.'

Gunnar quirked an eyebrow but waited patiently whilst I dashed back to the house for Fluffy. 'You can come,' I said, and he gave a pleased bark and chased his tail for a moment. A smile pulled at my lips. 'I'm glad you're happy, but can you hold still for half a minute so I can get this vest on you?'

He stopped his zoomies and stood still while I kitted him out. Shadow padded up and looked at me appealingly. 'You can't come. You won't wear your vest.' I held up the new one that Connor had ordered for him after the last one had been melted off him.

Shadow gave a vehement hiss then turned and walked towards the bathroom to sulk, making sure to show me his asshole as he went. Cats.

Fluffy and I climbed into the SUV and we set off. I was excited to see the mine; I'd never been to that part of Portlock and I was keen to explore. Besides, I knew nothing about chromite and rectifying that seemed like a good idea. A quick Google search taught me that it was the prime ingredient in chromium and used in the manufacture of steel, glass, copper and cement. It had a tonne of uses and I guessed that made it profitable.

'Penny for your thoughts, doc.' Gunnar interrupted my thoughts with a Bugs Bunny reference. He thought he was being funny, which was adorable. For that reason, I let it slide.

'I don't think they're worth that,' I said wryly. 'I'm just looking up chromite and plugging a hole in my knowledge before we get there.'

He gave a noncommittal grunt and left me to my internet search. I Googled 'mining in Portlock' and discovered that there used to be two mines: the Reef Mine and the Chrome Mine. Only the latter was still running.

Gunnar interrupted my search. 'Tell me about Shadow,' he demanded. 'What happened? You said he was stranger than usual?'

I put down my phone and thought back to the incident in the basement of the State Trooper Academy. Rogue MIB agents had captured Connor, Sidnee and me, planning to send us to a black ops site to experiment on us. The pricks were a secretive subset of the MIB and were behind the deadly drug, fisheye. We'd turned the tables on them, kicking ass and taking names. Shadow had stepped up and stopped one of them from fleeing the scene.

'Shadow raced ahead of the agent who was escaping and transformed into a two-hundred-kilo version of himself. His smoky coat vanished and he looked like a regular silvery lynx in colouring – though not in size. He was huge! It was crazy.' Shadow's transformation had been helpful for sure, but a little unnerving.

'He what?' Gunnar asked, aghast.

I leaned against the car door and twisted to look at him. 'After we cuffed the MIB bastard, Shadow shrank back to his regular size. And get this – when he did, his shadow seeped back until his coat was smoky again.' I gave a heavy sigh. 'Gunnar, what the fuck is my cat?'

Gunnar grimaced. 'I've got no idea, Bunny, but I sure am glad he's on our team.'

'Me too.' I sat in silence a while, my anxieties stewing inside me. 'Gunnar, what if—'

'Stop there. I know what you're going to say.'

'You do?'

It was my boss's turn to sigh. 'It hasn't escaped any of us that Shadow has a lot of powers like the beast beyond the barrier. You even told us about seeing a giant lynx behind the beast's smoke.'

'Yeah.'

'I think they're related somehow, but everything I've seen of Shadow makes me think he's good people. Maybe the beast started out the same a long time ago but something happened to change it. I don't have any answers, just theories, but I don't think that we should tar Shadow with the beast's brush. We all have the opportunity to be more than our parents were.'

I nodded solemnly; I certainly hoped so, because my parents sucked. My mum had even shoved me in front of a bus once to try and make my magic manifest; it hadn't and I'd broken some bones instead. That was something I didn't think I could ever forgive, no matter the rash of apologies she'd made of late. Maybe with time, I could rise past it. And Gunnar was right: we each carved our way in life. Even if we used the imperfect tools our parents had given us, we could still build something spectacular. Shadow deserved that chance, too.

Gunnar might be right, but we were both wilfully ignoring the alternative: Shadow was only a juvenile right now, but there was a real risk that he might grow up to become *exactly* like the beast beyond the barrier.

There was a distinct possibility that we might have already invited the enemy in.

Chapter 2

The Chrome Mine was beyond Kamluck Logging in a place I'd never been before around the back of the mountain. Kamluck – and Connor – were my usual destination.

I looked around with interest as we rolled into the area. The mine looked old but well maintained. The wooden buildings that pushed up the mountain were on stilts in some places, halfway into the earth and surrounded by thick forest, like almost everything in Portlock.

We pulled into a car park where the signage pointed to the main office and I collected our trusty black bag from the back seat before we headed into the office to meet Thomas. Apparently the deadly human had his fingers in a lot of pies around town: he owned the only taxi company in Portlock, hunted naughty supernats and apparently co-owned the mine, together with the two female council members, Liv and Calliope.

The office was rustic like its exterior but there was a bevy of modern conveniences nestled inside the ancient timber: computers, signage, climate control. The mine seemed to be in good working order as far as I could see, not that I had anything to judge it against. At least it wasn't a shambolic mess.

Of course, we hadn't gone inside it yet. Maybe inside it was in a real state. Maybe that's why Helmud Henderson had died from a heart attack. The thought made me uneasy. 'The mine's safe, right?' I muttered to Gunnar. 'Like, it's not going to collapse on our heads?'

Gunnar grinned. 'You're a vampire, you'll be fine. Connor would find you eventually.'

I grimaced. I was a hybrid vampire and I didn't think I'd do as well as he thought; for starters, as a hybrid I still had to breathe and that might be tricky in a collapsed mine. I tried not to think about it. As Nana would have said, no point in borrowing trouble.

Fluffy sniffed around but nothing appeared to set off his spidey senses. He returned to my side and I gave him a pat for a job well done.

Thomas was talking to what I assumed was a dwarf. The dwarves kept themselves to themselves and it was rare to see one in town. I'd had a full class about dwarves at the academy, and a lot of it had been about their strengths and weaknesses. Apparently they were irascible, prone to fights and especially sensitive about comments related to their small stature. When fights between dwarves broke out, most often it was fisticuffs and not a cause for concern. They didn't usually wear weapons so their bust-ups were rarely deadly. Even so, they were very handy with a pick and an axe.

Their culture was secretive and they were hyper-protective about their dead. The academy had taught us that we wouldn't be able to take custody of a dead dwarf's body because it had to be released immediately to the family. An autopsy was a complete no-no, meaning that cases involving them were far harder to work. Luckily, Helmud Henderson was wholly human, though he'd obviously known about the supernat world because he'd been hired by the dwarves.

Thomas was talking to a dwarf about four feet tall with a wild scrub of hair that had been forced – incompetently – into a couple of braids. His long red beard was so full that only his eyes, nose and a hint of lip showed through, which made it tricky to read his facial expressions. He was dressed in brown denim overalls over a thick flannel shirt with a heavy denim jacket on top and wearing brown steel-toed leather boots. He didn't have gloves and I could see that his hands were large and callused.

He glared at Gunnar and then at me with his copper-coloured eyes. I guessed it wasn't *that* hard to read his expression after all: this one had a clear 'fuck off' vibe.

Gunnar shook Thomas's hand then offered his huge paw to the dwarf who glanced at it, curled his lip and promptly ignored it. The Nomo let his hand fall, his expression mild and unoffended by the dwarf's blatant rudeness. He turned to his friend instead. 'Thomas, thanks for letting us examine the scene of death. Sorry for the inconvenience.'

Thomas nodded. 'No problem. We want this solved so everything can go back to normal. This is Leif Ericsson, the mine supervisor.' He turned to Leif. 'This is the Nomo, Gunnar Johanssen, and Bunny Barrington, Nomo Officer.'

Leif didn't acknowledge us but continued to look surly and bored. I addressed him politely. 'Leif, what can you tell us about the death?'

He stared at me blankly and gave no indication that he was going to reply. Oh-kay, then. I pushed some more. 'For example, it would be helpful if you could tell us who discovered the body. How long did it remain undiscovered? A timeline of his activities would be great – and anything else you think could be relevant.'

Leif grimaced, but this time he started to answer, albeit grudgingly. 'The inspector came in and started the inspection. At some point, he stepped into a shaft he shouldn't have and lost his guide, a miner by the name of Aaberg Allan. They were separated for less than fifteen minutes, and when Allan found him he was already dead. That's all I know. We called the ambulance and they took the body.' He shrugged. 'Never saw anything, but there's no way he dropped dead without help.' He leaned forward. 'It was the hag. I know it was.'

'Tell me about the hag,' I prompted.

His lips pursed under his shaggy beard. 'We have a hag that lives on the mine property. She's tried to shut us down several times in the past, insists we're on her territory and we're disturbing her. Things have been quiet recently, but it's clear that's set to change.'

'Have you spoken to her?'

'Not since the 1920s.'

I blinked. 'Have you seen her since then? I mean, are you sure she's still alive?' I was also wondering how long dwarves lived for, but given how tetchy he was it didn't seem prudent to ask. I looked him over; he didn't look a day over fifty, if that.

Leif barked a single derisive laugh and shot me a supercilious look. 'Hags are *immortal,*' he sneered. 'Unless they're killed,' he added, 'and it's almost impossible to kill one.' The suggestion that he'd tried to do so hung in the air.

'Do you know how we can contact her?' I pressed. Gunnar was standing back, letting me ask the questions, but he leaned in to hear the answer.

Leif shrugged. 'I can show you one of the known entrances to her den, but you take your life into your own hands if you try to get her attention. You could end up like Helmud – and don't say I didn't warn you.'

It wasn't a nice thought but I was determined; if Leif was convinced that this hag had killed Helmud then we needed to speak to her despite his dire warnings. 'After we're done examining the scene here, I'd be grateful if you'd show us to the entrance of her den,' I told him.

'Your funeral,' he groused, stalking off in a visible huff.

Thomas gestured that we needed to follow the grouchy dwarf. He led us out of the office and up a series of wooden steps. I guessed we were climbing the mountain to the mine lift; at least I hoped we were because if there wasn't a lift my thighs were going to *burn*.

At the entrance to another building, Leif stopped briefly to make sure we were following then opened the door. The place was full of lockers, coveralls and hard hats and was obviously where the miners prepared for work. There was also a bathroom and a small break room.

Leif gave Gunnar and me mining helmets, complete with head lamps, and showed us how to adjust the fit; Thomas grabbed his own helmet and adjusted it like a pro. Next Leif walked down a longish corridor to the lift room. He didn't check to see if we were following; he was a really nice fellow.

'Are any of you claustrophobic?' Thomas asked.

I didn't know if I was, but the thought of plunging down into the depths of the earth wasn't something I was feeling warm and fuzzy about – but who would? I shrugged. Fluffy gave an almost inaudible whine; he wasn't thrilled at the idea either.

'You and me both, bud,' I murmured. 'Stay close.' He pressed into my leg and I gave him a reassuring pat.

I was relieved to see the lift, but that relief was instantly washed away when I realised how rickety it was: it was an open cage with steel mesh over the inner cart with a single bulb hanging from the top for illumination. You could even see the cables that ran it. I gulped. I liked my lifts to be a mystery, a shiny box with mirrors and good lighting, maybe some nice lift music. This shit didn't look safe and my stomach clenched.

Leif opened the first part of the cage, then the lift door and stepped inside. We followed. I had a sudden urge to blurt out something about another appointment but I stomped on it. The cage door slid shut with an ominous clang.

The dwarf picked up a device that hung by a thick metal-bound cord and hit a button. The lift lurched downwards and we headed into the cold dark depths below.

Yay.

Chapter 3

Even with my lower-than-human body temperature, my breath puffed out in clouds as we approached the level where the inspector had died. Fluffy pranced a bit and I wondered if he was cold or nervous; as he was wearing his vest, I was betting the latter.

He wasn't the only one: even Gunnar looked a little spooked. Maybe the deep dark wasn't his favourite place to go. I could tell immediately that it wasn't mine. Vampires needed the dark but this was *too* dark: there were no stars, no moon – it was *unnaturally* dark. I could see well enough thanks to my supernatural vision, but I'd have preferred a little more light. Besides, I was a weird-ass vampire that actually *liked* the sun, and thanks to my charmed necklace I was able to enjoy it often enough.

The tiny circle of our headlamps and the weak lighting in the shaft felt fragile. Ignoring the rest of us quivering behind him, Leif marched along. Thomas also looked comfortable – but I had yet to see him ever look *un*comfortable, even when he'd been faced with the beast beyond the barrier. Thomas took 'cool under pressure' to a whole new level – and since he part owned the mine, he was probably familiar with its tunnels.

As we walked down a long wide corridor, I realised I hadn't seen another miner or any other people and I wondered why. It wasn't meal time, although when you worked in the dark I guessed your meal times could be anytime depending on your shift. Had the miners been cleared out because of us? Nosiness demanded that I ask.

'Thomas, where are the miners?'

Leif answered before Thomas could. 'Cleared out,' he grunted. 'The inspector didn't finish this section, so we can't mine here until a new inspector comes and completes it. We're haemorrhaging money through lost time.'

At first my mind said, *That makes sense*, then part of my lizard brain woke up with a definite zing of fear. 'Erm ... in that case is it safe for *us* to be here?' My voice came out just a shade too high.

Leif shrugged. 'Wasn't safe for the inspector.'

What a dick reply. Ice-cold fingers ran down my spine and I looked at every nook and cranny as I waited for the earth to collapse on top of me. Perhaps I did have a touch of claustrophobia after all because all I could think about was the ceiling falling in and covering me in tonnes of earth and rock.

Thomas must have noticed my discomfort because he said, 'It's safe to walk through. It's protocol for mining, that's all.' That alleviated a little of my panic – but not all of it.

Leif stopped suddenly and pointed to where the corridor split. 'This way.' He took the left passageway. After a few metres we moved into a side corridor; it ended in a large room that looked more like a natural cavern than something man- or dwarf-made.

Leif pointed. 'This is where the body was found.' He stepped back and leaned against a rough-hewn wall. Thomas joined him so we could get an unobstructed view.

Time had passed and the ground was hard, so not even an impression of the body remained. There were some scuffs and a partial wheel mark, where presumably the gurney had been used to remove the body, but nothing else. No clues, no blood, and if there was hair I couldn't find it. I dropped to my hands and knees to examine the dirt more closely.

'Do you see anything unusual?' Gunnar asked me quietly.

I sighed and shook my head. 'No, nothing. Only that one wheel scuff from the gurney.' I stood up and brushed off my hands. 'I don't see anything that would suggest this was murder. Do you?'

'Unless something unusual comes back after the autopsy, it appears he just collapsed and died.'

'Fluffy, scent,' I called and gestured to the area. Obligingly, he sniffed around, his tail held low and showing no signs of excitement. Then, as he came closer to one of the walls, he gave a low whine.

'Hag,' Leif said firmly. 'She travels through the ground. That's what your dog's smelling. It's proof she was here!'

I couldn't help raising my eyebrows. It was clear that Fluffy had smelled something unusual, but whatever it was it didn't look like it had come into the cavern. My dog had pointedly sniffed at the walls, not at the ground. Luckily, I could ask him about it later when I persuaded him to have some human time.

Fluffy gave a small yip, returned to my side and pressed into my legs again. I gave him a pat and some praise, then I frowned and turned to our grumpy guide. 'Leif, why do you think the inspector was murdered?' As far as I could see, absolutely nothing pointed to foul play.

'She's *here,*' he insisted. He cupped his hand to his ear and pressed it against the wall he was leaning against and gestured for us to do the same.

I leaned in – and then I heard a slight scratching noise. I was pretty sure I knew the answer, but I asked anyway. 'What's the scratching sound?'

Leif looked at me scornfully. 'You wanted to know where the entrance to the hag's den is. Well, it's right here. She did it.'

I searched the wall but there was no sign of a door. Gunnar and I looked at each other before I turned back to Leif. 'Where's the entrance?'

'She can pass through earth without hindrance because it's her natural element. This is where she enters the mine. She doesn't need a *door*,' he sneered.

'How do I knock so I can speak with her?' I asked stubbornly.

'Call to her if you dare, but wait until after I leave. I'm not dying for the sake of your curiosity.'

I stared at him for a beat. 'How do I call her, then?'

Leif grimaced. 'You're a fool with a death wish.'

Thomas grunted, 'She's a Nomo officer. Show some damned respect.'

'Sure thing, *boss*.' Leif's tone was faintly sarcastic. 'Officer Death Wish, you just need to call the hag's name three times and offer her a gift.'

'What is her name?'

Leif looked nervously at the wall, then leaned towards me and whispered, 'Matilda.'

Great. One step forward – but I had nothing with me I could offer as a gift. 'Gunnar, do you have anything we can give her?'

He shook his head. 'What kind of a gift do you offer a hag?' he asked Leif.

'Don't know. I don't go looking for her. The others say she's fond of sweets – at least, that's what gets stolen most from the lockers. She's a menace.' A menace with a sweet tooth, a girl after my own heart.

I didn't want to risk her wrath by summoning her when I was empty handed. I turned to Thomas. 'Would you mind if we came back? We'd really like to talk to her.'

'Your funeral,' Leif muttered.

Thomas ignored him. 'Sure. I'll come back with you.'

I really hated putting a human in danger but of everyone in this cave – hags excluded – Thomas was the most dangerous person I knew. He'd be fine. 'Thanks, Thomas. Are there any particular sweets she likes?' I asked.

'Doughnuts,' Leif answered immediately.

Good to know.

The dwarf led us back to the lift and I followed him eagerly; I couldn't wait to feel the sun on my face.

Hag or no hag, the mine wasn't my favourite place.

Chapter 4

I wanted to buy some doughnuts and return to the mine immediately, but the universe had other plans because there were no decent ones left in the bakery. It was late afternoon and the only two in the display case were old and dry; if I offered her those, the hag would be sure to slit my throat.

I put in an order for a dozen fresh doughnuts to collect in the morning then texted Thomas and arranged a time to meet him. Technically I'd be off shift but the Nomo's office didn't really keep to strict hours; we worked when we had to and rested when we didn't. Gunnar was still visibly tired after being run ragged for nine weeks whilst Sidnee and I were at the academy, so it seemed only fair that I put in any extra hours he required.

As Gunnar drove us back into town, I called Connor. 'Hey,' he answered warmly.

'Hi,' I replied as a huge smile crossed my face. 'How are you?' Connor was working hard these days, paying the price for taking nearly a week off work to visit me at the academy.

'I'm good,' he assured me. 'What about you? I heard you caught a new case.'

'Yeah,' I sighed. 'I'm not quite sure what the deal is with it yet.'

'I heard he choked himself to death in the mine. Some sort of sex thing.'

I snorted. 'The Portlock rumour mill is ridiculous. It was nothing like that – a heart attack, maybe.'

'Maybe? You're not sure?'

'No signs of foul play ... and yet...' I trailed off.

'Your gut says otherwise.' He knew me so well.

'Yeah. I'm going to be pulling a few extra hours.'

'What's new?' he teased lightly, but there was no acrimony in his voice. With his own company to run, plus being head of the vampires in Portlock, Connor knew what it was to be busy. 'I've got to go,' he said reluctantly. 'John's here.'

John was the vampire who'd helped rescue me from the clutches of the vampire king in London. I owed him big time for his help. 'Good. Tell him I said hi.'

'Will do. Love you, Doe.'

'Love you.' We rang off.

Gunnar slid me a glance. 'You two seem happy.'

I beamed. 'We are.'

'Good. I had my reservations at first, but he's good for you.'

It surprised me how much his validation meant to me. 'He is.'

When we arrived back at the office, a person was waiting for us – or, more precisely, waiting for *me*. As I put down the black bag, Gunnar escaped to his office. Sidnee had picked up Shadow for me and sat at her desk with the cat on her lap. I gave her a questioning look as I glanced at the woman sitting in the waiting area. She shrugged.

'Are you Officer Bunny?' the woman asked as she looked me over.

'Yes. How may I help you?' I was curious why she'd waited for me when she could have given the information to Sidnee if there had been a crime. Did she have some sort of prejudice against mermaids? The thought made me bristle.

'My name is Hayleigh Farnsworth. I read about you in the paper – you know, how the Fanged Flopsy solved that werewolf case. I was wondering if you could help me.'

Great: that whole Fanged Flopsy thing was going to follow me to the grave, and since I was a vampire, that might be a very long time. 'Sure. Can you tell me what you need help with, Hayleigh?'

Hayleigh was middle-aged, with mousy brown hair pulled back in a tight bun on top of her head. She was shapely, albeit she had a little extra timber, and was dressed in a sweatshirt, a blue rain jacket and baggy pants. I couldn't tell what type of supernat she was – and there was the outside possibility that she was human.

She dug around in her huge, purple bag and pulled out a crumpled sheet of paper. She handed it to me. I smoothed it out: it was a photo that had clearly been printed at home. It was dark – it must have used up most of her ink to print it – and it showed a heavily forested area with a darker blob in the centre of the trees. I couldn't make out anything clearly.

I looked up at her. 'What am I looking at?'

She sighed. 'I thought *you'd* be able to see it.' She lowered her voice and waggled her eyebrows. 'You know, with your extra powers and stuff from the government experimentation.'

I wanted to roll my eyes but I didn't; I just waited patiently. One of the things that the academy had taught us was that silence was a powerful tool; if you maintained it long enough, the other person would feel uncomfortable and try to fill it.

Hayleigh looked around as though someone might be watching. No one was except Sidnee, who was hiding her head behind her computer screen and trying not to smile. She leaned over the counter and whispered, 'It's bigfoot. He's trying to get in my house and ... you know ... ravish me.' She didn't actually seem that upset at the prospect, maybe just a little nervous.

I blinked. Several times. 'Bigfoot?' I knew the creatures existed – in fact I'd had a run in with more than one nantinaq. They were scary and territorial and *outside* the barrier, and they definitely wouldn't be after her body. But what if one had come inside the barrier? Was there a rip? I couldn't afford to ignore Hayleigh's claims, even though the whole thing seemed absurd.

'Yeah, you know, tall hairy, big feet, big—' she went on.

I interjected hastily before she could tell me about anything else big. 'I know what you're talking about!' I really did.

'Can you come and look around? See if you can find him? I live alone.'

I looked at Sidnee, who'd started to cough in an attempt to disguise her amusement, then I looked at the pink slips for callbacks on my desk. I nodded, 'Sure, I'll come by in an hour. What's your address?'

She wrote it down on a sticky note before she left. The moment the door closed, Sidnee couldn't contain her snickers. 'Banged by bigfoot! Imagine!'

'I'd rather not,' I admitted. 'Bigfoot is real. And terrifying. If one did get inside the barrier, I'd rather know now than worry that the barrier is failing again.'

That sobered her right up. 'You're right. I didn't think about that. I don't think it is, though. She strikes me as a lonely woman and this is a cry for help.'

'Then I'd better give it to her, hadn't I?'

'Yeah, you're right. If I were lonely and scared, I'd want someone to check on anything creepy. Especially spiders.' She shuddered.

'Well this isn't spiders, so guess what? You get to come with me.' I needed back-up on the off chance that it really *was* the nantinaq: one of us to try and fight it and one of us to get the word out that the barrier was down.

Sidnee held up both hands in surrender. 'I'll never laugh at you again,' she said, only a little huffy.

Fluffy barked. 'Yeah, you're going too, and so is Shadow,' I told him. If a nantinaq was on this side, Shadow would be the biggest help with his special brand of weird smoky magic. It was going to be a total circus, but needs must.

I checked the pink slips on my desk; nothing was pressing, and most requests could be completed with a few phone calls. I hurried through them and was done in thirty minutes.

I wasn't looking forward to the visit at bigfoot lady's place, but it seemed expedient to get to it. 'Are you ready, Sidnee?' I asked.

'Yeah, but we should wait until April gets here. She's due in five minutes.'

She was right; it was best not to leave Gunnar here alone in case something big came in. 'Good idea.'

I tidied my desk. The damage that Stan had done whilst cursed into his polar bear form was completely gone, though we no longer had a lowered ceiling. That made the room more spacious, if a little less refined.

The door opened and April Arctos, bear shifter and mum extraordinaire, breezed in. 'Hi, ladies! I'm so glad to see you both back!'

'Thanks, April,' we said together, then looked at each other and started laughing.

'Well, at least you're in sync.' April plopped down her big handbag on her desk. 'It was crazy here while you were at the academy.'

'I'm so sorry!' I said, and Sidnee echoed me.

April waved us away. 'No worries, ladies. We knew why you were gone. Nothing we couldn't handle.' She grinned, 'But as I said, happy as heck to see you again.'

'Back at you. We're heading out but if you need us, call!' I insisted.

'You got it!'

I grabbed Fluffy's lead and Sidnee scooped up Shadow, who was almost too large to carry, then we climbed in the Nomo SUV and headed out to find ourselves a potentially randy bigfoot.

Chapter 5

Hayleigh lived in a modest ranch-style home with an attached garage adjoining a forested part of town. Her nearest neighbours were hidden by trees, so I could see how she might easily feel lonely and isolated.

When Sidnee and I knocked on her front door, she opened it with so much enthusiasm that she startled me. 'I'm so glad you are here!' She was almost bouncing on the balls of her feet as she motioned for us to enter, all the while scanning the area. Once we were inside, she shut the door so hurriedly that Fluffy almost lost his tail.

'If you could show us...' I started, but Hayleigh didn't wait for me to finish my sentence

'If you look out here, you'll see where I keep seeing the bigfoot.' She paused. 'Well, eyes watching me. I haven't actually *seen* it, per se.'

Now she tells us! I thought, but we were there now so we might as well check out the place.

We followed her to a large family room at the rear of the house with picture windows that framed the forest like a living portrait. 'My ex-husband liked to look at the woods,' she said, as though she needed to explain the view. 'I've ordered blinds so *he* won't watch me.'

I looked at Sidnee then back at Hayleigh. 'How about we search your house – make sure there aren't any intruders – and then look into the woods out back?' I suggested. 'Does that sound okay?'

She looked relieved. 'Yes, that would be good.'

'Great. Is there anything else you're concerned about?'

Hayleigh seemed to shrink into herself. 'No, that's all.'

I felt bad for her. Apparently her husband had left her and she was scared and alone. Life was tough sometimes.

'Do you want to show us around, or just have us search? We're happy to do whichever will make you the most comfortable,' Sidnee said gently.

'You go on ahead. I'll wait here.'

'Fluffy can stay with you, if you want,' I offered.

Fluffy walked over to her and leaned against her legs as she lowered herself into a comfortable chair. She started to pat him. Hayleigh totally needed a big dog of her own; maybe it would help with the fear and the loneliness.

The house was spacious, though it wasn't huge like Connor's place, with three bedrooms and two bathrooms.

It was tidy but cluttered with furniture. The first bedroom was obviously for guests, and its mustiness suggested it was seldom used. We checked the closet and under the bed then moved on.

The next room was an office, but it looked like it had recently been stripped of its furniture. Dents in the carpet showed where a larger desk had once stood; now an old table and kitchen chair occupied the space. Maybe it had been her husband's workspace.

I noticed a framed 'Employee of the Month' certificate on the wall from the Chrome Mine. 'Hey,' I said to Sidnee. 'Look. I wonder if Hayleigh met Helmud.'

She raised her eyebrows. 'Maybe she can shed some light on your dead guy.'

'It might be worth asking her when we've dealt with her nantinaq issue,' I agreed.

We checked the closet but nothing seemed out of place. The last room we checked was Hayleigh's bedroom. Half the cupboards had been cleared out and she hadn't moved anything into them yet. Sidnee and I shared a sympathetic glance. Poor woman: perhaps on some level she still hoped her husband would return.

Looking at her side of the bedroom quickly showed us why she was bigfoot obsessed. Her reading material took up her bedside table, the space next to and under the bed. She must have had the largest collection of bigfoot romance books ever.

Sidnee pointed to a book, *Banged by Bigfoot,* and flipped it open. She read for a few moments then fanned herself. 'Okay, that's surprisingly hot. This bigfoot has a big—'

I held up a hand. 'I don't need you to finish that sentence. I'm more of a fade-to-black girl – you know, leave it to my imagination.'

Sidnee shook her head. 'Nah, I like it painted out for me.' She flashed me a mischievous smile. 'For some reason, I've been reading a tonne of military based age-gap contemporary fiction.'

I laughed. 'How much older than you is Thomas?'

'Old enough,' she said dreamily.

We grinned at each other, then hurried down to Hayleigh who was still happily stroking Fluffy. 'The house is clear,' I announced. 'No one is here.' I paused. 'We'll check in the woods in a minute, but I wondered if you could answer a few questions about the Chrome Mine.'

She blinked. 'Sure, but I don't know how much help I'll be. I'm just HR.'

'Did you meet Helmud Henderson?'

Her expression clouded. 'I did, actually – I did his induction paperwork before he went into the mine. He seemed very nice.' She touched a hand to her heart. 'He had a fiancée. I keep thinking about that poor woman.'

I frowned; that was interesting because we had Helmud's father down as his next of kin. I'd have to see if Gunnar had a number for the fiancée.

'He got real emotional talking about her,' Hayleigh admitted. 'It was so romantic.' She sighed. 'Poor Helmud. He got the days muddled up – he turned up at the mine a day early. I didn't have the heart to send him away after he'd travelled in from Anchorage, so I just let him get on with his job. And now I keep thinking that if I hadn't, he might have been around people when he had his heart attack...'

'You can't blame yourself,' Sidnee soothed. 'You couldn't have foreseen that.'

'Absolutely,' I chimed in. 'And it was his fault for getting muddled up.' I patted Hayleigh's shoulder. 'We'll go and check the woods now.'

Hayleigh smiled gratefully, her hands still tangled in Fluffy's fur; he was valiantly putting up with belly scratches and a side order of baby talk. 'Have you thought of getting a dog?' I asked gently.

She gazed at Fluffy, her eyes contemplative. 'No, but having him here like this sure is comforting.'

'You never know, the animal shelter might have a large dog. Maybe it would be nice to have company.'

'Perhaps I'll go look,' she said noncommittally.

Sidnee and I went through the back door. 'You know there is no bigfoot or nantinaq here, right?' Sidnee rolled her eyes. 'Besides the ones in her monster-porn books.'

I wagged my finger at her. 'Don't kink-shame! Don't yuck someone's else's yum. Each to their own and all that.'

'Is this your way of telling me you read space romance? Aliens with all sorts of tentacles covered with suckers...'

I snorted but my cheeks warmed. 'Not yet, but the day is young.' I tried to get into a businesslike mindset. 'I'm going to grab Shadow from the car. Worst case scenario, he gets a nice walk.'

'I think that's the best case scenario,' Sidnee pointed out.

'Good point.'

I opened the car door and Shadow jumped down with a judgemental yowl to show he hadn't liked being left behind, but he trotted after us obediently enough – for a cat. We crossed into the back garden and Shadow continued to follow us with only one essential detour to swat at a raven that had been cheeky enough to land and watch us. The raven evaded him with ease, then returned to his perch on an old stump with a vibe that said, *'nah nah nah nah nah nah'*. Shadow ignored him.

We scanned the backyard but it was typical for the area: mostly overgrown and untended. Other than an overturned wheelbarrow and a stack of wood under a roof built to protect it from the weather, it was empty.

As we walked towards the edge of the woods, Shadow bounded ahead to chase a squirrel. He didn't appear concerned or cautious, and I counted that as a good sign; previously he'd reacted when the beast was around.

I put my finger to my lips in a 'shush' sign and signalled to Sidnee that we should spread out a little. We melted into the woods.

This patch of forest was thick and spooky. The bright lights from the house faded from view as I scanned the surrounding area. Nothing. A broken branch sounded like a shot to my left and I jumped. A whispered 'Sorry' from Sidnee made me smile and calmed my heart, which had felt like it wanted to give an extra beat.

When I heard rustling up ahead, I unsnapped my holster and drew my service weapon. I kept it down, pressed against my leg.

'I don't see anything,' Sidnee muttered.

I rolled my eyes; so much for being quiet and sneaking up on anything.

Suddenly Shadow yowled and backed up so that his short tail was touching me. He was staring into the woods. 'Sidnee!' I called. She was only a few meters away from me but she heard the panic in my voice and started to run to me – just as the woods in front of me exploded into a mass of thick brown fur.

Fuck!

Chapter 6

A bear! An actual fucking bear! I squealed, dropped back and lifted my service weapon to face the enormous creature in front of me. It took one look at my gun and slid to a stop, then it lifted its paws. It would have been comical if I hadn't just nearly shit myself.

Clearly this wasn't a normal animal so it had to be shifter. I dropped my weapon down to my side but didn't re-holster it. 'Who are you, and why are you tormenting Hayleigh?' I yelled.

Sidnee joined me, her breath ragged with exertion and panic. She put her hands on her hips and glared at the bear too. It shrank into itself and morphed from a huge beast into a thin, scraggly, middle-aged looking man. I kept my eyes firmly on his face since he was butt naked; I still wasn't accustomed to the nonchalance of shifter nakedness and I really didn't want to see a strange man's junk. The only dangling equipment I wanted to see was Connor's – not that I got to see it dangling all that often.

'I'm not tormenting her,' the man said hesitantly, rubbing the back of his neck. He had pale blond hair and looked as though he'd been trying to grow a beard but couldn't find enough energy for the hair to appear. He seemed a little shy – not about his nakedness, since he made no move to cover his meat and vegetables – and didn't meet my eyes when he spoke. He was tall, but his nervousness made him seem much smaller than he actually was. But that bear *hadn't* been shy; he'd been prowling through the woods intent on doing who-knew-what to Hayleigh.

Much to the man's alarm, Shadow stalked around him. I slapped my leg in a half-arsed effort to call him to me fully expecting nothing to happen, but Shadow promptly came and sat next to me as though he were a trained dog.

Huh.

I put my gun back in its holster, stroked my cat for a job well done and folded my arms. 'Hayleigh thinks a bigfoot is going to ravish her. But it's you she keeps seeing, isn't it?'

Looking ashamed, the man nodded his head.

'So start explaining or I'm taking you in for stalking and intent to cause bodily harm.' I was bluffing because there wasn't really anything I could pin on him, but the threat seemed to scare him.

He looked at me, eyes wide with panic. 'Please don't!' he blurted. 'I'd never hurt Hayleigh. I love her. I'm her husband, Ray Farnsworth.'

Sidnee snorted derisively. 'Her husband left her. That doesn't sound too much like true love.'

The bear shifter seemed to collapse in on himself even further. 'I–I did leave, but it's not because I don't love her. Things had grown stale between us. She's ... bored with me. She loves these smutty romance books – she spends *hours* reading them and I can't compete with that.'

As he gestured down at his junk, I followed the gesture then berated myself for looking. Ack. I couldn't unsee that. I tore my eyes back to his face, wondering how I'd got sucked into this fiasco.

He continued, 'I told her I'd leave her unless she gave up reading those books. She didn't, so I went.' He shrugged. 'It's important to follow through so people know you mean what you say.'

'Sure,' I interrupted. 'So maybe you should be careful about what you say!' His shoulders slumped. I held up a hand. 'Let me just make sure I'm clear on the situation. Your wife likes books and you made her choose between you and them?'

'Yes.'

'And you were surprised when you lost?' I shook my head in disbelief. What an idiot. I glared at him. 'Everyone deserves books. Books are knowledge and fun and escapism. It's not okay for anyone to dictate what books someone reads and when.' I paused. 'Except school teachers – I guess they have to specify books to read for exams. But apart from that, fictional dictatorship is an absolute no-no. Do you hear me?'

Ray nodded mutely.

Sidnee huffed. 'Good Lord, this is an easy fix. Are your clothes nearby?' Ray nodded and pointed to a tree. 'Well, go get dressed,' she instructed, shooing him with her hands.

He went and dressed; when he returned, he was wearing fishing gear: brown Xtra-Tuf boots, jeans and a sweatshirt with a rain jacket slung over it.

'Now, we're going to talk with your wife.' Sidnee's tone brooked no argument. He slumped further but followed us obediently.

I stopped to put Shadow in the vehicle, which the cat protested loudly about, then we all walked to the front door and knocked. Hayleigh flung it open again. 'What...?' She stopped dead when she spied her erstwhile husband. 'Ray!' She looked gobsmacked, then she burst into tears and ran inside the house.

We followed her and guided Ray firmly to the sofa. 'You stay here,' I growled. I prowled down the hallway to find Hayleigh, leaving Fluffy and Sidnee guarding him in case his crimes were far greater than the bookish sins he'd confessed to.

I knocked lightly on the bedroom door. 'Hayleigh? Are you alright?'

Uncontrolled sobbing was the only response. I sighed and opened the door. She'd wanted the police and now she had them; I was solving this damned mess so that I could tick it off my list. 'Has he hurt you physically?' I asked gently.

She stopped mid-sob. 'Goodness no, never! But he,' her lip wobbled, 'left me!'

So he wasn't an abusive asshole just an inconsiderate one. 'Come on, let's go into the living room and work this out.'

'He left me!' She started sobbing again.

I stifled a sigh. Was this what I'd spent nine weeks at the academy for? It wasn't police work, it was social work – but then again, the two were often intertwined. I softened my voice. 'Hayleigh, he regrets it deeply. Let's talk to him.'

Hayleigh looked up then wiped away the tears with her sleeve and stood. Some hiccups followed, but they had stopped by the time we entered the living room. Her face was blotchy but her eyes had a hopeful light that I hoped was warranted. If Ray fucked this up now, it was on him.

I led her to sit across from her husband. 'This little fiasco is because you two need to communicate. Ray says he gave you an ultimatum and followed through. It was a stupid thing to do and he accepts that now. Don't you?' I slid a fierce glare at Ray.

He nodded frantically.

'Good. Ray screwed up. He's sorry.' I looked sternly at him. 'Tell her what you told us.'

He blanched, leaned forward and stared at his hands, which he was rapidly clasping and unclasping. He looked up at Hayleigh then back down again.

'I'm sorry, Haze, I–I just felt like you didn't care about me. You only cared about your books and those sexy primal animals. I thought maybe if I left, it would make you realise you had your own one at home. You didn't seem to miss me but I – I really missed you. I couldn't stand being away from you so I watched you from out there in my bear skin, just to check on you. I swear I didn't mean to scare you. I'm sorry.'

Hayleigh's mouth hung open for a beat. 'Ray! Why didn't you just come back home?' Her voice softened. 'I've missed you so much.'

His head shot up. 'You have?'

She stood up and threw herself at her husband. He caught her and there was a lot of mumbling and kissing; when things got a bit gropey, it was definitely time for us to leave.

I cleared my throat awkwardly. 'We'll see ourselves out.'

Sidnee grinned as she stood up. 'Our work here is done.'

The couple ignored us. I cleared my throat more loudly so that they would look at me then I said firmly, 'We don't want to be called back here. Work your shit out – and get a dog.' I addressed that last part to Hayleigh.

Hands clasped, they smiled at us. 'Thank you, Fanged Flopsy!' Hayleigh beamed at me.

Oh boy. It almost hurt not to roll my eyes. 'You're welcome.' I nodded at Fluffy, and Sidnee. 'Let's go.' I hoped that the couple could work it out and be happy together. Stupid decisions led to weird shit in this town.

Back in the Nomo vehicle, Sidnee said, 'That was weird but sort of ... cute,'

'Yeah. At least there was no nantinaq or beast from beyond, and I like an easy case we can cross off. It makes me feel like an achiever.'

'True. Maybe I'll write a book about all the crazy stuff around here, call it nonfiction and see what kind of reaction I get.'

'You'll get a visit from the MIB,' I warned darkly.

She perked right up, 'Oooh, speaking of sexy former MIB officers—'

'We really weren't,' I interrupted, amused.

Sidnee blithely ignored me. 'I've got a date tomorrow night with Thomas!'

I put the SUV in gear and backed out of the driveway. 'Really? Things are moving along?'

Finally!

'He's so careful of me. I get it, I know I'm a mess. Part of me is terrified, and the other part wants to climb that man like a tree.'

I grinned. 'Listen, only you can decide where you want to go.'

'I know.' She grimaced. 'After the whole Chris mess, I just... I don't really trust myself. My judgement, you know?'

I did know, but Thomas was different. 'Thomas isn't Chris. He's a good man underneath all the weaponry. He isn't dealing drugs, he's a pillar of the community and a council member. And he is so gentle with you.' I paused. 'So loving.'

She hit me. 'Don't use the L word.'

I grinned. 'It doesn't bite.'

She looked out the window. 'Sometimes it does.'

I changed the subject. 'Let's go see what turned up while we were gone, and then in...' I glanced at the clock on the dash '...five hours, I'll get my doughnuts and talk to a hag.'

Chapter 7

I had to deal with two more calls before it was time to collect the doughnuts. The jobs were the everyday humdrum stuff that passed the time: a first-time teenage shoplifter at the hardware store, and a minor disturbance between two guests at the hotel. An appearance and a finger wagging was all that was required of me; the teen had been sullen but reluctantly apologetic, and the guests slightly panicked at being seen by the eyes of the law.

I'd still called the shoplifter's parents and she was totally getting it in the neck, though she wouldn't have a criminal record, which her parents were endlessly grateful for. Gunnar often let the kids have one strike for free, an attitude I'd also adopted. We all made mistakes, particularly in the vicious grip of teen hormones and existential angst.

After those issues were dealt with, I dug a little more into our deceased guy, Helmud. There was no mention anywhere of a fiancée so I checked Gunnar's notes of his call with Helmud's father, but the dad hadn't mentioned a fiancée either. Had Helmud lied to Hayleigh? Maybe she'd hit on him and he hadn't wanted to hurt her feelings? It was a possibility.

I did a quick internet search. Helmud had made headlines not that long ago for closing down a mine because of safety breaches. The Chrome Mine had looked a little worn, but I hadn't seen any red flags – then again, I knew absolutely nothing about mines; the flags could have been glittery rainbows and I still wouldn't have seen them.

If Helmud had been killed – and that was a big if – could someone at the Chrome Mine be responsible? One of the owners: Calliope, Liv or Thomas? They were all killers and I could easily see one of them dispatching Helmud to stop him shutting down the mine if there *were* safety concerns. It was all a bit of a stretch, but I believed Liv would be capable of it. *And* she was a necromancer; she could probably kill someone without leaving a mark on their body.

Suddenly, the thought didn't seem so far-fetched after all.

My phone alarm blared to warn me it was nearly time to meet the hag, Matilda. I wondered if she'd been given that name at birth or if she'd chosen it for herself when English became prevalent on the peninsula. If she was friendly enough for a chat, I'd ask her later. Between the lesson at the academy that taught us hags were powerful and deadly elementals with metal teeth and claws, and Leif's obvious fear of her, I was feeling a tad wary.

I took Fluffy and Shadow home first, fed them then asked Fluffy, 'Can you be Reggie, please? Just for a moment?' He looked at me with soulful eyes, but didn't shift. 'For me?' I pressed softly.

Fluffy sighed audibly, then a moment later Reggie was crouching in front of me. I smiled at him. 'Hey, kiddo.' He launched himself into my arms and I hugged him right back. 'It's good to see you,' I murmured into his lank, dark hair.

His hug tightened but he still didn't speak. Eventually, though, he pulled back to look at me and raised a questioning eyebrow. 'I wanted to talk about the crime scene,' I told him – plus it was a good excuse to spend a few moments with him in human form.

'Sure,' he croaked. 'What do you need to know?'

'Any signs of foul play? You growled at the wall...'

'The stench of *something*. There was a metallic tang to it... I'm betting it was the hag.' He shuddered. 'She was right there on the other side of the wall listening to us.'

'Was the same scent at the site of the death?'

Reggie shook his head. 'Nothing on the ground, just a hint of her on the air.' He paused. 'But she reeked. Really, really reeked. So prepare yourself.'

I smiled ruefully. 'Thanks for that. I need to plug my nose before I speak to her, huh?'

'At the least,' he said seriously.

'Anything else you can tell me about the crime scene?'

'There were a bunch of recent scents but very few of them were dwarven. Dwarfs have an almost earthy tone to them and these didn't.'

Huh. Leif had given me the impression that the area wasn't used much, yet Reggie was telling me it was Grand Central Station. 'Anyone familiar?' I asked. Surely he would have mentioned if he'd smelled Liv there.

'I've smelled one of the scents before but I couldn't tell you where, or who it belonged to. But one of them was familiar.'

That didn't rule out Liv; then again, there was still nothing to suggest foul play. Maybe the poor guy really had just keeled over when the stress of recently closing down a mine had come back to haunt him. And yet... Something was niggling at me but I didn't know what.

I needed a cause of death.

'All right. Thanks, Reggie, that was more helpful than you know. Do you mind keeping Shadow company for me while I step out?' I slid him a sidelong glance. 'As a human?' I tacked on lightly. 'Just for a bit? He loves to be stroked. And then,' I added as a final incentive, 'you can pick what's on TV...?'

Reggie licked his lips. 'Yeah, okay – for a bit.'

I resisted the urge to do a fist pump. 'Cool. I'll grab you a soft drink and some biscuits.'

'Maybe a cup of tea?' he asked hopefully.

I ruffled his hair. 'You got it. One brew coming up.'

I made him a quick cuppa, shoved a few biscuits on a plate and took them through. He was sitting bolt upright on the sofa watching TV. I put the tea down on a side table and shoved a blanket at him. 'Here,' I said firmly, pushing him gently back into the cushions. 'Snuggle up.'

He sank a little more into the cushions and dragged the blanket onto his lap.

'See you later, Reggie.' I kissed his cheek and waltzed out. I really hoped that I would see him later, but I suspected that on my return my canine companion would be back.

For once, I hoped that I was wrong.

Chapter 8

I locked the front door behind me; I wanted Reggie to be safe and sound whilst I was out though he had a key for emergencies. My home didn't have a great track record for being safe, but Connor had made sure this current house was warded to the hilt.

Gunnar was waiting for me outside with the SUV's motor running. 'Sorry I kept you waiting,' I apologised. 'I asked Reggie to talk to me.'

'And did he?'

I smiled. 'He did.' As we drove to the store, I gave Gunnar a brief rundown of everything Reggie had told me.

'Interesting.' Gunnar pulled up outside the bakery and I ran in to grab my box of doughnuts.

When I jumped back into the vehicle a minute later, it was immediately filled with the wonderful scent of sugary, yeasty goodness. My stomach grumbled; I wasn't even hungry but they smelled so good that I was sorely tempted to devour the lot. The hag didn't need a gift *that* badly, right?

Gunnar sighed and looked longingly at the box. 'We should have ordered an extra dozen.'

I laughed. 'Yeah, I was thinking the same.' I paused a moment. 'Gunnar, can I pick your brains?'

He looked at me wryly. 'Sure. It doesn't feel like there's much there these days but go ahead and shoot.'

'What do you know about hags?'

'Not a whole lot – they're insular creatures. I knew there was one in Portlock but that's all. I've never met her and I didn't even know that she lived by the mine.'

I'd hoped for more. 'They mentioned them at the academy. They're earth elementals, meaning she can use the power of the earth to do pretty much anything she wants with the ground. They have metal teeth and metal claws, and their appearance can range from looking fairly humanoid to downright monstrous. I think that if the hag really wanted the mine closed, she could probably make it happen by simply collapsing the tunnels.'

Gunnar rubbed his chin thoughtfully. 'You have a point. So why would she need to kill the inspector?'

I shrugged. 'She could have had another reason but I think it eliminates one motive, unless she's a magical dud or something. He might have pissed her off in her own home, or she could have killed him accidentally.' I paused. 'Or he may have died of natural causes.'

'I hear a "but",' Gunnar chuckled.

'Yeah, well... I can't help but feel something is off, even if I can't put my finger on what.'

'I feel the same. Nothing points to murder and yet... I like how your mind works, Bunny.' He winked. 'It works like mine. Keep it up.'

I intended to – if we lived through our conversation with Matilda. I was nervous: this would be my first chat with something that had never ever been close to human. My brief conversations with the beast beyond the barrier had consisted of me screaming and running away, and not much else. The beast had rarely replied. Some people had no manners.

Gunnar pulled into the mine's car park and my heart gave a solid beat in protest as a sudden wash of nerves engulfed me. Maybe it was because we were meeting an unknown creature but it might have been due to the prospect of going down into the dark depths of the earth again. It turned out I wasn't a big fan of that. It wasn't bad enough to call it claustrophobia – I wasn't terrified – but I was distinctly not *keen*.

Thomas met us in the office before taking us to the storeroom for our hard hats, then he led us to the lift. 'You ready for this?' he asked me, quirking an eyebrow.

I hadn't put on my poker face so my fear must have been showing. I rectified that immediately. 'Yeah, I'm good,' I lied, though he didn't look convinced. It was like bolting the barn door after the keelut had already escaped.

I focused on the box of doughnuts, inhaling their vanilla scent. They did a good job of distracting me until Thomas hit the button and we lurched downward. 'Do you know if the hag speaks English?' I asked as we dropped steadily into the bowels of the earth.

'I've never met her,' he admitted. 'But the dwarves have hinted that she's spoken to them. We conducted a full risk assessment when we found out she lived there but she refused to meet with us. In the end Liv concluded she wasn't a threat to us.'

'What about the other dwarves? Are they as terrified of her as Leif is?'

'Oh, they are,' Thomas confirmed. 'But it hasn't stopped her from talking to them.'

'What about?'

He shrugged. 'They aren't very forthcoming, but I grasped she was warning them to stay out of certain areas.'

I knew I'd probably regret asking, but I did anyway. 'She was warning them to keep them safe? Areas of instability, right?'

He chuckled. 'No, she was warning them to stay away from the parts of the land that she's claimed.'

Damn it. Why couldn't she have been a Good Samaritan hag?

As the lift juddered to a stop, the wires screamed in protest. Thomas didn't bat an eyelid; he merely opened the gate and ushered us out. Like before, the silence and dark were absolute until he switched on the weak lights that were wired permanently into the mine. I shivered, despite their wavering light and reached up to turn off the lamp on my helmet. Better to conserve it for if shit got pear-shaped.

Gunnar noticed me tremble. 'You cold?'

I shook my head. 'No, just spooked. Turns out I'm not a huge fan of tunnels.'

He grunted. 'Me neither.'

Thomas ignored us as he led us to the cave where Helmud had been found; I doubted he was ever afraid. I took a deep breath. 'I guess this is it. I'll do the honours. Are you ready?'

Both men indicated they were. I held the doughnuts out in front of me and yelled, as instructed by Leif, 'Matilda, Matilda, Matilda! We come bearing gifts!'

Chapter 9

We waited a few minutes but no hag appeared. I looked at Thomas. 'Did I do it wrong?' I asked dubiously.

'I've never called her, but you did exactly what Leif told you to do,' he replied. I noticed that his hands were hanging loose at his sides, he was balancing on his toes and his knees were soft. He was tensed for an attack, prepared to act – and act quickly. That didn't improve my mood.

A soft scratching noise came from the cavern wall nearest to us and we stepped back cautiously. Suddenly there were knives in Thomas's hands and Gunnar had unsnapped his service weapon holster. I did nothing because I was holding the doughnuts; imagine that on my tombstone.

I was strung tighter than a violin string. I swallowed, my mouth drier than the sands of Liv's original home. *You are a vampire, get it together*, I chided myself, then for good measure I added, *and a witch*.

Feeling inside for the burning ball of heat that lived in my centre, I comforted myself with its roaring presence. If my teeth, speed and strength were nothing against the hag, at least I had flames. I called to the magic, getting it ready for release.

The scratching grew louder.

I shifted on my feet. The cold from the mine seeped through to my bones and I yearned to let my fire out to warm me.

The scratching stopped abruptly. One moment the cavern wall was there, the next it had vanished in a puff of dirt and the strangest creature I'd ever seen was standing before us. I was glad I'd secured that poker face or I'd have been gaping. Even so, I was blinking rapidly, as if the blinks could make the vision in front of me go away.

'Who calls I?' The rasping voice sounded as if the hag smoked fifty cigarettes a day. A chill ran down my spine and I wished to hell that I had my weapon in my hand rather than diabetes in a box.

I cleared my throat, trying to keep my nerves from my voice. 'I do.' I wiggled the doughnut box in what I hoped was an enticing manner but it may have just looked like I was having a small fit. 'I've brought you some treats and I wish to ask you some questions in exchange.'

Despite her unusual appearance, the hag was no more than five feet tall; that made her seem childlike, though I knew she was far from it because elementals were long-lived. Her hair looked like fine willow sticks and hung below her waist. Her large, pointed ears poked through it and flicked at any sound.

She was wearing animal skins and her feet were bare. Her nails were bright silver and her shiny metallic teeth were all the same length and pointed like a carnivore's, which made her maw strangely reminiscent of a shark. That wasn't the best comparison to leap to mind whilst my stomach was still rigid with nerves.

She sniffed like an animal then lunged forward. Thomas leapt in front of me with his knives. This situation was about to go to heck in a hand basket. 'Stop!' I ordered them both.

Thomas froze, glanced at me and stepped back obediently but his knives were still out. The hag looked at him warily and bared her terrifying teeth. I felt the tingle that indicated magic was rising and saw that the earth around us was swirling in little dust clouds. I had to do something fast or this encounter wouldn't end well.

'These are for you.' I thrust the box towards her, opened the lid – and the swirling dust around us settled. Matilda sniffed the air again, her mouse-like nose whiffling as she scented the doughnuts. Then, in a lightning-fast move, she snatched the box and dashed back into the hole in the wall. Okay, then.

The only positive was the fact she didn't close the hole behind her. The sound of paper tearing and food being devoured reached us and we exchanged uneasy glances.

It didn't take her long to eat the dozen doughnuts and she didn't offer us a single one, which was outrageous. I made a note that manners weren't her thing. Moments later the remains of the pink bakery box came sailing out of the hole. It looked like she'd tried to take a couple of bites out of that, too, but decided it wasn't very appetising. The doughnuts were gone, though. *Every last tasty morsel*, I thought mournfully.

She poked her head back out and pointed a metal-encased finger at me. 'You. Come!' she commanded before disappearing back into the tunnel. It was clear that I, and I alone, was meant to follow her.

Gunnar put a hand on my arm and lowered his voice. 'Bunny, that isn't a good idea.'

Thomas echoed him. 'I can't protect you if you go in there. If anything happened to you on my watch, Sidnee would never forgive me.'

I shook my head. 'We have to know,' I said firmly. 'This is how we find out what really happened.'

'We won't find out shit if you don't come back,' Thomas objected.

I wanted to shrug off the comments, but the thought of following Matilda really didn't fill me with the warm and fuzzies. I couldn't pass through earth like her. I had a gun, but if I killed her I'd never get back through the wall again. If I offended her or said something she didn't like, I'd be completely screwed. That didn't feel great but bravery isn't about not being scared; it's about continuing even though you *are* scared.

In the end my sense of duty and my insatiable curiosity won. It seemed likely that my need to solve a mystery would kill me someday; I just hoped it wouldn't be today. 'It's okay, I'll be fine,' I said out loud to reassure them and myself.

'Bunny, please don't go,' Gunnar murmured, but I noted that he didn't order me not to. He could have pulled rank but he didn't because he wanted to know the truth as much as I did, even if his common sense told him it wasn't a good idea. We really were peas in a pod – an idiotic, suicidal pod.

'I'm going in,' I said with as much bravado as I could muster. I paused. 'If I don't come out, take care of everyone.' I paused again. 'And thanks, Gunnar – for everything.' I couldn't say more or I wouldn't have been able to do this.

Like a curious cat, I stooped low and walked into the earthen hole after the hag. Like a cat, I hoped I had a few lives left.

Chapter 10

The scent of damp earth was all around me. I jumped and tried to suppress the jolt of panic when the 'door' behind me disappeared and I was plunged into total darkness. *Think, Bunny!*

I reached up and fumbled with my helmet to flick on my headlamp. Relief flowed through me as it came on; it was meagre and underpowered but definitely *light*. I was still in a tunnel with an unknown threat, but at least now I could see her coming for me. Surely that would be better, right?

The hag's small form shuffled in front of me. Her head was down and her back was hunched so she was an ideal size for the tunnel, but she had failed to consider her tall guest and I had to stoop low as I walked forward. I was several inches taller than my guide and my back was already protesting.

I was completely disoriented in the narrow tunnels. I was panting, but I told myself that it was from the exercise rather than from fear and being in a tight space at another creature's mercy.

Because the darkness and being underground messed with my senses, I had no idea how long we walked. When the hag finally came to an open space, I stumbled. She had led me to her home and apparently she was willing to let me in. Huh.

Of all the things I'd expected, it wasn't this. Old lanterns lit the cavernous space and cast a dim glow in the cave and I could see that she even had some furniture. Matilda waved me past her and I started forward. As I lifted my head, my headlamp illuminated more of the space.

Oh fuck.

The walls of the cavern were lined with skulls. Human skulls. My knees buckled. As I collapsed into the chair next to me, I heard the hag cackle. 'You should have had sugary snack, little girl,' she said. 'You so weak.'

I ignored her taunts and pointed to the skulls. 'They gave me a turn,' I admitted honestly. My heart had given three solid beats: I was in vampire tachycardia.

She looked at the skulls and laughed harder; her wheezy bark reminded me of a seal. As she sat on another chair, I noticed the mismatched nature of the furniture. Had she stolen castoffs from places around town? She seemed to like the overstuffed type.

The hag explained, 'Those from graves. I move out of way.' Well, that was a relief because I'd immediately thought of cannibalism. 'Food?' she offered. 'Drink?'

I blinked and tried not to let my eyes linger on the skulls. 'No, thank you. I've just eaten,' I lied.

She grunted. 'Fine. You want talk, so talk.'

'Sure. I'm Bunny, by the way. I'm an officer at the Nomo's office.'

'Why Bunny? Is it because you jump like rabbit?' She giggled.

Great, even the non-humans were comedians. 'I've always had carrots in my fridge,' I explained, pulling out a well-worn story. 'So everyone calls me Bunny.'

She snorted. 'Carrots for rodents. You rodent?'

I eyed her flatly and ignored her comment. 'I called you because there was a dead body in that mine shaft we were just in. You might be our only witness to the death. The dwarves told me that you had an entrance there and might have seen something.' I left off the whole 'the dwarves thought you did it' part. I really wanted to get out of there alive.

She frowned. 'Dwarves hate Matilda.'

I had a million questions but I didn't dare ask them yet because I had no feel for Matilda. I could tell that her magic was strong – it grated just out of reach like electricity in the air. She'd been friendly enough so far, but that didn't mean she *was*.

'They don't *hate* you,' I said firmly. Dislike and fear, yes, but hatred was arguable.

She seemed mollified. 'I not see dead man.'

Bummer: there went my easy solve. 'No problem. Have you noticed anything different in the mine?'

'Strange smell,' she said finally. 'Three moons ago. I leave, not like.'

That sent my mind racing. A strange smell? Some weird mine gas, perhaps? Did the inspector die from poison gas? If so, was it natural or man-made? I groaned inwardly to myself; if Stan was here, he'd be joking about farts. It was a good thing he was absent.

'Were you near that shaft when you smelled it or somewhere else?' I asked.

She cocked her head in thought and scratched her large, bulbous nose. 'I not close.'

So there went that idea. This was going nowhere; if she'd done anything to the inspector, she wasn't going to simply admit it.

The skulls were giving weight to some of Leif's fears, though, and our brief chat hadn't ruled her out as a suspect. I had to tread carefully; I wanted to get home to Connor in one piece. 'Thank you for your hospitality, Matilda. I should go back.' I stood.

Her eyes narrowed at me. 'Sit. Matilda ask questions now.'

I sat abruptly and forced a smile to my lips. 'Sure. I'm so sorry – go ahead.'

She pursed her lips. 'Matilda want more sugary snack. You bring here?'

I wasn't sure if she was asking if I'd brought them today or if I'd bring more. 'Yes, I brought them today.'

'Tell dwarves Matilda want more. They give.'

'I will tell them,' I promised. 'But I can't guarantee they'll listen.'

'They listen. I no bother them, they do what Matilda say.'

Sounded like a protection scam to me, but whatever was going on seemed to be working. The dwarves had been running this mine for over a century, so I guessed they knew the cost of doing business. From the little I'd learned at the academy, hags were territorial and could be vicious. Since it was pretty certain that she'd been there first, a daily box of doughnuts seemed a small price if she was allowing the miners to work there.

'I'll let them know.'

She bared her teeth in a terrifying smile. 'Good. Come.'

She stood up. I had no choice but to follow hastily down the corridor she seemed to create effortlessly as she moved through the ground. Where did the earth *go?* Was it moved elsewhere as she walked, then pulled back into place when she was done? Or was it compressed somehow?

A huge wave of relief crashed through me as she led me back to the shaft where Gunnar and Thomas were waiting. The mine no longer felt like it was closing in; in fact, it felt positively spacious compared to her cramped tunnels. The hag waved me through and, as I stepped out, the 'door' disappeared behind me. Just like that, Matilda was gone. Not so much as a ta-ta.

Gunnar rushed up to me. 'Are you okay?' His eyes were a little wild.

I nodded. 'Yep. She really just wanted a private chat.' I paused. 'I got the feeling that she wanted to show off her home to someone – she enjoyed my reaction.'

Gunnar blew out a long breath. 'You were gone too long. I thought I'd lost you.' He pulled me into a warm bear hug.

My heart swelled. It was nice to know I'd be missed; of course, Gunnar wasn't the only one who cared. Connor would have torn this place apart if I hadn't come back.

I hugged my boss until he finally released me, still scanning my face for signs of injury or distress. I smiled reassuringly. 'Honestly, I'm fine. Matilda was quite a good host – she even offered me food and drink. To be honest, I wondered why the dwarves are so afraid of her.'

'Apparently, she's mellowed,' Thomas said. 'She and the dwarves began their relationship quite contentiously. This is her territory and the mine had a rough start until they reached a compromise.'

'Well, I don't know anything about that – but she wants a dozen doughnuts to be delivered daily.'

He nodded. 'I'll arrange that with the bakery. Small price to pay.'

I thought for a moment. 'She seemed okay ... content, you know? Of course, I'm not familiar with any other hags so I could be completely misreading her.'

'I wouldn't assume anything about her. She isn't human – she doesn't think like we do,' Thomas cautioned.

I shrugged. 'If we're being picky, I'm not human either.'

'No, but you *were*. And you're humanoid. She's not.'

'I suppose. But did you know she has furniture in her cosy little cave?'

He looked genuinely taken aback. 'She does? Where did she get it?'

'I'm assuming she's raided local cast-offs. You know, someone puts out a chair with a "free to a good home" sign.'

There was one other thing that I was pretty sure I should mention. 'As well as the furniture, her cave is lined with skulls. She said they were from graves. Is there a graveyard around here?' I hadn't seen one but I hadn't explored this area yet; for all I knew, there was a graveyard just over the hill.

Thomas shook his head, not in denial, but in consternation. 'Now I think I know why the dwarves fear the hag.'

'Why?' I pried.

His expression was grim. 'She's keeping their dead hostage.'

Chapter 11

As we returned to the lift, I couldn't stop thinking about that last statement. 'Thomas,' I said, 'treat me like an ignorant supernatural. How does anyone – apart from Liv – hold the dead hostage?'

'The dwarves have very specific rules to allow them to pass into their afterlife,' he explained as the lift clanked, whirred and jerked along. Talking helped me stop worrying about its obvious fragility, so I encouraged him to continue with a 'go on' gesture.

'According to dwarven lore, the bodies of the dead have to be kept whole for them to be released to the afterlife. If the hag is taking their heads, she's keeping them from moving on and trapping their spirits forever on the mortal plane.'

I shivered. Having just dealt with a poltergeist and the trapped banshee spirits in the barrier gems, I could go a long time without dealing with any more spirits – Aoife excluded. 'I don't know,' I said finally. 'The skulls looked human.'

Thomas shrugged. 'There's no visible difference between human skulls and dwarven ones. You wouldn't be able to tell.'

That was all well and good but one question remained. 'So how did she get them?' As soon as it left my mouth, I realised it was a dumb question: Matilda passed through earth like it was air; no doubt she simply took them directly from the dwarves' graves.

To my surprise Thomas said, 'That's a good question. The dwarves burn their dead within twenty-four hours of death if they can, then they scatter the ashes. If the heads *are* dwarven, she must have taken them shortly after death.'

That was a macabre picture that I didn't want to dwell on. As the lift finally lurched to a stop I asked, 'What do they do with the bodies if they can't be burnt whole?'

He shrugged and pushed the button to open the doors. 'I don't know, but I wonder if they're keeping them somewhere in the mine until they can be reunited with their heads. How many skulls did you see?'

I hadn't counted them but there were a lot. 'I'm not sure. Hundreds, maybe?'

'Hundreds?' Thomas sounded surprised. He shook his head slowly. 'Not possible. Dwarves live a long time and they've only been in Portlock since the early 1800s. I wouldn't have thought a hundred dwarves have lived here in that time so they can't all be dwarf skulls.'

'Then who do the others belong to?'

Thomas stared at me. 'I don't know, Bunny. Are you sure they were all humanoid?'

I thought back. Were *all* of the skulls human looking? That had been my initial view, for sure, and they certainly hadn't been animal skulls, but I'd only glanced at them. 'I'm no expert and the lighting was dim. They were either human – or they looked human to me.'

Gunnar's expression was grim. 'Short of digging up graves all over the peninsula, we might never know where she got them.'

That itched under my skin: I *had* to know. A mystery was afoot – several in this case – and I needed to get to the bottom of all of them.

When we went into the locker room to return our helmets, Leif was waiting for us. 'She did it, didn't she?' he asked eagerly.

I shook my head. 'I don't think so – and as we said previously, the inspector might not have been murdered. We'll know more when we get the autopsy results.' I looked at Thomas, wondering if I should mention the skulls to Leif. He gave a tiny shake of his head.

'She wants a box of doughnuts delivered to that cavern daily,' he said. 'I'll set up the order if you can have someone drop it off.' I noted that Thomas didn't ask Leif so much as told him.

Leif made a sound that was suspiciously close to a growl. 'Fine.' He stalked off.

'Did I put him in a bad mood by not believing him about the hag?' I asked.

Thomas looked amused. 'Nah, he's always like that.'

'Don't worry, Bunny Rabbit. Dwarves don't like anyone,' Gunnar added. 'It's nothing personal.'

'I'm picking up on that,' I said wryly.

I followed my boss out to the SUV and we drove off. Through the rear-view mirror I watched the mine disappear, relieved that I wouldn't need to go back into the bowels of the earth again for quite some time.

The journey home seemed to fly by, mostly because the adrenaline from the adventure had receded and I was beyond bone weary. It was after my bedtime and then some. Gunnar dropped me at my house, idling at the curb until I was inside safely with the doors locked. When I waved to him through the window, he roared off.

The TV was on but Fluffy and Shadow were asleep on the sofa. I sighed. Reggie hadn't lasted long in human form. I scrubbed my tired eyes and tried to feel like I wasn't failing him.

I woke and fed them and let them out to do their business, then I made myself a glass of warmed blood and a much-needed cup of tea and slice of toast. I was the walking dead in more ways than one. Finally I put the animals to bed again and gratefully collapsed onto my bed.

Tired as I was, my mind was spinning round and round. I needed more information about hags; I had a tiny bit of knowledge from my time at the academy and hints from the dwarves, but that was all. Even Connor and Gunnar knew little about them and they were both old. I only knew three people who were older: Mrs. Wright, the oldest original resident of Portlock; Calliope Galanis, an ancient water dragon that had pissed off Homer, and Liv Fox.

Liv and Calliope were so ancient that they might know something; they were also on the suspect list for Helmud's death because they could both have killed him without leaving a mark. Calliope could just have shifted and scared the bejasus out of him.

I sighed. Neither woman was currently on Team Bunny because I'd accused Calliope's lover of being a drug dealer and I'd arrested Liv for attempted murder. Admittedly,

Liv had reached out to me recently for help in earning Gunnar's forgiveness; maybe she'd be willing to talk to me.

I yawned and reached up to stroke my new daylight charm, an emerald pendant that Connor had given me for Christmas. I smiled a little as I thought about him. I'd have called him, but it was firmly daytime and I didn't want to wake him up.

But I fell asleep with him on my mind, and I definitely had sweet dreams.

Chapter 12

I woke when Shadow, all ten kilos of him, landed firmly in the middle of my guts. 'Oof.'

He yowled, soundly telling me off, then gave me his characteristic lynx bark, 'mrow', which was easily translated from cat to the English equivalent of, 'Get up and feed me now, you lazy human oaf!' The half-grown lynx was probably in the middle of another growth spurt because he was always hungry, though the vet insisted I was feeding him enough.

'I'm getting up!' I yawned and tried to ignore his weight. I closed my eyes again for a moment and he let out another yowl as close to my ear as possible.

I cracked open one eye and stared at him. 'You're not letting me fall back to sleep, are you?' I huffed loudly, picked him up and set him down next to me so I could get out of the covers. Damned cat. He accurately read my movements and jumped down to run to the kitchen to wait for me. Pussy-whipped usually meant something else, but in this context it meant that Shadow had me exactly where he wanted me. I couldn't help feeling that he'd trained me far more than I'd trained him.

Meanwhile, a sleepy Fluffy had padded in. Seeing that there were no villains making his companion screech, he turned and trotted back to the kitchen. Presumably he wanted to give me some privacy as I got dressed – but it could also have been to wait for his own food.

I needed a shower to blast away the sleep, so I turned the water to hot and luxuriated in the new vanilla-scented body wash that Connor had given me. The bottle had cost a wince-inducing amount but it made my skin feel buttery soft so I tried to ignore the price tag. I shouldn't have Googled it. Live and learn.

I dried my ash-blonde hair and dressed in sensible clothes, then went to deal with my impatient pets. As soon as I entered the kitchen Shadow wound through my legs, purring loudly and asking politely to be fed.

'Purring is a much nicer way to wake me,' I grumped. 'Jumping on me is not. Just for future reference.' Even so, I hurriedly filled their bowls and changed their water before I switched on the kettle for my tea. I yawned as I prepared a cup of blood, then plugged my nose and glugged it back. I was starving, so I made breakfast and settled in to eat it with my first glorious cuppa of the day.

My phone rang as I was cleaning up. Because I'd assumed it would be Connor, I was surprised when the screen said that it was Gunnar. Uh-oh. 'Hey, Gunnar, what's wrong?'

He was silent for a moment then he sighed heavily. 'We've had a murder. A definite one this time.'

'Any details?'

'Not over the phone,' he said gruffly. 'Come to the office and I'll fill you in. I've called Sidnee.'

I covered the night shift, April worked the day shift and Sidnee covered the in-between, but we often worked at the same time if there was a serious crime. April would be going home right now but she could come in early to cover the end of Sidnee's shift if she had to; alternatively, Sig could cover by CCTV. We all worked more hours than we were supposed to but we were still short-handed. We really needed Reggie to be Reggie sometimes so he could help out too, but the last thing he needed was pressure.

'Okay, Gunnar, I'll be there in ten.'

'See you then.' He hung up.

I turned to my canine companion. 'Fluffy, we have a murder to solve. Are you game?'

He barked a yes. I patted his head and started to pull on my winter layers; vampire or not, it was colder than a lawyer's soul so I put on coat, boots and gloves – and this time, I remembered to wear my cleats.

It was still snowing and only the main streets seemed to get ploughed consistently. I wasn't used to that much snow; despite movies that showed wonderful wintery landscapes, it rarely snowed in the UK.

I grabbed Fluffy's lead and plonked Shadow in his pram, which he was quickly outgrowing. I wondered if they made prams for a twenty-kilo pet. I didn't even know how big he would get; I'd read that male lynxes were around twenty kilos, but Shadow was an unknown cryptid that looked like a lynx with a melanistic coat. Who knew what he *really* was – or how big he would grow?

I opened the door to find that my front step and sidewalk had been shovelled. I blinked in surprise and looked around for the identity of my fairy snow shoveller. Sure enough a familiar white truck was parked across the street with a shovel handle sticking out of the back.

I beamed and waved as I walked over. Connor was in the cab, talking on his phone. He hung up and got out of the truck to greet me, a warm smile on his gorgeous features. It took my breath away.

Butterflies fluttered in my stomach as he leaned down to give me a very thorough good-morning kiss; it was all too easy to get lost in his arms. Despite the cold, he was wearing a flannel shirt with the sleeves rolled up because he knew I got so damned dreamy over those forearms of his. *Murder, Bunny,* I reminded myself. *There's been a murder.*

It was a real effort to pull away from the safety of his arms. 'Hey, thank you for the shovelling. You didn't have to do that.'

He gave me that crooked smile I adored and shrugged like it was no biggie. 'I was in town and I saw it hadn't been done. Plus, it was my chance to see you before work.' He winked. 'You smell good enough to eat,' he murmured, and suddenly my vanilla scent reminded me of Matilda and her doughnuts. I gave him a quick rundown of the previous day's adventures, ending with, 'And now there's been a murder.'

His brow furrowed. 'Who's dead?'

'I don't have any details yet – I just got the call. But I have to head in early. Sorry about that.'

He smiled ruefully. 'I never appreciated how hard it would be to date law enforcement. Getting our schedules to align is harder than solving a Rubik cube blindfolded.'

'Have you ever solved one?' I asked. 'Normally, I mean. Because I'm not sure you need to add the blindfolded part to that sentence.'

'Maybe not. Well, I'm glad I got to see you.' He eyed me up and down. 'You're a treat for sore eyes. You look great.'

I grinned as warmth filled me. 'You do, too.'

'How about after work, you and me, Garden of Eat'n?'

I beamed. 'Can't wait.'

He kissed me again and climbed into his truck. 'Oh, I want you to know that John's settling in well. I'm going to ask him to be my third.'

'Third?' I was surprised and pleased. John clearly knew his shit and evidently he was a first-rate minion, but even so he was leapfrogging a tonne of competent vampires. I knew that was because Connor really appreciated the fact that John had pretty much saved my life.

'Yeah, he'll fill in for Margrave when he isn't available.'

'Thanks for doing that,' I said softly. 'It means a lot to me.' I leaned in for another kiss through his window.

What a great way to start my day. I should have been maudlin because of the murder but I positively bounced into the Nomo's office. I'd seen my mate, and my friend John was being taken care of. This was already a good day, dead person notwithstanding.

Sidnee was already there, so I settled Shadow then she, Fluffy and I went into Gunnar's office. 'What's up, boss?' she asked, plopping into one of the two chairs in front of his massive desk. I took the other chair and we looked at him expectantly.

'Well it's a bit of a messy situation, which is why we aren't already over there.' Gunnar stopped and steepled his fingers.

'What's the situation?' I asked impatiently.

'The murder is at the mine. I'm waiting for Thomas to act as a go-between. As soon as he calls, we'll head over.'

I leaned forward. 'Why? Who's dead?'

Gunnar shook his head. 'We aren't sure. All we know is it's a dwarf ... and he's missing his head.'

Chapter 13

We travelled in silence, lost in our own thoughts. It seemed obvious to me that the missing head pointed directly to Matilda's involvement, but had she killed the dwarf or just taken the head after he'd been killed? Either way, I was sure the dwarves were going to accuse her.

She was the obvious culprit, yet I still had my doubts. I hadn't found anything malicious or threatening about Matilda, and it all seemed just a little too neat, too convenient, for my liking. We had only just learned that she was possibly holding the dwarves' souls hostage… My gut told me that even if she *had* taken the head it was after the dwarf had already died.

Still, I couldn't ignore the possibility that Matilda could be the killer. My next thought was that if she *was* guilty, how the hell would we arrest and hold her? She was, quite literally, a force of nature and no bars would contain her; we'd need some wards, possibly of the deadly variety – and that meant Liv.

I couldn't shake the feeling that something was going on at the mine. A second death made Helmud's seem even more suspicious, but what was the purpose in killing a mine inspector and then a miner? What motive could someone have? My mind continued racing in unhelpful circles until, before I knew it, we were pulling into the car park.

Sidnee tapped me on the shoulder. 'What are you thinking about?'

I shrugged. 'A few things, I guess. If the dwarves insist Matilda did it, how will we arrest her and keep a hold of her?'

'Magic-cancelling cuffs will work on her, the same as anyone else,' Gunnar said. 'If anything, they work too well on an elemental, or so I've been reading. Because an elemental's whole being is magical, they can't wear the cuffs for too long or the consequences can be deadly. If we end up arresting her, we'll need to cuff her and get her into the warded cell quickly. No diversions.'

'You've been doing some reading up?' I asked.

'Sigrid,' he admitted. 'She looked at some book last night after I asked her about hags. It talked about elementals in a general way rather than specifically about hags, but I'm guessing what it says will apply to her.' He patted the cuffs at his hip. 'You both got yours?'

'Got 'em,' Sidnee confirmed.

'Me too,' I chimed in.

'All right then. Let's see who's dead.'

He parked up and we climbed out of the SUV. As we walked over to the mining office, I wasn't sure who we'd meet but I hoped it would be Thomas again because I trusted him. I respected Liv and Calliope, but the trust wasn't quite there yet – they were both deadly and scary. Thomas was deadly but in a human way and somehow that was more familiar.

We opened the door to find all three mine owners waiting. 'Hi ladies,' I greeted Liv and Calliope. 'Good to see you.'

Calliope Galanis's long blue hair was neatly braided; it never seemed to fade – I was fairly positive that the colour was natural because I'd never seen her at the salon. The earthy surroundings at the mine seemed like a direct opposite to her own watery nature, and she was casting her eyes around frequently like she was looking for a way out. This wasn't her happy place. That made two of us.

By contrast, Liv looked totally at ease. Like Calliope, she was wearing a business suit, though hers was a dark colour that seemed to fade into her skin and made the silver streak in her afro pop. She'd painted her lips a deep blood red. Her beauty would have been truly remarkable were it not for the coldness in her eyes when she looked at me; obviously I was still not her favourite person. She was carrying a huge bag; evidently, she was planning on doing some necromancy.

I really needed to get back on her good side; sure, she'd accidentally kidnapped my mum, but my mother wasn't my favourite person and Liv hadn't been in control of her actions. I was working on forgiving and forgetting – both Mum and Liv.

'Besides the dead body,' I started, 'are there any issues at the mine we should be aware of?'

'Is the dead body not enough?' Liv asked drolly.

'Sure – but you have a dead inspector, too. We'll be treating the deaths as connected until we receive evidence to the contrary. So, was there something that someone didn't want Helmud to find?'

Calliope snorted with amusement. 'Someone like the owners? Are we suspects, Bunny?'

'We're just making enquiries, Calliope,' Gunnar said smoothly. 'That's our job.'

'Indeed,' she drawled. 'To my knowledge the mine is operating profitably and well. We have had no issues and there is nothing we need to hide from you – or an inspector. Liv?'

Liv shrugged, 'I'm a silent partner. I don't deal with any day-to-day issues, that's Thomas and Leif's role. If there was a problem, I wouldn't know about it.'

Thomas nodded. 'That's true. Neither Liv nor Calliope come to the mine regularly.'

'And you?'

'I come here every couple of days. Having the boss around at different intervals keeps everyone on their toes. I do the same with my cab company. Keeping an irregular schedule keeps employees honest.'

'And did you know of any issues?'

'None, other than the ones we've discussed,' he said carefully. 'The miners and the hag don't get on, but other than that the mine is doing well. If that's all your questions for now, we'll go to the site of the murder.'

'Sure,' I responded easily. No doubt we'd have more questions once we'd assessed the crime scene.

'Leif will meet us there.' Thomas paused to meet our eyes. 'I know I don't have to caution you about the sticky nature of the dwarven culture in this regard. They aren't going to release the body to the Nomo's office, and I doubt we'll be allowed to take samples from the deceased. If they say no, don't push it. If we act respectfully they *may* allow us to use magic on the body. That's likely the only way that we'll get any answers.'

Liv looked smug; she liked being essential. 'Yes, I could raise the body if the soul remains, which seems likely given dwarven lore.'

I pursed my lips. 'Won't it be tricky to get information from a body with no mouth?'

'That's not the way it works, *rodent*.'

'Can you just *not*?' Gunnar said to her through clenched teeth.

She blinked and some of her bullshit seemed to drain away. 'Right,' she said quietly.

Gunnar didn't look at her as he went on, 'Let's see the body and the crime scene before you start raising the dead.'

'You got it. I'll follow your lead.' Liv's eyes were suddenly downcast. It made me nervous.

Since we were agreed on a course of action, Thomas led us out of the office to collect the safety gear then we went into the rickety lift and down into the mine. My now-familiar surge of anxiety rose as the chains clanked and we started to descend. I squared my shoulders. I had no choice this time: this was work. This was my duty and my fear wouldn't stop me from doing it.

I braced myself. *Once more unto the breach, dear friends,* I thought as the darkness swallowed us whole.

Chapter 14

Thankfully this body wasn't as far away as Helmud's had been. We walked down a shaft from the main entrance and into a branch where a number of dwarves stood guard around the corpse. He was lying on the ground only a few steps from the entrance, facing the aperture as if he'd been trying to escape; he'd have been lying face down – if he'd had a face. The bloody stump of his neck stared at us and the scent of blood overwhelmed me for a moment.

My stomach gave a loud and audible growl. 'Sorry,' I said faintly, my face reddening.

'Skipping meals and eating Connor instead?' Liv sassed. 'I approve.'

My face warmed further.

'Okay, Bunny?' Gunnar was studying me, making sure I wasn't about to go into a blood frenzy.

I forced a smile. 'Totally fine. I guess that slice of bread just didn't cut it this morning.' I stomped on my embarrassment and made myself think about business. I turned to my currently canine friend. 'Fluffy, scent.'

He started to sniff the area as I squatted down to look at the corpse. The dead miner was dressed like all the other dwarves: coveralls, sturdy boots and gloves. His hard hat had been discarded nearby. A small pool of blood had soaked the dirt floor around him where his head should have been: it appeared he'd been killed in situ and the body hadn't been moved. If that was true, this wasn't a staged crime scene.

I took evidence bags from the black bag so I could collect a blood sample but before I could start, Leif appeared. He nodded to the other dwarves, but his gaze lit with fire as he turned towards us. 'Don't you dare!' he snarled at me. He strode over and ripped the bag from my hand. 'The body and all its fluid must remain intact!'

Thomas had said the dwarves had been difficult, but this was a murder. I stared at Leif. 'I understand your culture dictates the entire body must be burned, but surely a drop of blood won't make a difference? Without it, I can't test for drugs or poisons.'

Leif continued glaring at me. 'Alfgar did *not* take drugs.'

'Perhaps not willingly – that's the point of the test. We need to determine if the murderer gave him something.'

He snorted. 'She didn't give him anything, she just cut off his head!'

'She?' Sidnee said quietly.

'The hag!' He waved his arms wildly. 'I don't know why you're here! We know who did this! And now we can get rid of her for good, like we should have done when we first came here.' He slid a reproachful gaze to one of the older dwarves who was standing by the body.

Gunnar kept his voice level. 'There is nothing here to indicate that the murder was carried out by the hag.'

'The head is missing!' Leif roared. 'She has taken so much from us! This will be the last time. Our dead deserve to rest!' His chest was heaving.

'Damn right,' one of the other dwarves grunted.

'And you are?' I asked.

'Delvin Simonson,' he grunted. 'Alfgar's cousin. And now I can't burn him or sing his song.' His voice warbled with emotion. 'It's not right. We should burn *her* and her damned den!'

'We need to recover the heads first so that they may be laid to rest whole,' the elderly dwarf said sagely. His back was bowed, his dark brown beard mottled with grey, and he was leaning on a gnarled stick. He was eyeing Fluffy with concern, as were his companions. Cat people, then.

'And you are?' I asked.

'This is Baldred Simonson, our most honourable and venerated elder,' Delvin explained a shade haughtily.

Baldred patted his hand gently. 'I can introduce myself, son.'

'Alfgar is your nephew?' Sidnee asked.

'Indeed.' Baldred sighed and tugged his dark beard. 'It is a sad day.'

'We're sorry to intrude on your grief,' I offered.

'And yet you do it all the same,' Leif snapped.

'Justice waits for no one,' Gunnar said mildly. 'The killer could be anyone, that's why we must investigate. Now, is there any reason someone would want you to shut down?'

'Yeah,' Leif retorted. 'The hag. She wants us out.'

I grimaced; Leif was a broken record and I didn't think he was right. Matilda had wanted them to stay out of certain areas and she'd seemed more than happy to have some daily doughnuts. She hadn't seemed in a hurry to get rid of the dwarves.

Gunnar sighed. 'Anyone else?'

Leif glared at him. 'We know who did this and we know why. She thinks she can intimidate us into leaving, and with some factions that will work.'

'Some counsel leaving the mine,' Baldred agreed. 'The heads being stolen has stirred up much bad feeling over the last year.'

I frowned. 'The heads being stolen is a recent thing?' Matilda had quite a collection in her cave; if the dwarves were long lived, she couldn't have taken that many skulls in the last year.

Delvin nodded. 'It is wrong! Three have passed and had their heads taken before the proper burning. And now this is four – and it is Alfgar, no less.' He shook his head sadly as he turned to his father. 'We cannot let his soul wander lost.'

Baldred patted his arm again. 'All will be well. We will talk when we are alone.' He looked pointedly at us.

I cleared my throat and tried to return to the matter in hand. 'When I spoke to the hag, she mentioned there was an odd smell around the same time the inspector died. Have you noticed any gas? Has anyone else complained of strange smells?'

Leif's jaw tightened; he obviously didn't want to answer but Baldred jerked his head, telling him to do so. 'There is no poisonous gas in this mine,' he said finally.

I knew nothing about chromite mining, so I couldn't argue. 'But did anyone report a strange smell?'

'Yes, a couple of miners did,' Leif admitted. 'We sent in a testing device but it showed nothing.'

Maybe it had been a coincidence, a weird pocket of something that smelled bad that had since dissipated. Even so, I looked at Thomas, Liv and Calliope. 'We'll need a copy of that report.'

Leif threw up his hands in frustration. 'Why are you wasting our time? It's the *hag*.'

'I'm sorry, Leif, but we have to investigate,' Gunnar said. 'We can't accuse anyone without *evidence*. As well as the report, we'll need a list of all workers in this section at the time of death, as well as anyone else that had access to this area.'

Leif looked to Baldred who nodded, before replying huffily, 'Fine. I'll email you.' He yanked on his long beard angrily.

Since Baldred was being agreeable, maybe I could make one more little push. 'We need to examine the body. The small amount of blood by the missing head suggests it could have been removed immediately after death, but we can't assume that decapitation was the cause of death. The pool of blood is too small and there's no arterial spray. I need to examine the body.'

Delvin grunted, 'Examine it, if you must, but Alfgar stays here under dwarf supervision.'

'Could we take him to a better-lit place like the locker room?'

Delvin shook his head firmly but Baldred countered with a nod. 'Yes,' he said. 'That's acceptable, Leif?'

Leif nodded grimly. 'Yes, Elder Baldred.' He glared at us. 'I'll be right back. Don't touch him until I return.'

'May I take photos before the scene is disturbed?' Sidnee asked.

Baldred nodded again and Sidnee got busy, taking dozens of photos of the body and the cavern in general. She also took some more general shots showing the route to the body and the direction in which the deceased had been walking.

'What do you think?' Gunnar asked me quietly as she worked.

I hesitated. 'I'm not sure yet, but my gut doesn't like the hag for this. I can't put my finger on why. But whether it's her or not, we'll find out who killed Alfgar.'

Gunnar smiled at me with satisfaction. 'Damn right we will.'

Chapter 15

Leif came back with four more dwarves and a stretcher. We backed away as they reverently loaded up the body and carried it away. Another dwarf carefully shovelled the earth that had soaked up the blood into a sack and took that away as well. Sidnee took photos to document their actions.

Liv was smirking at me from the other side of the cavern; of course she was. She'd been a tiny bit nicer during Christmas, but now that the festive season was winding down it seemed that her acerbic self was returning with a vengeance. She was obviously still angry at me for the whole arresting her thing.

I smiled back calmly. I was kind of looking forward to seeing her do her necromantic thing. I crossed my fingers that the dwarves would allow her to raise the dead body, though it felt like a pipe dream at that moment. If the soul really was trapped without the head then the chances were good she'd be able to do it – if they'd let her.

We followed Leif and his helpers to the locker room and they set the stretcher in a space between the rows of lockers. The miners departed, leaving Leif and a couple of other dwarves to oversee the examination.

Fluffy came in quietly. He hadn't indicated that he'd smelled anything unusual, but it was a new place with many strange odours and people; anyway, I didn't think he'd indicate anything was amiss with all the dwarves around. Maybe he'd tell us more later when he was in human form. For now he hung back, sensing that the dwarves were wary of him.

'Leif,' I asked, 'did you know Alfgar well? What was his full name?'

'Of course I knew him well.' He seemed determined to find fault with everything I said. 'I know all of my crew well. His full name was Alfgar Simonson.'

'Thank you.' I gestured for Fluffy to stand at my side as we went over every inch of the body. Sidnee started at the feet and I started at the neck stub. Lucky me.

I quickly found a stray hair just below Alfgar's shoulder blade, plucked it up with my tweezers and went to put it in an evidence bag. 'What are you doing?' Leif protested.

'Collecting evidence!' I was beginning to lose patience. 'What colour was Alfgar's hair?'

'Brown.'

'This hair is red, so it doesn't belong to the body. It is evidence.'

Leif looked shocked. 'No, that can't be.'

I raised my eyebrows. 'What can't be?'

'The h-hag,' he stuttered. 'She doesn't have red hair.'

'No, she doesn't. But it's a single hair and he could have picked it up anywhere during the day. We'll consider it together with the other evidence we obtain. However, we will want to interview any of the workers on the list who have red hair.'

'Red is a very common dwarven hair colour,' Delvin interjected. His own hair was red. 'My father's brown hair is considered rare.'

'Thank you for that insight.' I wanted to groan; naturally red hair would be a dime a dozen here. We wouldn't want it to be too easy, right?

Leif was visibly shaken; he'd been so sure that the hag was guilty because he obviously hated her.

'I've got something,' Sidnee said excitedly and I looked up. 'There's some dirt in his boot treads that doesn't match the mine surface.'

'Let me see that,' Leif insisted.

Sidnee stood back as he squinted at the bottom of Alfgar's boot. Finally he stood back and nodded. 'That dirt is from the tailings site.' My hasty Googling on the way to the mines last time had taught me that 'tailings' was the term given to the waste product of mining. The tailings site was essentially the mine's dump.

'Was Alfgar often there?' Gunnar asked.

Leif looked upset. 'No. There was no reason for him to be. He didn't work the tailings.' As Sidnee scraped the dirt into a bag, he watched with narrowed eyes, but he didn't protest.

Once we'd finished with the front of the body, we asked for Baldred's permission to turn him. He gave it and Leif supervised Gunnar and I as we gently rotated the body.

Although we looked carefully at every inch of Alfgar, Leif wouldn't let us strip him to look for bruising or injection sites, and annoyingly Baldred upheld his objection. We had nothing but a bit of dirt and a single hair; however, they might help the dwarves drop Matilda as a suspect. I wasn't holding my breath, though; Leif seemed fanatical in his hatred of the hag.

He was frowning. 'She could have still set this up. I wouldn't put it past her.'

'Really? You think she has a TV down there and watches all the forensic cop shows?' Sidnee sassed. 'You think she knows about DNA evidence and planted the red hair?'

Leif's face turned purple. I didn't say anything though I did grin at Sidnee's comment.

We finished what little we were allowed to do then Gunnar looked pointedly at Liv. His gaze wasn't friendly; subsumed by evil spirits or not, she was still on his shit list for trying to harm Sigrid. I thought I'd seen a crack in his armour over Christmas when Liv had given him a sincere apology, but now I wasn't so sure.

She took his meaning. 'Leif, I suspect I can raise the body and ask it some salient questions. Would you allow that? I won't destroy anything in the process.'

Baldred nodded before Leif could reply. 'That will be acceptable. It would seem the most expeditious way of finding the murderer.'

Leif frowned darkly. 'You swear that all parts of him will be preserved?'

Unused to being questioned, Liv raised an elegant eyebrow. 'Of course.'

'Father!' Delvin objected vehemently. 'That is out of the question!'

Baldred shot his son a quelling glance before turning back to us. 'Proceed.'

Huh. I really hadn't thought they'd allow it – but why not? Maybe Alfgar could tell us where his head was, and then he could move on to the afterlife.

'I will go and prepare.' Liv sauntered out.

'I have no need to watch this,' Calliope said. She fixed Leif with a hard stare. 'Keep me up to date.'

He grimaced, his default expression. 'Yes, Miss Galanis.'

Calliope waved goodbye to Gunnar, ignored Sidnee and me, then went back to the office that she apparently kept at the mine. Maybe she came here when the stench of the fish plant became too much for her.

'Leif will oversee matters here,' Baldred said, leaning heavily on his cane. 'I will go and speak with our people.'

'I'll stay to oversee things here,' Delvin objected tightly.

'No, no.' Baldred patted his son's hand. 'Leif will do it. I have need of you.'

Reluctantly Delvin offered an arm, which the elderly dwarf took, and the two of them made their way slowly out of the room. Clearly Baldred had no desire to see an animated corpse and I got that, but frankly I was excited at seeing Liv do her thing. I'd only seen one failed attempt and her work with the barrier gems, so this was new.

She came back a few moments later, her hair tied back and her face serene. She set down her heavy bag on the floor next to the body then started pulling out objects; it was clearly a Mary Poppins' bag because no way could an ordinary bag hold so much.

She encircled the stretcher with candles, crystals and herbs then shot us a sharp look. 'Stay back.' She eyed

Fluffy. 'The mutt too.' Fluffy growled at her and she winked cheekily at him. She loved nothing more than getting a reaction.

Liv placed crystals on Alfgar, one on each hand and foot, one on his belly button, others on his chest and above the neck where the forehead should have been – if it hadn't been missing. Next she sprinkled the body with herbs, raised her hands above her head, threw back her head and started to chant.

Her oily magic pulled at me, tangling in my guts and urging me forward with its slimy fingers. Shuddering, I stepped back. Her death magic called to the undead parts of me and I wondered what it would do if I were a full vampire. Liv clearly knew I was different because her magic didn't control me like it should have done.

As the hum of the magic increased, I shook my head to clear it and focused on Liv; I didn't want to miss this. Unfortunately she was speaking in a language I'd never heard; it was probably a dead language because Liv was ancient. I knew she'd been born somewhere in or near Egypt, but every language evolved with time. I doubted even an Egyptian would understand the ancient tongue she was now using.

A hot wind swept through the room, blowing our hair and stirring the skirt of Liv's power suit. She lowered her hands, then raised them again and spoke the only word that I'd understood so far: 'Rise!'

I shuddered and tried not to gape as the headless corpse sat up and swung its legs over the edge of the stretcher.

Fuck me.

Chapter 16

'Speak!' Liv commanded.

I looked at the headless corpse in confusion. The head was gone and the vocal cords sliced through, so how could Alfgar possibly speak?

'Who did this to you?' Liv asked, her forceful voice demanding an answer.

'I did not see. My killer struck me from behind.' A deep booming voice came from Liv's mouth and filled the space. Oh, that was freaky. It sounded *nothing* like her.

If I was freaking out, I dreaded to think what Leif was doing. I looked at him and, sure enough, he looked beyond queasy as he leaned against the wall.

'Where were you killed?' Liv asked.

'The tailings,' came the response.

The blood had pooled around the dwarf where he'd been found – had it all been a set up, then? Was it even *his* blood? Because if not, we were dealing with someone truly sophisticated, and I couldn't help but feel that was *not* Matilda. The hag wouldn't know anything about forensics; she wouldn't know enough about a crime scene to try and fake a pool of blood to make it seem like *that* had been the scene of death.

Everything, even down to the way the body had been positioned as if Algar had been running away, was a set up.

'Why were you at the tailings?' Liv asked.

I nodded approval, impressed that she remembered that Alfgar wasn't supposed to be there.

'I was given a note. If I didn't come to the tailings by 5pm, they would kill my family.'

'Who gave you the note?'

'I don't know. I found it in my locker. But they included a photo of my family and I was afraid for them. I complied.'

Liv addressed us hastily between gritted teeth. 'I can't hold him much longer – it is far more difficult without the body being whole. What other questions do you have?'

'Where is the note now?' I asked urgently. We might get prints. Liv repeated my words.

'Still in my locker. I tossed it back inside.'

'Was anyone else at the tailings site when you arrived?' Gunnar asked and Liv echoed his words.

'I saw someone from a distance. I don't know who it was.'

'Who took your head?' Leif asked urgently.

'Who. Took. Your. Head?' Liv managed; she was panting now.

Poor Alfgar freaked out. 'My head is gone?' His words were a panicked shriek. The body reached up to feel above itself then a bloodcurdling scream ripped out of Liv. We all jumped.

'Did you have any enemies?' Sidnee asked, but Liv didn't repeat the question. Her eyes rolled back into her head and she crumpled to the floor. Alfgar's body also went limp and slumped over. Leif leapt forward to stop it toppling forward and crashing to the ground.

Leif hurriedly arranged the body so it wouldn't slip off the stretcher as I raced to Liv. Gunnar hung back, seemingly unconcerned about the necromancer's faint. As Sidnee and I helped her up, her eyes flared open. There was a flash of annoyance in them when she registered that Gunnar had not come running, and I wondered if the faint had been a feint.

'Did you get your answers?' Liv asked.

'As many as he knew the answer to.' I looked at her admiringly. 'That was brilliant,' I said honestly. It had been totally fascinating and by far the least disgusting thing I'd seen her do. The last time she'd done something, she'd killed a goat.

She waved a limp hand. 'I'll bill you.'

'Of course you will,' Sidnee muttered sourly.

I didn't blame Liv for charging for her time; she wasn't one to do anything out of the goodness of her heart – I wasn't sure she even had one. I just said, 'Thank you.' Liv nodded and took a deep breath. While she recovered, we picked up her supplies and put them carefully in her bag.

Leif returned a few moments later, shoved a broom at me and gestured at the mass of herbs scattered on the floor. Apparently, in his eyes I was an officer of the law *and* a cleaner. I had grown up with cleaners dusting every corner of my parents' mansion and many of them had been far kinder to me than my own mother had been, so I had no issue with taking the broom from him and sweeping like a pro.

After I'd finished, I handed Leif the broom. 'You heard Alfgar. He was killed at the tailings and moved here. That means the blood pooling around him probably wasn't his. Let me take a sample from the blood in the sack so we can know for sure.'

Nostrils flaring, Leif's hands flew to his hips. 'Absolutely not! We cannot risk it. I will not have him denied the afterlife because of your insatiable curiosity! We have done enough, been more than reasonable. It was the hag!'

I studied him. 'You don't really believe that,' I said softly. 'We both know she isn't smart enough, let alone to plant notes in lockers. Talking of lockers, which was Alfgar's?'

Leif reluctantly walked me over to a locker that was closed and locked. He pulled out a cell phone and scrolled through something, presumably to retrieve a master code, then he unlocked the door.

I pulled on a new set of gloves and started bagging the contents. Refreshingly, Leif didn't complain though that may have been due to the fact that there wasn't much in there: Alfgar's street clothing and shoes, a few pictures taped up, toiletries and the threatening note in an envelope with the photo of his family, just as he'd said.

The photo showed a dwarf whom I assumed was Alfgar on the arm of a human red-headed woman with three red-headed children of varying ages. My heart panged for them: they didn't know that their father was dead and I was *not* looking forward to that conversation. I sealed up the note and photo carefully.

When the locker was empty, I turned back to the mardy dwarf next to me. 'What will you do with the body?' I asked nosily.

Leif squinted at me, as though wondering if I would come back and steal it. 'We'll keep it in the freezer until the head is found then we will complete the funeral rites.

Now, I have to inform his family.' He shrank as though the weight of the world were on him.

'We can do that if you wish. It's one of our duties at the Nomo's office,' I offered gently.

He shook his head. 'It's a dwarf matter. It is right that I do it.'

I didn't argue because so far arguing with Leif had gained us absolutely nothing. I needed another way to get his help. 'Do you have any CCTV at the tailings site?' I asked.

'No, because there's nothing valuable there. We take the trucks back to the warehouse at night and lock up our gear. We've never had a need until now.'

'What about the corridor where we found the body? Any cameras?'

He shook his head. 'We usually place cameras where we are actively working. This is an old corridor – we mainly just pass through it.'

The murderer clearly knew the mine well; it was looking more and more like they could be another miner, though I still couldn't rule out Matilda until I'd spoken to her. 'Besides dwarves, who else works in the mine?'

'Plenty of people,' Leif groused. 'We have mixed crews, not all dwarves. We have a few humans, shifters, vamps like you and even a couple of magic users.'

So tonnes of people; this was going to be complicated and I'd be pissing off every group in town by the end of it. Yay. Making friends everywhere I went. 'What can you tell us about his home life? He was worried about his family?'

Leif looked momentarily stumped. 'I don't know what to say. We usually keep our families private.'

'He had a wife? Children?' I'd seen the photo inside the locker so I knew that already, but I wanted to see if Leif did.

He pressed his lips together. 'Alfgar was in a mixed marriage to a human woman, Sarah. And yes, they have three children.'

'Are mixed marriages common?' Sidnee added.

'No.' His face carefully blank, he gave no other explanation.

That piqued my curiosity, especially since Sidnee had experienced discrimination because of her mixed race. 'Did he have trouble because of the mixed marriage? Any bullying of his children?'

Leif folded his arms. 'A dwarf would not do this,' he insisted. 'To remove the head like that ... it is the most heinous of sins.'

'We have to start with the people familiar with the mine. We aren't pointing specifically at the dwarves, but we need to look at everyone. Please answer the question. Did Alfgar face difficulty because of his mixed marriage?'

Leif blew out a breath. 'Yeah, some. No one liked that he married outside of his race. It's not natural.'

'Is there anyone who was particularly vicious about it?'

He dragged his toe on the ground as he considered his options. 'Yeah,' he said finally. 'He reported an altercation with Faran Ashton.'

'Does he work in the mine?'

He nodded.

'What race is he?'

Leif sighed. 'He's a dwarf.' He looked up with fire in his eyes. 'No dwarf would remove another dwarf's head,' he insisted once more. 'They know what it means – the consequences. It's impossible.'

Yet we had a headless dwarf. I wasn't so sure that it *was* impossible.

Chapter 17

It was strange leaving the body behind, but we couldn't do anything about it. If we went all law and order on them, the dwarves would shut down and disappear and we'd get nowhere. Sometimes the human world was much easier than the paranormal one: in the human world law and order was more black or white and applied to everyone; in the supernat world, each faction had its own rules and regulations. It made things messy.

We were headed to the tailings site, hoping to find the real crime scene. Thomas was meeting us there; he'd already been in the wind when we'd finished up with Alfgar.

'Thoughts?' Gunnar asked, once we were back on the road.

'I think a dwarf is definitely involved, although not necessarily the killer,' Sidnee said.

'A miner certainly,' I agreed. 'Leif was pretty vitriolic about the head removal thing, though he seemed certain no dwarf would do it.'

'You'd think a doctor would never kill a patient but it happens,' Sidnee said darkly. 'Shit happens. Life isn't fair.'

I grimaced: she was having another of her downward spirals. I texted Thomas discreetly, letting him know that she needed some TLC. I hoped she'd do the same for me if I was feeling blue.

Gunnar looked in the rearview mirror. 'Reggie,' he asked, deliberately using Fluffy's human name, 'have you got anything?'

I looked over my shoulder at my dog. He cocked his head but didn't indicate anything, nor did he shift to join the discussion. I tried to hide my disappointment. 'What do you think, boss?' I asked Gunnar.

'I'm with Sidnee. I'd be surprised if the hag is involved. She doesn't seem like the message sending type. She'd just kill and be done with it.'

'I agree. However, she could have taken the head after the fact.'

'Indeed,' he grunted.

'This is such a mess.' I sighed. 'We have one hair, a little dirt and a note. Alfgar could have picked up the stupid hair anywhere – hell, it could be one of his wife's. She's a redhead. And he was killed at the tailings pile. How much do you want to bet that Leif has radioed ahead and the dwarves have already found any blood there and taken it?'

Gunnar nodded. 'I'm not fool enough to take that bet. Thomas said he'd meet us though, so we're hustling. Maybe – just maybe – we'll get there before they interfere with our damned crime scene.' He thumped the steering wheel in frustration then pressed the pedal to the metal.

The SUV roared forward. We'd left the paved section and were on a well-used gravel road. We passed a huge truck full of dirt and kept on chugging around the mine, up a hill and then back down to a desolate looking valley. It was just the other side of the mine, but the hill and valley made it more of a journey than if we'd just been able to walk as the crow flies. Thomas's dark-green truck was up ahead, so we pulled in next to him and I climbed out with our trusty black bag in tow.

Thomas looked as prepared as ever with a rucksack slung across both shoulders and a plethora of weapons strapped to him. Despite his deadly nature, he opened Sidnee's car door and held a gentlemanly hand out to her. 'Miss Fletcher,' he greeted her with a soft smile.

She hit him playfully. 'Sidnee,' she cooed.

His smile widened. 'Miss Sidnee.'

She laughed, and I felt a smile tug at my own lips. He was *so* good for her. I tried not to watch as he took her hand and raised it to his lips to brush a kiss against the back of it. If she wasn't swooning, I sure was.

I texted Connor. *I want a kiss on my hand next time you see me. xxx*

The response was immediate. *I'll kiss you wherever you want, as long as I also get to kiss wherever I want. Xx*

My cheeks heated. *Deal! xx*

I slipped my phone back into my pocket and tried to focus on work.

I let my Fluffy out of the car, sure that this was where he would shine. We weren't sure where the murder had taken place and his nose was already full of Alfgar's scent. 'Okay, bud, time to find a murder site. You ready?'

He jumped a little on his front feet and barked. I adjusted his vest since it was skewed and flashed him an approving grin. 'Hunt.' He didn't really need commands because he understood what I wanted, but after our demonstrations at the police academy I thought we should be more professional, if only to maintain the illusion to outsiders that Fluffy was really nothing more than a dog.

He started from where we were, working in an arcing pattern with his nose to the ground. Gunnar and I walked slowly behind him, staying out of his way as he searched for any scent that might indicate where the murder had taken place. Sidnee and Thomas followed, and I noted approvingly that he had slipped a protective arm around her slender waist.

Things were starting to cook between them and I was pleased to see it. She deserved a happy ever after, or at the very least some phenomenal sex and a few orgasms. I'd bet any money that Thomas was an attentive lover; he was a man who missed nothing.

Fluffy let out a bark and wagged his tail excitedly. We were in a flat valley dotted with small hills of gritty dirt and gravel. Everything was an even gunmetal grey mixed with brown; it was ugly and unremarkable to my uneducated eye.

My dog continued to work his way at ground level. I'd thought he was on to something, but now I wasn't so sure; this was a large area and it could take him a while to search it all. I'd need to give him a break in a while – he deserved a snack and some water.

'Thomas,' I asked belatedly, 'are any of these materials going to be bad for Fluffy?' I'd read on my phone about the possibility of toxicity with some types of chromite.

'No, I promise he'll be fine,' he said reassuringly. 'Our mine is checked continually. We've never detected any hexavalent chromium – that's the dangerous kind.

Everything here has been tested, and it's stable and nontoxic.' He waited a beat. 'Though I still wouldn't recommend eating it.'

Sidnee burst out laughing, and Thomas looked faintly pleased. Huh. That was a joke? He was always so stoic that he was difficult to read at times but apparently Sidnee knew him well enough to recognise his joking face, or maybe she'd genuinely found his remark funny. Stan's sense of humour was off, too; I blamed Sigrid and Gunnar.

'No eating. Got it,' I replied, giving a thumbs up.

Fluffy disappeared between two hills of tailings and I moved forward to keep him in my sight. He gave a sharp bark, whirled towards me excitedly and gave me three more clear barks in rapid succession. 'We're up,' I called to the others as I ran towards him.

When I reached him, he was sitting and staring pointedly at a spot on the ground. I patted him. 'Good boy.'

Gunnar took the camera and started taking photographs of the area as I scanned the ground for any obvious clues. The place Fluffy was staring at looked exactly the same as everywhere else and I couldn't see any bloodstains. If Alfgar's head had been removed here, I'd have expected to see something.

I squatted down and used the flashlight on my phone to scan the earth more closely; although the area was lit by bright halogen lamps, they threw odd shadows between the two hills. There was still nothing to be seen, not to my eyes anyway – which gave me an idea.

'Sidnee, can you do a partial shift and look around with your mer vision?' I asked.

She brightened. Her mer eyes could see extremely well in the dark and she had an increased colour spectrum. 'Sure!' She was bouncing on her toes, excited to help in a way only she could.

Before she said anything else, Thomas was reaching into his rucksack and pulling out a bottle of water. She beamed at him. 'Thank you.' With the water close to her, when she smiled again she revealed teeth like a shark's – not unlike the hag's – and her eyes were as black and flat as a great white's.

When Sidnee went mer, her nature changed, too. She leaned into Thomas, her whole body sinuous and sensuous as she sniffed up his neck and gave a soft clicking noise I'd never heard before. Thomas held himself still as the woman he desired above all others wrapped herself around him like a stripper round a pole. She ground up against him and leaned in, then she went on tiptoes and lightly nipped his ear. He inhaled sharply and couldn't hold back a low groan.

Abruptly, Sidnee seemed to remember what she was *supposed* to be doing – and it wasn't taunting poor Thomas. She took a deep breath and, with a visible effort, turned away. His expression was carefully neutral but he couldn't bank the heat in his eyes, and he was definitely staring at her ass when she exaggerated the swing of her hips as she sauntered to the scene of the crime. His breathing was faster, and he took the rucksack off his shoulders to hold casually in front of him. Heh-heh-heh. Yes, things were really starting to cook between them.

Sidnee crouched next to me and stared at the ground. 'There,' she pointed.

I looked around for a stone to mark the spot. 'What is it? Blood?' I asked, seeing nothing.

She sniffed. 'Not blood, not sure what it is.' Her speech was a little muffled. As a mer, she spoke underwater with a series of high-pitched sounds and clicks; her teeth weren't that conducive to English. 'It's green, I think.'

'Hold on.' I retrieved a small spade and an evidence bag. 'I'll let you get it since you can see it.' She nodded then removed my marker and scraped a tiny bit of whatever it was into the bag. 'Anything else?' I asked.

She blinked and her eyes went back to their usual warm brown. 'No, there's nothing. This site is very clean. Too clean,' she added.

'Dammit.'

'Yeah.' she smiled. 'I wonder what that was? It was almost neon green in my mer sight. I've never seen anything like it.'

I shrugged and picked up the bag. 'We'll have to hope the lab can identify it.'

We walked back to Gunnar and Thomas. 'What did you find?' my boss asked.

I looked at Sidnee. It was her explanation to give. 'Not sure,' she admitted. 'Some sort of green substance. There wasn't much and we don't know what it is.'

Gunnar picked up the evidence bag and stared at it. 'I don't see anything but dirt.' He looked at us curiously.

'Sidnee could see it but I can't,' I told him. 'It's only neon green in another spectrum of light that we can't see. We'll have to send it to one of the labs.'

He looked at Sidnee. 'Great work, kid.' She beamed, displaying her perfectly white, human-shaped teeth. Gunnar put the evidence in our black bag and I put the bag in the SUV.

'Are you going home or back to work?' Sidnee asked Thomas as we busied ourselves.

'Home, I think. You want a ride?' His voice was still a little husky, and I wondered what kind of ride he was offering.

She smouldered at him. 'Oh yeah,' she purred at him. 'I definitely do.'

Thanks to my vampire hearing, I heard his muttered, 'Thank God.' I stifled a giggle with a lot of effort.

'Thomas is giving me a ride,' Sidnee said loudly to Gunnar and me.

I grinned. 'Enjoy.'

She winked. 'See you later.' She gave a finger wave and climbed into Thomas's truck. As she slid all the way over to lean up against him, I smirked. She was off shift and I was still on, so I hoped she had fun – but it made me miss Connor even more.

Gunnar and I talked a bit about our case on the way back to town, though there wasn't much to say. I wanted to get a better look at the note, dust it for prints and look at it under the microscope; it was pretty much our only real clue apart from the weird substance Sidnee had found. We had the red hair that we could send to the lab and maybe it would have a follicle attached to get a DNA profile; it wasn't likely, but it was possible.

Once I received the emailed staff list from Leif, I'd have a tonne of miners to interview – including Faran Ashton, the dwarf who'd hated Alfgar because of his choice of a human partner. I also needed another tête-a-tête with our resident hag.

I'd take doughnuts again so that she wouldn't be tempted to take my head.

Chapter 18

Back in the office, I sank into my chair and checked my email. Nothing yet. I grimaced; I supposed it would take time for Leif to put together his list and he probably slept at night. I checked the time. It was approaching my 'lunch' time with Connor at the Garden of Eat'n.

Yep. That took my mind off the murder. My stomach full of butterflies of excitement and anticipation, I studied my reflection in the bathroom mirror. My hair was coming out of its braid and my mascara was slightly smeared. I cleaned up, unfastened the braid and brushed my hair. After a moment's thought, I decided to leave it down; Connor liked it loose and I could plait it again after lunch for work. That would be more professional and it would be out of my face if things got physical.

Grimacing, I plugged my nose and quickly downed a cup of blood, then I petted the animals and told them I'd be back soon. Shadow ignored me as usual. Gunnar had gone home for the night so I put up the sign, set the work phones to divert to my mobile then walked to the diner. Connor liked to pick me up, but it was only a block away and the walk did me good.

I was grateful for the cleats and my warm winter coat; it was snowing hard and there'd been another couple of inches since I'd come back from the mine. No one was about and the night was inky black, the clouds adding another layer of darkness, but the streetlights reflecting off the snow combined with my vampire eyesight meant it was as light as day to me.

Connor was standing outside the diner, watching for me; behind him were Margrave and John. I smiled and waved as I approached. Connor had a professional relationship with Margrave in contrast to the easy friendship he'd shared with his previous second, Juan. In some ways, I felt like Connor was subconsciously punishing Margrave simply for not being Juan.

Margrave looked at me sternly but gave me a nod in greeting. John grinned and waved back at me; he was looking much better since I'd last seen him. He'd been a broken and grieving man but clearly having a job had done wonders for him. People dealt with grief in different ways, and for some people keeping busy was essential. I was grateful that Connor had given him a job, and such an important one too, because I owed John. He'd been through more abuse from the vampire king of Europe than I had but that experience still linked us: a shared past, a shared trauma.

I smiled at Connor, my eyes drinking in the sight of his tousled dark curls and his icy-blue eyes. As I drew closer, he surprised me by reaching out to take my hand and sweeping a courtly bow. He looked up and met my eyes as he lifted my hand to his lips and gently brushed a light kiss across it.

I felt a jolt of desire so strong that I nearly moaned. I pulled him up and pressed against him like Sidnee had done to Thomas and found his mouth with my own; his lips were cool but his mouth was hot and the differing temperatures and the rocketing desire made my mind blank.

The snow swirled around as we kissed in the doorway of the diner. I could have gone on kissing him forever if someone hadn't chosen that moment to exit. 'Well I never,' she harrumphed. 'Excuse me!'

I pulled back and we moved aside so the impatient diner could leave. Obviously a member of the pearl-clutching brigade, she huffed loudly as she went.

'Hey.' I smiled at my mate.

'Hey,' he responded, giving a slow grin that melted my insides all over again.

'We should go inside.'

'We should,' he agreed, but didn't move.

'One more kiss?' I suggested.

'For luck,' he agreed. We found each other again and I moaned into his mouth as his tongue swept against mine in the way that I loved.

Then my stomach rumbled and I pulled back reluctantly. 'Feed me,' I insisted. Connor's eyes darkened and I knew he was thinking something filthy. I hit him lightly. 'Not like that. With food.'

He grinned. 'Your wish is my command, my lady.'

He held open the door and the warmth of the diner hit me like a blast. I looked over his shoulder at his followers. 'Are they eating with us?'

'They're eating, but not with us.'

'What's going on?' I asked, concerned. 'Why two bodyguards?' I looked around to see if there was a threat close by.

Connor laughed. 'Nothing – no more than usual, anyway, John is shadowing Margrave for a week before he officially becomes my third. He knows the ropes but he needs to learn the way *I* do things.'

'Sounds good.'

When we'd sat down, a harried-looking waitress dropped off the menus. 'So are you doing the chicken fried steak or the halibut today?' Connor grinned.

I laughed: I guessed I was a little predictable. 'Hey, in my defence I've been in Sitka. I missed my favourite Garden of Eat'n meals!'

He chuckled and set aside the menu. 'I'm having the chicken fried steak.'

'That's what you *always* have! Let's be brave and choose something new.' I glanced at the menu, determined to eat something different. I could order a beef steak, but I wasn't feeling it; the other options were a chicken sandwich or a half a fried chicken, but one seemed like too little and the other seemed like too much.

The waitress came by with water and asked if we were ready to order. Connor looked at me. 'Are we trying something new?'

I laughed and shook my head. 'Nope.' I looked at the waitress, 'I'll have the chicken fried steak.'

'Make it two,' Connor added.

She left and we laughed together. 'If it ain't broke, don't fix it.' I reached out to take his hands. John and Margrave were sitting behind us. I leaned over the table and whispered to Connor, 'How is he doing?'

Connor raised an eyebrow. 'John?' he whispered back.

'Yeah. Spill the tea,' I said, using one of Sidnee's favourite phrases.

'He's doing fine. It took a while to get his papers done so he could work legally, but he learns fast and he did something similar in England, so it's not a stretch for him. He's a good man and he's eager to prove himself.'

I beamed at my mate. 'I don't have to tell you how much I owe him.'

'You don't – I owe him too, for sending you to me. Don't worry, I'll take care of him.'

'Isn't it his job to take care of you?' I teased.

He gave me the single-shoulder shrug. 'My position requires them but I can take care of myself.'

'I know.' A memory of him coldly cutting throats because I was in danger flashed through my mind. Yes, my mate could take care of himself all right, and me too if the need arose, though I was learning to be dangerous too. We were turning into a power couple. I tried to think of a name for us and burst out laughing as one came to mind.

Connor raised an eyebrow in question.

'I thought of a couples' name for us.'

'Do tell.'

'Connor and Bunny, together become ... Cunny.'

He gave a proper belly laugh. 'Let's hope that doesn't catch on.'

The waitress returned with our Cokes; I drank tea with my lunch at home, but I'd quickly learned not to order it in an American restaurant because you got a sad-sack, flavourless tea bag and often creamer instead of milk. I shuddered at the thought.

'What did you discover at the mine?' Connor asked casually, although his eyes were alight with interest.

Normally I wouldn't have shared details of a case but, as a council member, Connor was *technically* one of my bosses so I filled him in. I told him that I doubted the killer was the hag, but that I couldn't formally rule her out.

He grunted at that last bit, but didn't have time to say anything before the waitress returned with the food. Once she'd gone again, he said, 'It seems complicated. Be careful of the hag.'

I shoved a bite of steak into my mouth covered with potatoes and white gravy. Yum. I waved my fork. 'She should be careful of me. I'm a force of nature, too.'

He grinned. 'That you are. You'll figure it out. You must be happy – you love a good mystery.'

'I do,' I agreed. 'But I feel for his family. He had a human wife and mixed kids and apparently their relationship was a bit of a no-no in dwarven culture. I'm not sure how much support they'll get.' We ate in silence for a few moments. 'Do you think Liv or Calliope would know anything about hags? That they'd share with me, I mean?'

'Maybe. Are they speaking to you yet?' Connor grinned.

'No, not really. But this is work so they have to, right?'

He snorted. 'Calliope still holds a grudge against Homer who's been dead for what – nearly three thousand years!'

I groaned. 'I never thought I'd say this, but I actually think Liv might be the more reasonable of the two.'

'Well, she did come through for you at the mine.'

'Yeah, whereas Calliope just looked bored and annoyed. I'll call Liv when I get back to work. I don't think the Queen of the Dead ever sleeps.'

'I dare you to call her that to her face!'

'Not a chance in hell.'

Connor snickered. 'Wise.'

We finished our meal about the time my lunch hour ended. Connor insisted on walking me back to work, not that I resisted in the slightest. He came in for a minute to check on Fluffy and Shadow and give them both some affection. Shadow pretended to ignore him but then, when Fluffy was getting all the attention, he wound himself around Connor's ankles: he hated to be ignored.

Connor kissed me goodbye, another heated kiss that warmed me in all the right places. 'I'll see you later,' he murmured. 'No matter what time you finish work, you call me.'

'You got something planned for later?' I teased.

'Team-building exercises. We're going to play a communication game.'

'Oh?' I asked, a little breathlessly. 'How's that going to work?'

He kissed me again. 'I'll explain later but just know that you're going to need phrases like, "harder" and "just like that" in your repertoire.'

'I like the sound of the game already.'

'Me too,' he groaned. With one last kiss he left, taking his entourage with him.

'How am I supposed to concentrate now?' I complained to my animal friends.

Once Connor had left, I bit the bullet and called Liv. 'Bunny,' she answered flatly. 'Haven't I done enough for you tonight?'

I ignored that. 'I didn't get a chance to ask you earlier in earshot of the dwarves, but do you know anything about hags?'

'Quite a bit, actually.' She paused for a moment. 'But I'm tired. I'll talk to you tomorrow.' She hung up.

Typical Liv: it was a total power move. She'd work with me – eventually – but it would always be on her terms.

Chapter 19

It was a quiet night, which happened once in a while. After I'd completed all my work, I started doodling on my sticky notes and that triggered an itch in my brain. Two deaths at the mine: what could be the motivation for *both* deaths? They didn't seem linked at first blush. The first victim – *if* he was a victim and that still hadn't been established – was a human, an inspector, not a miner. He'd kept his head. The second victim was a dwarf, a miner and had been found headless. The only thing they had in common was the mine itself. Something was going on there and I needed to work out what.

I decided to check the evidence locker and look through Helmud's belongings. Predictably there was a phone that we didn't know the code for, but there was also a paper diary. I opened it up and flipped to the dates around the murder. There in red pen was *Inspection of Chrome Mine* and a red arrow across several pages, making it clear he would be in the mine for a week.

I frowned. Hayleigh had said he'd arrived a day early, but according to this he'd been aware of the correct date. Why had he come a day earlier than planned. Had he been hoping for some kind of unofficial access? If he suspected something was going on at the mine, there was no note of it.

I flicked through the long book but only one other entry gave me pause. *Wedding Day!* was written in a feminine hand with numerous hearts drawn round it. So he *did* have a fiancée!

I pulled out my phone and dialled Helmud's father but there was no response. I left a quick message requesting a call back then put Helmud's effects away and returned to my desk. I started researching chromite; I knew very little about it and it was time to rectify that. I'd done a quick Google before, but I needed to go deeper.

If someone was trying to send a message, what would that message be? Was it environmental? Mines could be controversial for putting toxins into the environment, but Thomas had said the mine tailings weren't toxic. Was it about money? Almost *everything* was about money, so I pushed that to the top of my list of motivations.

My shift was nearly up and I'd had no email from Leif. Tired and fed up, I toyed with the idea of calling Liv but figured she'd take my head off after having only four hours sleep. I'd call her later when I woke up.

I was yawning when April came in. The bear shifter gave me a warm smile and bustled over to give me a hug. 'Morning, Bunny!'

'Morning, April. How are you doing?'

'Great, thanks.'

'How's Russell?' I asked. Her son Russell had been tangled up with some drugs and unsavoury characters, including Sidnee's slimeball ex, Chris Jubatus.

She gave a bright smile. 'He's doing much better, thank you. He's been talking to me so much more lately.'

'I'm glad to hear it.'

She'd put her son in counselling. He'd gone through some horrible stuff: his friend Skylark had been kidnapped and Russell had felt partially responsible despite the blame not lying at the adolescents' doors. It was promising that he was keen to take responsibility for his actions; he'd even come to the office a few times with his mum and helped her do some filing.

I held up my pile of pink slips and ran through them, as well as doing the rest of the hand-off items; there wasn't much because the night had been painfully slow. Next I rang Connor to let him know I was finishing on time then grabbed my coat and walked out with my cat pram and dog into the dark snowy morning.

The brisk walk did me good, pumping some fresh life into my veins. I was glad to see Connor's truck and the lights on when I got home, and the warmth rolled out when I unlocked the door. He'd even turned on the heating for me. 'Hey,' I called out.

'In here,' he shouted, from the kitchen. I hung up my coat, kicked off my boots and padded into the house. The sun had yet to rise and Connor had lit the kitchen solely with candles. 'Well now,' I said approvingly. 'Isn't this romantic?'

'That's what I was shooting for.'

'Objective achieved,' I confirmed.

'I hope pancakes are okay. I figured we'd had a big lunch.'

I brightened. 'Absolutely. Pancakes are fantastic!'

He'd already made the batter and now that I was home he started frying pancakes like a pro. He knew I preferred them thin like crepes, rather than the thick American-style ones. He made us one each and filled them with fruit, chocolate sauce and cream whilst I fed the animals.

'Yum!' I said happily as he laid the plate before me. The candlelight flickered, casting a soft glow in the room, and I realised that this was the perfect day. Okay, so the headless talking-corpse thing had been a bit grim, but I had a mystery afoot and a date with the most delicious guy ever. How had I got so lucky?

Fluffy and Shadow had taken themselves off for a snooze in the lounge, discreetly giving us some privacy. After we'd eaten, Connor made us another crepe each and we wolfed them down. 'More?' he asked.

I pushed back my plate. 'No, that was perfect. Thanks so much.'

'You're welcome. I love to see your face light up when you eat.' He grinned impishly. 'I love seeing pleasure on your face, however I put it there.'

'Yeah? You got any other ideas on how to put it there?'

His smile widened. 'One or two.' He snagged the can of whipped cream from the kitchen counter. 'Come on. It's time to communicate.'

'Communication *is* important in any relationship,' I agreed primly as I followed him.

Connor paused on the way to switch the TV on for the pets. 'Soundproofing?' I murmured.

'Sometimes we communicate loudly,' he replied with a wink.

I was laughing as he tugged me into our bedroom.

Chapter 20

My phone rang exactly one minute after my alarm went off: Sidnee. She knew my schedule as well as she knew her own.

Still snuggling into Connor, I swiped to answer. 'Hey, Sidnee, what's up?' I yawned into the phone. Shadow clearly had heard me move and padded into the room. The moment he appeared, he started to scream loudly at me; hungry cats were difficult to ignore. 'Just a minute, buddy,' I said to the impatient lynx.

Sidnee laughed. 'I heard that. Give Shadow an ear scritch from me.'

'Will do.' I yawned again. Abruptly I realised why she was calling so early. 'How did things go with you and Thomas?'

'Amazing!' The word burst out like she couldn't contain it anymore. 'Oh my God, he is so good in bed, Bunny. Like ... the best ever.'

Connor rolled out of bed. 'I don't need to hear this,' he murmured as he pressed a kiss to my bare shoulder. Sometimes vampire hearing was a pain in the ass; no phone conversation was ever private. He strolled buck-naked into the bathroom and moments later I heard the shower.

I stifled a grin and focused on Sidnee. 'I am *so* happy for you. So are you and Thomas moving forward?'

'Yes – and I have a plan.'

'Yeah?'

'I'm going to throw a fabulous New Year's Eve party, and we're going to out ourselves as a couple then the whole town will know.'

'Is Thomas okay with that?' I asked cautiously. He often struck me as a private man.

'He is if it's what I want.'

'And is it?'

'You bet! I want to scream from the rooftops that he's mine.'

'Okay. So, a party?'

'Yes!'

I instantly visualised my best friend bouncing on her toes the way she did when she was excited, but I wanted to groan. At Sidnee's last party, I'd made a complete fool of myself. I'd drunk too much and apparently treated the whole town to a table dance, complete with some

karaoke-level singing. But since she was my best friend…
'Sounds great. Do you need help with anything?'

'Yes! What I need for you to do is to show up with your party on and bring Connor. I got the rest.'

Sidnee did love to throw a party and she was great at it. 'That I can do,' I promised. 'Where are you holding it?'

'The hotel. They have the best facilities.' That was where she'd thrown the last one, too.

'Can you get it all ready in three days?' I asked incredulously.

She snickered. 'I've had the idea for a while – about a New Year's Eve party, anyway. I wasn't sure if I'd follow through, but I booked it and started planning while we were in Sitka. I needed something to look forward to.'

I got that; the academy had been tough. Long hours, little-to-no down time, and a rampaging poltergeist. Yeah, a party was just what we deserved, a reason to let our hair down.

I laughed. 'I hear you. I'm excited for it already.'

'Me too!' she said brightly. 'Now, get ready and get your ass into the office. I need some coffee and girl time before the town wakes up and things get crazy.'

I laughed again; things always got crazy. 'I'm getting up,' I promised. 'See you soon.'

If I hurried, Sidnee and I would cross over for a couple of hours. I fed my animals and jumped in the shower, which had been newly vacated by Connor. By the time I was dressed, he'd made us each a hot drink – coffee for him, tea for me – and several rounds of toast.

I held my nose and forced down some blood before wolfing his offerings, then Connor drove us all to the office, stopping to get us more drinks on the way and a takeout cup for Sidnee. He dropped me outside the office and drove off to Kamluck with a promise to see me later.

'Thirsty?' I asked Sidnee as I breezed in.

'You read my mind!' she exclaimed.

I stifled a grin; she had demanded that I get her a cup of joe on the way in so it was hardly surprising that I'd done so.

'Let me dump this crap, then gimme!'

'Any calls yet?' I asked.

'Just one complaint that the snow plough hadn't been down their street. I don't know what they want me to do – arrest the driver?' She rolled her eyes. 'Then nothing would get done.'

'Can you imagine? The whole town would be calling to yell at us.' I could tell she was bursting to tell me about Thomas. 'Well?' I finally asked, waggling my eyebrows.

She grinned. 'Oh my God, Bunny! Why did I wait so long to get with him properly?'

'Better to be sure, isn't it?' I pointed out. 'And to be in a good place yourself.'

She smiled dreamily. 'You're right, and I *am* sure now. I worried at first that it was just a knee-jerk reaction, a rebound thing after Chris, you know? But it wasn't. What we have, it's real. He's so patient with me, so kind.' She licked her lips. 'This feels anti-feminist to say...'

'Hey! This is a judgement-free zone. Say what's in your heart. I don't care what label you want to stick on it.'

'After all I've been through, I feel like he can protect me and I like that. He makes me feel safe.' She made a face. 'And I know I should make myself feel safe, I should be strong enough alone—'

I held up a hand to stop her. 'There is absolutely *nothing* wrong about wanting a strong partner in life, feminist or not.'

She smiled. 'Thanks, Bunny.'

Shadow was stalking around the office flicking a pen around the floor. His game was interrupted by the door opening, flinging the pen across the room. He chased it happily. The newcomer blinked, nonplussed at the sight of the unofficial Nomo cat. I stood up and went to the counter. 'Mayor Finau, how are you this evening?'

Of all the council members, I saw him the least. I still wasn't sure what supernatural creature he was, if any.

'I'm well enough,' he said, but his voice was tight with anger. 'But I do have a crime to report.'

I found the clipboard and a pen so he could fill out a report and pulled out my notepad. 'What happened?'

'Someone has stolen my boat. If we hurry, we can follow him. I have a tracker on it.'

Water chases weren't my wheelhouse. 'Okay, let me call Gunnar. I can't run a boat.' I hurried to my desk to call my boss. The Nomo's boat had recently been fixed after being dented by a pissed-off selkie and it was at our slip at the south harbour.

'What's up?' Gunnar answered his mobile abruptly. The office never rang during our time off unless there was a problem.

'Gunnar, we need you down at the south harbour. Someone has taken Mayor Finau's fishing boat, and we have limited time to track it.'

'Again?' He sighed audibly. 'On my way. Meet you there.'

Again? I studied the mayor. Mafu's nostrils were flared and his chin was up; he was battling his anger, but it was still riding him. 'It's probably too late anyway,' he spat. 'He'll be miles away by now.'

'He?' I questioned, surprised. 'Do you know who took it?'

'Yeah,' he muttered darkly. 'Damn right I do.'

I raised an eyebrow and waited for him to tell me. When he didn't elaborate, I asked, 'Well, who took it?'

'My son-in-law.'

I blinked. Okay, this was weird. Family borrowed stuff from each other all the time, so why was Mafu so upset? 'He took it without your permission?' I asked carefully.

'Damn right he did. That prick!'

'Does he live in Portlock? Will he be returning home?'

Some of Mafu's anger drained away and he gave a long sigh. 'Yeah, the good-for-nothing prick lives here. He'll be back.' He grimaced and rubbed his forehead. 'I'm sorry. I'm not thinking straight. Ring Gunnar, won't you? Stand him down. This is a family matter, not a police one.'

His one-eighty took me completely by surprise but nevertheless I picked up Wilson, the office phone, and rang Gunnar back. He answered instantly. 'Stand down?' he asked, his tone resigned.

'Yup.'

He huffed. 'On my way to the office then, see you shortly.'

Mafu slumped into one of our plastic visitor chairs. I went round the counter and sat next to him. 'What's going on?'

The big man gave a sigh that seemed to deflate him completely. He shook his head. 'Family drama.' He slapped his hands on his thick thighs and stood up again. 'I'm sorry, I shouldn't have wasted your time.'

'That's okay,' I said faintly. 'No harm done.' Plus, he was the mayor. 'If you do need help, let us know,' I offered lamely. He nodded briskly and walked out.

'What was that all about?' I asked Sidnee.

'Beats me. I knew he didn't like his son-in-law, but not enough to press charges.'

Soon afterwards, Gunnar came in the back. 'Where's Mafu?' he asked, scanning the waiting area.

'Umm, he left. He sends apologies,' I told him.

He shook his head with annoyance. 'He does this at least twice a year. Let me guess – it was his son-in-law?'

'Yep,' Sidnee confirmed.

'Twice a year, I tell you, it's his car or his boat or some tool. They fight like cats and dogs.' He looked down at Shadow and Fluffy who were curled up together on the dog bed. 'Or most cats and dogs.'

'So do I write up a report?' I asked.

Gunnar sighed. 'Nope, let this one go.' He grimaced. 'Like all the others. But I *am* going to have words with the mayor because he can't keep doing this. At least this time he changed his mind quickly – sometimes I spend hours following up before he drops it. It has to stop.'

'Okay, no report.' I hesitated a second and Gunnar saw it.

'What?' he asked.

'I'm about to call Liv. She said she knew a lot about hags. Do you want to listen in?'

His face grew ruddier and his lips pressed together. 'I do not. You can take notes for me.'

'Okay, I'll do that.'

Sidnee started to pack up. 'I'll leave you to it. Have a great night.'

'You too!'

She grinned. 'You bet I will!'

I waved my beaming bestie out then waited until Gunnar was in his office before I dialled our resident queen of death.

Chapter 21

Liv answered my call right away. 'Hello, Bunny.' Her voice was flat and unwelcoming.

'Is now a good time?' I asked optimistically.

'I guess. What do you want to know?'

I rolled my eyes. She knew what I wanted to know but she was making me work for it. 'Hags,' I specified.

'I know *that,* Bunny. What do you *specifically* want to know about them?' Her tone was rude.

'Everything, really. I'll tell you what I've learned already, but it's not a whole lot. I know that they're earth elementals and I've seen a demonstration of what that looks like. I know they have metal teeth and nails, and they're immortal.' I paused. 'Ours also has an insane sweet tooth, but I'm not sure if that's specific to Matilda or not. What else is important?'

'Well, if a hag bites or scratches you, you'll get a terrible infection worse than you'd get from your little cat. Hags have nasty bugs on their teeth and nails.' She sniffed. 'I can't imagine living in all that dirt is very hygienic.' She took a breath.

Before she could start again, I asked, 'Is it true that they are immortal? Like, they can't be killed?'

She was silent for a moment. 'What are you contemplating?' she asked guardedly.

'It's not me, it's the dwarves. They want the hag gone, and with the death of one of their own they might be looking for a chance to get rid of her for good. Is that possible?'

'I think it'd be easier to drive her off, but yes. Hags can be killed. It isn't easy, but I've heard it has been done.'

'How?'

I pictured her eyes narrowing because she sounded a little annoyed. 'You use the opposite element.' It felt like she wanted to add a 'well duh' to the end of the sentence.

I ignored that. 'Pretend I'm a new supernatural. What is the opposite element to earth?'

'Well, if the opposite of fire is water, what's left?' she asked, mocking me. She wasn't a teacher, that was for sure.

'Air?'

'You're brighter than I thought.' Deadpan.

I stuck my tongue out at the phone. 'Okay, so killing someone with air? That sounds impossible.'

'It's very difficult,' she agreed. 'You'd almost certainly need an air elemental of equal strength to the hag. An air witch isn't going to do the job.'

'Is there an air elemental in town?'

'I have no idea. They don't announce themselves and you wouldn't recognize one. I doubt the dwarves could, either.'

'What do air elementals look like?'

'Like the wind. They are largely incorporeal – they rarely take a physical form.'

'Oh.'

'Anyway, even if you could see them they'd look odd to you.'

'Odd how?'

I could hear Liv's annoyance. 'Odd, only vaguely humanoid. Imagine a sort of humanish face, long flowing hair, antlers, clawed hands, white eyes made of shiny smoke – sort of iridescent, like a rainbow and an aurora had a baby.'

'Got it, not human or remotely so. But I probably won't ever see one.'

'Exactly.'

I frowned. 'So, how do you know what one looks like?'

This time I swear I heard her eyes roll. 'Obviously,' she started tightly, 'someone has seen one and told someone else.'

I ignored that and her shitty tone. 'Is there anything else you know that would help me understand the hag better?'

'They think like the earth, they aren't going to think like a human. If you can understand rock and dirt supporting all life, then you'll be fine.' She paused. 'I've often thought you're as dumb as a box of rocks, so fingers crossed you'll be a natural.'

I sighed. 'I let you in my home at Christmas,' I pointed out. 'No need to be a total bitch.' The words snapped out of me before I could stop them. Oops.

'You let me into *Connor*'s home,' she corrected, though her voice was a shade softer. 'How's Gunnar?'

'Fine. Happy with Sigrid,' I added pointedly. I decided to refocus on the case; the quicker we were done, the quicker I could stop speaking to the snarky necromancer. 'What's the best way to ask a hag for help?'

She was quiet for a beat. 'I think like most beings, you simply need to find something she wants and trade for it.'

'How do I do that?'

'How would I know? You're the detective. Go detect. I'm hanging up now. I'm busy.' The phone clicked off.

Actually, she'd talked longer than I'd expected. I tucked that away in the win box, despite her hostility.

Maybe I could get answers from Matilda herself with another box of doughnuts. Or, now she was getting them every day, I could find something else she liked: maybe some chocolate? Who didn't love chocolate?

I noticed that Wilson had a flashing light to indicate voicemail. I pressed the button, played the message – and went pale as I listened to it. It was from John: *This is Kamluck Logging, it's an urgent message requesting the presence of Officer Barrington.*

Oh my God – Connor!

Chapter 22

My floppy heart gave two solid beats as I grabbed my phone and dialled my mate. My call went directly to voicemail. Fuckity fuck-fuck.

I collected my coat, the vehicle keys and Fluffy then dashed out of the office, panic riding me. I should have called out to Gunnar and let him know where I was going but instead I just pounded the pavement to the SUV.

As I leapt into the Nomo vehicle, Fluffy jumped in through my open door and settled into the passenger seat, already alert and as worried as me. I fired up the engine, buckling my seatbelt as I tore out of the car park, then I did something I'd never done before: hit the lights and gunned it.

'Please let Connor be safe,' I begged the universe. I hadn't been raised particularly religious, but with everything I'd seen I was willing to believe in a higher power. Heck, with all the spirits I'd seen, it would be hard *not* to believe.

I raced the ten miles to Kamluck faster than I'd ever driven there before and pulled into the car park at the offices, a single wide trailer with faux-wood sides. Connor did his paperwork and met clients there, but mostly he worked outdoors with the men either logging or at the sawmill. He could be anywhere on the site.

Fluffy and I ran up the five metal stairs and flung open the office door. No one was there. Damn it! I scanned for signs of disorder or conflict. There was no blood, no evidence of fighting; both my eyes and my nose said everything was clean and hunky-dory. I looked at Fluffy for confirmation, but he didn't indicate anything unusual.

We went out the back door towards the large warehouse several yards away. It housed an employee breakroom and a showroom for flooring and the fancy treated wood that needed to stay dry. Most regular boards were stored outside under cover.

Both rooms were empty, which was unusual since a lot of Connor's employees were vampires and it was night time. Everyone should have been there hustling.

I yelled, 'Anyone in here?' but the only sounds I heard were my own voice and Fluffy's breathing. My tension rose and I tried to push down my panic. I'd know if Connor was hurt, right? We had a nascent bond so surely I'd know if he wasn't okay?

Fluffy and I raced to the bunkhouse. If John was off-shift he'd be there, and it had been his voice on the message. I pounded on the door, but didn't wait for an answer before yanking it open and shouting, 'John?'

There was a pause, then, 'Bunny?'

'Yeah!' I stepped in, relieved *someone* was around.

John came around the corner pulling on a shirt. 'You got here fast. I was going to meet you at the office.'

'What's wrong?' I asked, panting. 'What's going on?'

'I'm not sure. I was just told to get you here. Apparently it needs to be seen to be believed.'

'Is Connor alright?'

John studied me; my every emotion must have been scrolling across my face because he winced. 'He's fine! I'm sorry, Bunny, I didn't mean to frighten you. Connor's up the hill. His phone died and the snow has driven in rodents that have eaten all his charging cords. He told me to get you here pronto.'

My knees almost gave way in relief as I sent a silent thank you to the universe and waited for John to put his boots on. Now I knew Connor was okay my brain clicked into gear. I pulled out my phone and texted Gunnar to let him know what was going on.

I got a terse response: *Saw you tear out of the office. Checked Wilson, heard the message. I'm right behind you.* It made me grin to hear Gunnar call the office phone Wilson; my whimsy was obviously contagious.

By the time John was ready and we were walking out of the bunkroom, Gunnar was barrelling up the trail. 'Sorry,' I blurted before he could chew me out.

He pulled me into a hug. 'I'd be the same if it was Sigrid. Do we know what's the matter?'

'I'm not sure yet. John says we have to see it.'

'Connor is okay?'

John nodded. 'Yes.'

'Good.' Gunnar looked almost as relieved as I felt. He might like Connor but I knew he was more worried for me. That was an incredible feeling, one I was still getting used to; people genuinely cared about me.

John started walking up the hill towards the sawmill. I expected him to stop there but instead he kept going further than I'd ever been before. Roads and trails criss-crossed the hills. There were some old trees but most of them were replants from almost a century ago, and some were being logged. Connor's skill was apparent; he knew how to manage his resources in an ethical and sustainable way.

We followed a logging road so far that I wondered if we should have brought a vehicle, but John had to have a reason for bringing us on foot. Eventually I heard a low murmuring and we approached a crowd of loggers. Lights had been set up, although I doubted the vampires needed them. I certainly didn't.

As Connor's third, John had some authority and wasn't afraid to use it. 'Move out of the way, Nomo coming through,' he called as we edged through the crowd. The workers parted reluctantly.

On the other side of the gathering Connor, Margrave and a few more of Connor's vampire council were standing around something. Connor sensed me and turned around to meet my gaze. Although his eyes welcomed me, his face was serious but after the scare that I'd had it was just a relief that he was there. I'd been so panicked that seeing him made my legs wobble. I walked up to him, trying to look calm and casual even though I wanted to fly to him and wrap my arms around him.

Then I turned to look at what the crowd was staring at.

There were five poles thrust into the earth in front of one of Connor's huge tree-lifting, stripping and moving machines – I reminded myself to find out their proper name. On each of the poles was a skull. The centre one was still covered in flesh; its hair and beard were brown, and dried blood had darkened the colour around the bottom.

'Alfgar Simonson, I presume,' I said quietly.

The other skulls on the poles looked old; I guessed they'd been free of flesh for some time. But the skulls weren't the only thing of note. Written in the earth below the heads was a message: *Tell the dwarves they can have their heads if they leave the mine. They have 72 hours, then the heads will be destroyed and their dead will never rest.*

So many people were talking at once that it was hard to make out what was being said, but I made out one word that was being repeated by the assembled vampires: 'hag'. Great, now the dwarves *and* the vamps had it in for Matilda.

Gunnar, Connor and I walked away a little and put our heads together. 'When did you find them?' Gunnar asked grimly.

'My team saw them about forty minutes ago.'

'Are they new, or do you think they've been here a while?' I queried.

'New – they appeared after lunch. No one saw anything before that, and no one saw them being put here.'

I looked Connor in the eye. 'What do you think?'

'I think someone is fucking with the dwarves.'

'Gunnar?' I asked.

'I agree with Connor.'

'I don't think this is the hag,' I said slowly. 'When I went to her den, there were no books, no paper, no pens. She had furniture, sure, but nothing to read or write on. Do you know whether the hag has *ever* left a written message?'

Gunnar shook his head. 'Not to my knowledge.'

'Mine either,' Connor agreed, 'But I'm no expert. We'd be better off asking Thomas.'

I rang the hunter. He sounded slightly breathless when he answered and I heard Sidnee giggling in the background. My cheeks flushed as I tried to ignore the thought of what I might have just interrupted. 'Hey Thomas, sorry to bother you but I have a question about the hag.'

'Shoot.'

'Do you know if she can read or write?'

'She definitely can't,' he confirmed. 'The dwarves have tried to get her to sign contracts agreeing to areas they can both use but she refused on the grounds that she couldn't read or understand what they wanted her to sign.'

'Thanks, Thomas, I appreciate your time. You get back to ... whatever you were doing.'

He hung up without responding but not before I'd heard Sidnee giggle some more. Vampire hearing was a curse sometimes.

I looked at the others. 'According to Thomas, she can't read or write. Someone is definitely trying to set her up.'

Chapter 23

Connor sent his workers back to their jobs whilst I pulled out the camera and photographed the scene. Once it was thoroughly documented we pulled on gloves, collected the skulls and secured them. Gunnar had the gruesome honour of collecting Alfgar's head so it could be examined for evidence before being returned to the dwarves.

We knew they would demand it back as soon as they knew about it so we moved quickly; there would be no chance to send it to the lab. Gunnar opened the mouth and checked for anything unusual, any signs of poisoning, but there was nothing. It was the same with the eyes. Finding the head hadn't moved the case any further along, though hopefully it had brought Alfgar closer to the afterlife.

After we'd finished our examination, we put the physical remains in a body bag and collected the poles. The whole process was gruesome. As I packed away the skulls, I noticed some differences that pointed to them not being quite human: they were larger, a bit more pointed at the back, and the eye sockets were bigger than a human's. Were they dwarves?

I turned to Connor. 'Why do you think this ... *message* was placed here? Why not at the mine?'

He scrubbed his hands through his hair. 'I'm not sure. The mine is over this hill. It's a few miles, sure, but whoever is doing this is trying to make it look like it's the hag. She could pass through the earth easily. I think another reason is that more witnesses could add pressure on the dwarves to leave the mine.'

'Why would the vampires care?'

'Some work in the mines,' he explained. 'Working in darkened tunnels is pretty ideal for us.'

Not for me, I thought, shuddering. All that earth pressing down...

Connor continued, 'If the killer keeps targeting miners, there's a chance a vampire could be the next victim.'

'Are you going to order your people out, or put pressure on the dwarves to leave the mine?'

Connor smiled grimly. 'Neither. No one tells me how to look after my people. I'm going to help you find this fucker.'

'How?'

He thought for a moment. 'You have hundreds of miners to interview and only you, Gunnar and Sidnee to do it. How about I organise and coordinate their initial statements? I can ask for alibis for the times of death then I can bundle up a list of all those you three need to look at closer.'

I blinked. 'I could kiss you.' So I did.

He grinned. 'The next couple of days are going to be real busy, but another sleepover soon?'

'Yes, please. And Sidnee is throwing a New Year's Eve party, so that will be fun.'

'Jeans and shirt, or suited and booted?'

'The latter, I reckon.'

'Got it.' He leaned in and gave me a long kiss that made my toes curl. 'I'll start with the vampires I know, but fire me the list from Leif when it lands.'

'Thanks, Connor. I appreciate you helping us.'

He winked. 'Only doing my civic duty.'

'Well, I'll reward you in a very un-civic way.' I winked back.

'I look forward to it.'

I bent to pick up the black bag but Connor beat me, shouldered it and walked me back to the SUV. He put it in the back, opened the door for Fluffy, then eased me against the driver's door and kissed me breathless. 'Are you going to dance on the tables at Sidnee's New Year's party?' he murmured, his hot breath tickling the shell of my ear. 'Those are some of my favourite memories.'

My cheeks warmed. 'I was very drunk last time.'

He ran a light touch down my arm. 'Is that what it'll take to see those hypnotising hips again? Because I can get you some 'shine real easy.'

I laughed. 'I can take requests when we are alone, but I think drinking you under the table would be a lot more fun if I was under it with you.'

His eyes darkened. 'Most definitely.'

'I think I'll stick with bad karaoke and only a few drinks at this party. We'll let the others dance on the tables.'

He sneaked in one more kiss that I didn't resist in the slightest, then I slipped into the driver's seat and headed back to the office. I had a shit load to do; I didn't care that it was the middle of the night, I needed to get things moving.

As I drove, I rang Leif and chased up the list.

'You woke me,' he groused.

'Well now you're awake, you can send me the list of all the miners that you promised me.'

'I'll get it to you first thing tomorrow.'

'You'll get it to me now, and you'll contact them to tell them Connor Mackenzie and his team will be talking to them individually. Tell them to comply with his request for information and/or interviews.'

'This is nothing to do with him,' Leif hissed. 'It's a dwarf matter.'

'He gets kind of involved when people put heads on his lands. Alfgar's head was placed on a pole there.'

There was a long beat of silence. 'You have his head?' he said finally.

'Yes.'

'Where?'

'I'm taking it to the office. When you get me that list, you can come and get it.' Okay, I was playing hard ball, but technically it wasn't blackmail, right?

Leif hung up and moments later my phone buzzed with an email from him. I pulled over to open it: it was a list of names, addresses and phone numbers. That asshat had been sitting on it this whole time! He was such a jobsworth.

I stifled my irritation and sent the file on to Connor so he and his team could start work. I made a note in the file that I would deal with Faran Ashton myself since I knew he had a beef with Alfgar.

When I rang him, he answered with a decidedly grumpy, 'Hello?'

Just once I wanted one of the dwarves to model the chirpier behaviour of the dwarves from Snow White. Would it kill them to emulate Happy or Doc once in a while? 'Officer Bunny Barrington here, from the Nomo's office. We need you to come in for an interview.'

'Now? I just got in from my shift. I'm ready for bed.'

'Now. Come in your pyjamas, if you want.'

There was an incredulous silence. 'I'll be there in thirty,' he said finally and hung up.

Finally feeling like things were cooking, I slid my phone into my pocket and roared back to town.

Chapter 24

Back at the office, Wilson was flashing again. There was a message from Gunnar: *Caught a fender bender. Be back in a few.* I hoped no one had been hurt in the traffic collision.

'Shadow,' I called. 'We're home!' Fluffy and I went into the office to look for the sulky lynx. 'Shadow?' I called again then frowned at my dog. 'Help me find him?'

Fluffy put his nose to the floor and sniffed around, finally leading us back to Gunnar's office. I flipped on the lights and started searching. Besides Gunnar's massive desk and chair, were some file cabinets and a small round table with chairs. I checked them all.

Just as I was about to leave, I heard a loud raspy purr: Shadow *was* in the office. Uh-oh. He was lying on an empty tinfoil wrapper under the desk. He had discovered Gunnar's ham sandwich, which my boss must have abandoned when he rushed out of the office to join me at Kamluck.

I winced. 'Shadow, did you eat Gunnar's lunch?' He purred. Oh boy. 'Your funeral,' I muttered. Sigrid's food was sacred to Gunnar and I did *not* want to be in Shadow's paws when my boss found out what he'd done.

The bell on the front door rang; it wasn't Gunnar because he'd have come in the back. I went through to the front of the office and called out, 'Hello?'

'Hi.' A beautiful red-headed woman was standing there. She was small, not much taller than five feet, and her eyes were red-rimmed. I recognised her instantly from the photograph in the threatening note: Alfgar's wife. 'I'm Alana Simonson,' she said.

I softened my eyes and voice. 'Nice to meet you, Alana. I'm really sorry for your loss.'

'Thank you. The children are devastated – we all are.' She closed her eyes. 'Leif said you've ... located his head.'

'Yes,' I confirmed gently.

'I'd like to take it. We'll burn him later tonight, and then he'll...' She started to sob. 'He'll be free,' she managed.

'Of course,' I said. I hesitated then added, 'I know this is a difficult time, but I wondered if we could talk a little first?' I waited until she nodded then asked, 'Did Alfgar have any enemies?'

She shook her head. 'Al was such a kind, honest guy – he'd do anything for anyone. If something was wrong, he was always the first to volunteer to fix it. Honestly, he was salt of the earth.' Her bottom lip wobbled again as she tried to hold her shit together. 'I don't know how I'm going to live without him, raise our children without him.' She pressed the heels of her hands to her eyes. 'This is a nightmare.'

'I'm sorry,' I repeated uselessly. 'We're working hard to find out who did this to him.'

'We all know who did this to him.' She sounded rather bemused that I hadn't been let in on the secret. 'The hag,' she whispered, looking around in fear as if Matilda was going to melt out of the walls at the mention of her name.

I resisted the urge to tell her you had to say Matilda's name *three* times to summon her. Not everyone valued knowledge the way that I did. 'Have you ever spoken to her?' I asked.

Alana shuddered, 'Goodness, no.'

'Did Alfgar?'

'Absolutely not – he was petrified of her. Rightly so, it seems!'

'Did he talk about anyone being ... unkind about you?'

She blinked wide eyes. 'About me? Why would anyone be unkind about me?'

'You're not a dwarf,' I murmured.

'No, but I'm short like one! That's what attracted Al to me in the first place – that and my name. My parents call me Al, too – Al and Al, together forever.' Her voice hitched. 'We named all our children Al as well. Alexander, Ally, and Alistair.' She rubbed her chest like her heart hurt; I suspected that it did.

What was becoming clear was that Alfgar hadn't told his wife about the prejudice he'd faced from being in a mixed marriage; he'd been protecting her from reality, a reality I was about to dive into with Faran Ashton. Now I'd met Alana, I found I was quite ready to go toe-to-toe with the twat.

'Could I have Al now?' she pleaded. 'We'd like to burn him tonight,' she repeated.

'Of course.' I rose, retrieved the body-bag and passed it to her.

'Thank you,' she said, her voice barely audible, then she turned and walked away carrying her husband's head.

As she left, Gunnar swept in. 'Everything okay with the fender bender?' I asked.

'Yeah, just a little damage. No one was hurt.' He seemed in a good mood, which was great because I was about to ruin that.

'Cool. Er ... Shadow ate your lunch.'

Gunnar glared at the cat who was now sitting casually on Fluffy's bed, licking his paws. 'That little monster! This isn't the first time.'

'It's not?'

'No, he got in the habit while you were at the academy. I had to start locking everything up. I must have left too fast and didn't think about it.' He paused. 'I'm giving that cat a job. He owes me.'

'He does,' I agreed readily. 'Totally. He'll make it up to you.'

Gunnar looked at Shadow and sighed. 'He's a pain in the ass.' He turned to me, 'Anything to report?'

'A lot, actually.' I filled him in on Leif's email, Connor's plan and my brief meeting with Alana. 'Faran Ashton is due in any minute now.'

'Good.' Gunnar banged his hand down on the counter, making me jump. 'I hate bullies,' he growled. 'I'll sit in for that one.'

'No problem. I'll set things up.'

I hustled into the interview room, prepared the recording equipment and placed some water on the table together with three plastic cups. I wasn't a fan of bullies myself; I'd had my fair share of them growing up. Ignoring them, like my mum had advised me, had rarely put an end to the torment but Mum had never been willing – or able

– to intercede on my behalf. And now it was too late for any intercessions on Alfgar's behalf.

Yes, I was ready to talk to Faran Ashton.

Chapter 25

Ashton glared across the metal table at Gunnar and me. He'd turned up in his pyjamas: either it was sheer laziness on his part or it was a power move to show he wasn't taking us seriously.

'Thank you for coming in,' I said pleasantly. Gunnar was letting me take the lead; he was mostly there to observe and intimidate.

'You didn't give me a choice,' Faran bit out.

I smiled. 'I didn't, did I? We're here today to discuss the murder of Alfgar Simonson.'

He stared blankly. 'What is there to discuss? The hag killed him.'

'That is not a foregone conclusion,' Gunnar rumbled.

'Well, she's the one that keeps taking heads! And Alfgar's head was removed. Seems a pretty obvious conclusion to me!'

'The most obvious answer isn't always the right one,' I stated.

Faran snorted. 'No, it usually *is*, that's why there's a name for it – Occam's razor. Your education was lacking.'

I smiled. 'I am familiar with Occam's Razor, and my education was excellent. I have a degree in philosophy from a prestigious university in the UK. But beyond that, do you know what else I have?'

He didn't answer.

'I have this badge,' I tapped it. 'And that means you're the one answering my questions.' I paused a beat to let that sink in. 'How well did you know Alfgar?'

'Not well,' Faran admitted grudgingly. 'We were on different shifts. We crossed paths in the locker room is all.'

'Tell me about your altercation.'

'Which one?'

'Did you have so many altercations with the deceased that you don't know the one that I'm referring to?' I asked mildly. He shifted but didn't answer. 'You had an issue with him having a human wife, didn't you?' I persisted.

'Of course I did. Any self-respecting dwarf would. He was polluting the bloodline. Disgusting.' He sneered. 'Dwarf purity is sacrosanct. I'm not the only one that thinks that way, far from it. Alfgar was the aberration, not me. Baldred is too soft, insisting that love conquers all – including species divide.' He snorted. 'Things will be different when he's gone.' He pounded a finger on the desk. 'Mark my words.'

'Marked,' I said dryly. I was less interested in dwarven politics and more focused on my victim. 'When Alfgar was murdered, what were you doing?'

'Sleeping.'

'Any witnesses to that fact?'

'No, I live alone.'

I stifled the urge to point out that he couldn't even secure a *human* wife. 'You've got red hair,' I said instead.

He did a sarcastic slow clap. 'Congratulations on your powers of observations.'

I bit back a retort; my powers of observation were top drawer. 'A red hair was found on Alfgar's body.'

'So?' he sneered. 'He probably picked it up from his human bitch.'

'His what?' Gunnar growled.

Faran swallowed hard and shifted in his chair, but he didn't dare repeat himself in the face of Gunnar's glower.

'Can we have some of your hair?' I asked. 'To cross-reference it with the one we found?'

Faran folded his arms. 'Not without a warrant.'

Interesting. 'It behoves you to comply with this investigation,' I said.

'This "investigation" is a farce. The hag is behind the murders. You're working with the mine owners to cover it up, to force us to stay in the Chrome Mine when there's a deadly demon stalking us! We all know the truth!'

Matilda had intimidated me a little, yes, but I really didn't see her being a deadly demon; she'd actually seemed quite nice. A bit scary, perhaps, but nice.

'The only thing we're working on is finding the truth,' Gunnar asserted. He shot Faran a hard look. 'And you better believe we'll find it.'

The dwarf stood up. 'We're done here.' He wasn't under arrest, so there wasn't much we could do but watch him walk away.

'He's a keeper,' I said sarcastically.

'Not the most pleasant of fellows,' Gunnar agreed.

'He's got a chip on his shoulder big enough to dive off.'

Gunnar chuckled. 'That he does. Now, what are we going to do about my lack of lunch?'

'Go to the diner?' I suggested. The Garden of Eat'n catered to a paranormal town with a mix of nocturnal and diurnal supernaturals so it was open twenty-four hours a day, seven days a week – though it *had* closed on Christmas Day.

Gunnar considered the proposal and dismissed it. He picked up his phone. 'Hey, Sig,' he said warmly when his wife answered. 'The damned cat did it again.'

I heard her laughter and her loving response. 'I'll bring something over now.'

'And something for Bunny?'

'You got it. See you soon, BamBam.' They rang off.

'I'm surprised she's still up,' I commented.

'She tends to keep to nocturnal if I am so we can spend more time together. She only goes diurnal if the office needs more cover. It's been great having April because Sig and I have seen so much more of each other.'

I smiled. 'That's lovely. April was a great hire. She doesn't get intimidated by anyone.'

He grinned. 'No she doesn't!'

'I'll go type up some notes on our interview.'

'You do that. Sig won't be long.' Gunnar's tummy rumbled. 'Luckily for that greedy feline,' he groused.

He was right: it wasn't long before Sigrid bustled in with an oven dish filled with hot pasta and a happy Loki at her heels. The aroma made my mouth water. 'I love you,' I blurted out, making her laugh.

The hearth witch gathered me into her arms, 'And I you, Bunny Rabbit.' I let the nickname slide since she was bringing me food.

Loki said hi to Fluffy and Shadow and then started sniffing around the office. I warmed some blood and chugged it, looking forward to Sigrid's food. Gunnar found some bowls and we sat together, eating at our desks. We were actually way past lunchtime and had probably strolled right into dinner, but either way the pasta hit the spot.

We were all happily eating when Loki cocked his leg and peed on the leg of Sidnee's desk. 'Loki!' Sigrid chastened.

'That's why you're not allowed to come to the office,' Gunnar said to Loki. 'You're a bad dog. Why can't you be more like Fluffy?'

Fluffy looked pleased while Loki, totally unperturbed by his telling-off, chased his tail. Sigrid sighed, stopped eating and cleared up the puddle. 'Let's not mention this to Sidnee,' Gunnar suggested. 'She can be funny about germs.'

I grinned and mimed zipping my lips shut. Sigrid washed her hands and joined us again. 'How's Stan?' I asked as I wolfed down a huge mouthful.

She beamed. 'He's really doing well. He's even been on a few dates.'

'He has?' That was welcome news. Stan had held a torch for me for a while and it had felt awkward when I had firmly friend-zoned him. Even so, I hadn't missed the occasional lingering glance he'd sent my way, or the way his touch lasted a beat too long. If he was moving on from me, I was all for it. 'With whom?' I asked.

'With Anissa – you know, the shaman who helped us all when we were cursed by...' Sigrid trailed off, not wanting to finish the sentence by saying Liv.

Gunnar's expression darkened. 'Anissa!' I interrupted hastily. 'Whoa! That's lovely. I know she hasn't been with the father of her baby much beyond the conception, so he's not in the picture. But is Stan going to be okay stepping up to that?'

Stan often seemed like the immature baby brother I'd never wanted. I knew there was far more to him than that – you didn't get to be the leader of a faction like the shifters by being childish – and yet I couldn't quite see him taking on the role of stepdad.

'One step at a time!' Sigrid chastened me. 'They're enjoying each other. That might be all it is.' She paused and a smile crossed her face. 'But I don't think so!'

'They're well-matched,' Gunnar grunted. 'And with her magical skills, she'd be an asset to the shifters whether she can shift or not.'

'Is that a problem for them?' I asked, thinking of Faran and his insular thinking.

'It can be,' Gunnar conceded. 'But Stan will deal with it.' That note of pride in his voice always made me swell when it was directed at me, but now I felt a twinge of jealousy. Being an only child I'd never quite mastered the art of sharing, but I was determined to learn. Portlock Bunny was a far better Bunny than London Bunny had ever been, and I hadn't finished growing yet. Not by a long shot.

Chapter 26

Sidnee burst into the office with Thomas behind her then paused. 'Hey, no fair! I smell Sigrid's cooking!'

I laughed. 'You snooze, you lose!' When she shot me a faux glare, I conceded, 'There's some left in the kitchen.' She ran off.

Thomas looked amused. 'I've been abandoned for food.'

'Not just for any food,' I said. '*Sigrid*'s food.'

He nodded. 'Yeah, that's fair.'

I grinned. 'It's pasta. Just consider that Sidnee is carb loading for some more ... exercise later.' I winked. I paused and my smile faded. 'You're good for her, you know.'

His lips tipped up. 'I hope so. *She*'s good for *me*.'

'Good.' I felt a little awkward talking about their love life, so I changed the topic back to something I knew and adored: work. 'There's something weird going on at the mine, Thomas.' Even though he was one of the owners, I totally trusted him. 'The dwarves are all terrified of the hag, and someone is using Alfgar's death to point the finger at her. I'm thinking someone wants you to abandon the mine.'

He frowned. 'The mine has been in existence for over a century. Why now?'

I shrugged. 'A competitor, maybe? Has anyone offered to buy it from you recently?'

His frown deepened. 'No, nothing like that. Not as far as I know, anyway.'

Sidnee came back in holding a plate of pasta for Thomas. 'You *have* to try this.' She looked around. 'Where's Sig?'

I squelched down a grimace. 'She's in Gunnar's office, but honestly ... there have been noises. Don't go in.'

'Eww!' Sidnee covered her eyes. 'If they are having sex in his office, I am never going in there again!'

I laughed. 'Maybe not sex, maybe just some frottage,' I suggested, crossing my fingers.

Sidnee glared at me. 'These are my adoptive parents you're talking about. It's gross!'

I shrugged. 'I think it's kind of nice. I hope Connor and I still want to have desk sex when I'm their age.' I said *I* rather than *we*, because Connor was already goodness knew how old and he was definitely still game for desk sex.

'We were not having desk sex!' Sigrid blurted as she walked in looking scandalised. Her face reddened. 'I was just giving Gunnar a massage. His shoulders are super tight and I had to really put my weight into getting the knots out. That's why he was groaning!'

'Oh, thank God,' Sidnee burst out and we all laughed.

Sigrid went into the kitchen to get her dishes and Gunnar came out, ostentatiously rolling his shoulders. I slid a glance at Thomas and caught the small smile playing on his lips. We exchanged knowing glances. Sigrid and Gunnar had totally had office sex; it hadn't just been Gunnar's groans I'd heard. Damned vampire hearing.

I pushed down my snicker. 'Right, that's it. I'm tired. I'm clocking off. I'll be in early though,' I promised Sidnee.

'We'll give you a lift home,' Sigrid offered.

'Thanks, that would be great.'

We loaded up until the car was stuffed with humans and animals. The atmosphere was light and friendly and I realised I'd missed Sigrid. 'Sig,' I said quickly before I could change my mind. 'Coffee date soon?'

'Absolutely, Bunny.' She smiled. 'I'd love that. Now hop out, dear and we'll watch you until you're all safe and sound in your house.' I loved that small act of caring; I knew she'd see me safe and it was a lovely feeling.

I hopped out as instructed and made my way inside. No lights on, no heating on, no Connor's truck outside. I was surprised by how disappointed I felt but I was really tired; it would do me good to fall into bed without some fooling around. Even so... I blew out a breath. I had really wanted to fall asleep in his arms.

I bustled around feeding the animals and letting them out. I put the heating on for a couple of hours, made myself a cup of tea and phoned Connor. He didn't answer and I sighed; he must be busy.

I sat nursing my tea on the sofa next to Fluffy. 'Hey,' I said softly. 'You want to try and be Reggie for a bit?'

After a beat he shifted and the young man was sitting on the sofa with me. 'You want a brew?' I asked.

'That would be great.'

He followed me into the kitchen. I made him a cup of tea and put some biscuits on a plate because who didn't want those with their brew? We settled back on the sofa. It was still a little cool in the house so I grabbed a couple of blankets and put one over him. I caught his startled expression before he wiped it off his face; he wasn't used to being cared for.

I longed to dig into his story, to find out more about the man living in my home – albeit in dog form – but I knew that if I probed he'd retreat into Fluffy quicker than a wolf could howl. Work was a safe topic.

'The head thing was gross, huh?' I said. Not my best conversation opener, but at least it was relevant.

'Totally,' he agreed. 'The other skulls were old and smelled like bleach.'

'They'd been cleaned recently?'

'Yeah.'

I frowned and cast my mind back to Matilda's den. No bottles of bleach had been lying around, and there was no sign of running water. I doubted she knew what bleach was, let alone how to use it. 'Another thing to point away from the hag, then.'

Reggie nodded. 'Someone's trying to set her up.'

'They're not doing a very good job of it,' I huffed. 'I'm all-but certain the hag can't read, but I'll test her on it next time I see her. Did you catch any other interesting scents?'

He shook his head. 'With the vampires trampling all over the scene, I couldn't catch anything. Whatever had been there was gone. All I could smell was human and vampire – and decapitated dwarf head.'

I sighed. 'Bummer. At least Alfgar can be laid to rest now, so that's something.'

My phone lit up as Connor called. I looked at Reggie and he grinned. 'Take it.'

'Okay. You maybe want a shower or something while I'm chatting to him?'

'You trying to tell me that I smell?' he joked.

I was trying to give him more time in his human form, more time to remember who or what he really was. 'No! I just thought you might like one. A hot shower is one of my favourite things.'

He hesitated for a beat before nodding slowly. 'Okay.'

'Grab a fresh towel from the cupboard. You know how to work the taps?' He nodded and disappeared off.

I swiped to answer the phone. 'Hey!'

'Hi, Doe. Sorry I missed you. I'm already wading through dwarves.'

'That doesn't sound comfy!'

'Not at all. They're a prickly bunch, though by all accounts Alfgar wasn't.'

'Yeah, he seems like he wasn't the average dwarf. I'm wondering if that was part of the reason he was targeted.' I thought of Faran and his vitriol. 'He had a human wife.'

'There's been plenty of commentary on that.'

'You going to head over to mine later?' I asked hopefully.

'Sorry, Bunny, I'd better stay and supervise the interviews. We have a whole military operation going on here.'

I shuddered. 'Ugh, don't say that. It reminds me of the MIB.'

'Not all MIB are evil.'

'No, not all of them,' I conceded. 'Just a subset that are intent on kidnapping and destroying us and every other supernat on the planet.'

In my mind's eye, I could almost see Connor's shrug. 'There are bigots in every walk of life determined to destroy anything different from themselves.'

'Yes, but how do you defeat them?' I felt deflated. 'At times it feels like bigotry is everywhere. I mean those MIB guys were even on Sitka.'

'It's not prevalent, it's just that those types of people shout the loudest. Most people in this world want to live and let live. You start small, focus on your community. You educate, you raise awareness and, if you can, you keep standing up for what is right.'

'How did you get to be so wise?' I teased.

'I've lived through some interesting times,' he admitted.

'"May you live in interesting times" is actually a curse, isn't it?'

'It certainly feels like it at times, but afterwards you know that those challenges we face actually define us and make us stronger than ever. Dark times just mean that the light is coming. And it always comes, as sure as the sun.'

'The miners are having dark times,' I said. 'And the hag certainly is. Someone is targeting her through the mine. Does she have any natural enemies besides air elementals?'

'Not as far as I know. She keeps herself to herself. I've only ever seen her once, and that was from a distance.'

I gave Connor a brief rundown of Liv's information, albeit I wasn't confident that it was a hundred percent true. Before he could reply, I heard John in the background saying, 'The next interviewee is ready in room five.'

Connor sighed. 'I have to go. We're trying to get through as many as we can by this evening, prioritising the interviews around the miners' shifts.'

I closed my eyes. He was working around the clock to get this done for me, and he was already behind on his own work because he'd visited me at Sitka. 'I love you.' The words spilled directly from my heart.

'And I you, Bunny Barrington. Sleep well, Doe. Dream of me.'

We hung up and I sulked over a fresh cup of tea. The shower had finished long ago but I didn't want to intrude. I was just setting the cup down when Fluffy padded out of the bathroom looking clean and shiny. I tried to keep the disappointment off my face but Fluffy's low whimper made me realise I had failed.

'It's okay,' I said softly. 'It'll take time. And that's okay. I'm just... I'm here for you, okay?'

He jumped up next to me, laid his heavy head on my lap and looked up at me with doleful eyes. I stroked his head gently and let the movement soothe me, too.

He'd be okay one day. He had to be.

Chapter 27

I had fallen asleep on the sofa cuddled up with Fluffy when the blare of my phone jolted me awake. For a moment, I was utterly disorientated. Even with the shutters down, it was clearly daylight outside. I reached blearily for the phone and checked the time. I'd had four hours of sleep. Ugh.

It was the office. 'Sorry to wake you,' Sidnee said apologetically. 'But I could do with Fluffy's nose. There's been another murder.'

The last vestiges of sleep were wiped from me in an instant. 'Another murder? At the mine?' I asked.

'Where else?' She sighed. 'I'll pick you and Fluffy up in ten. We can let Gunnar sleep a little longer while we deal with it.'

'All right. See you soon.'

I fed the animals and ran around like a mad woman chucking on clothes. I brushed my hair and teeth and we were just about ready when Sidnee motored up in the

Nomo SUV. 'You'll have to stay here,' I said to Shadow. He hissed at me. I ignored him and put Fluffy's Nomo vest on him.

I opened the front door and Shadow pelted out. He stood by the Nomo car and yowled loudly and pointedly until Sidnee opened the door. I felt better about that: at least the half-grown lynx kitten was bossing me *and* Sidnee around.

Shadow had his own plastic crate, so when I put Fluffy in the car I pointedly opened its door. Evidently Shadow was just happy for a road trip because he climbed in. I closed the metal mesh door and he settled down like he was fully trained and not a cheeky little beast with a mind of his own.

'Thomas will meet us there,' Sidnee said as I buckled up. I was grateful for that because he had a better relationship with the dwarves than I did.

Finally ready, we headed to the Chrome Mine. It had warmed up and was raining lightly so the snow was turning to slush and ice in places. It was a mess, but luckily the roads had been cleared after the last snowfall.

Sidnee pulled into the mine and we went up to the office. Thomas and Leif were there, both stern-faced and serious as they should have been with a dead dwarf on their hands. Thomas pulled us aside. 'Look ladies, things are tense and they don't want you here.'

'We're the law Thomas, we have to investigate,' I insisted.

'I know, but stay on your toes. The dwarves are sure the hag is behind this and they aren't going to listen to anything else. Just ... tread carefully.' He looked at Sidnee. 'Both of you.'

He looked worried, and since Thomas generally appeared unperturbed I felt nervous. Maybe we should have called Gunnar. 'Should I call backup?' I asked.

Thomas shook his head. 'At this point I think more outsiders will make it worse.'

'I need to speak to Matilda again.'

'I figured. Let me find a location outside the mine. She won't be welcome inside it.'

'Yeah, sure. Thanks.'

Thomas signalled that we were ready and Leif led us to the locker room. We picked up hard hats and headed to the lift. This time, the murder victim's body was deep in an active working area and we passed miners who glared at me, even yelling obscenities at the Nomo's office and the hag. Leif stopped one aggressive dwarf that approached me with his pickaxe, but he was more threatening than serious.

I would have just flashed my teeth if they'd cooperated, but they didn't. I felt in my core for my molten heat, hoping it would be there if I needed it. It was burning away and I clung to it, unease rippling through me at the obvious aggression in the mine.

'The hag is asking for it,' a dwarf yelled as I passed. That was the nicest statement anyone had made. Hag-hatred was high.

'Thomas, does this body have its head?' I asked quietly once we were out of earshot of the miners. Leif was several steps ahead of us.

'I don't know. I was called before you, but no one said either way and I haven't seen it yet.'

As I nodded, Fluffy whined and cocked his head at one of the walls. I stopped. 'What is it, boy?' Then I heard the scratching sound. 'Shit, Thomas – the hag is coming through.'

Thomas's hands disappeared into his clothing and I knew he was retrieving a weapon or two. 'Leif,' he barked. 'Keep your miners back. The hag is coming in and we don't need more deaths.'

From what I could see of it under his helmet, Leif's face was grim. He looked around and I assumed it was for something to use as a weapon, but luckily there was nothing but loose rock.

The scratching sound grew louder and I saw the wall next to us dissolve as though it had never been there. Matilda stepped out. As she saw me, she either smiled or grimaced – I wasn't sure which, because my eyes were focused on her needle-sharp chrome teeth. Her twig-like hair was in even greater disarray than the last time I'd seen her, and her large, pointed ears were sagging beneath its weight.

'Matilda, how are you?' I greeted her. It always paid to be polite, no matter how nervous you were. In fact, I was at my most polite in terrifying situations – and this was an absolute powder keg. There was a dead body, caverns of angry dwarfs, and now the hag was strolling in to light the fuse.

She sniffed around and looked at me. 'No sugar snack?'

'I'm so sorry, I wasn't prepared – this trip was unexpected. I'll bring some next time I come,' I promised. 'Extra to make up for it.'

That seemed to mollify her; her nose wrinkled, but she didn't ask again. She looked briefly at Thomas, dismissed him and then snarled at Leif, 'No treat yet today. You promised. Box a day – or I smash skulls.'

If anyone else had said that, we'd have assumed it was a threat to the living but we knew she was talking about the dwarf skulls she was holding hostage. I imagined the dwarves wanted the remains of their dead as whole as possible; smashed skulls would be difficult to sort out.

Leif growled back, 'Don't you dare touch them, hag, or you will die!'

She cackled, mirth gleaming in her eyes. She knew that she'd be hard to kill; if Liv's tale was right, it took an elemental to kill an elemental. At the academy, our instructor had told us they'd been almost wiped out in the Middle Ages but there was no way to verify that, and it was possible that the information was inaccurate. Supernats were very close-mouthed about their histories.

'Bring sugar snack, dwarf. Matilda want.' As she lifted her hands and wiggled her fingers, her three-inch-long metal nails clicked together; it wouldn't have been a threatening gesture on a human, but on her it was.

Leif looked at her nails and finally jerked his head in an approximation of a nod. Finished with threatening him, Matilda looked at me. 'You no jump, Bunny.' She gave two hops and howled with laughter.

'Wait!' I said as she started to disappear into the wall. She paused, half-in, half-out. I pulled out my notepad and I wrote in big letters: *HAGS SUCK*. I showed it to her.

She looked at me curiously. 'What do wiggles mean?' she asked finally.

'You can't read?' I asked.

She shrugged. 'Have no need.'

'What do you do for fun?' I asked.

'Polish skulls.' She cackled again.

Oh boy. 'Did you know Alfgar Simonson?'

She looked at me blankly. 'I know Bunny.' She pointed at me. 'That is all.'

That made my heart ache a little. 'This is Thomas.' I pointed to the hunter and owner of the mine. 'And this is my friend, Sidnee. And this is my dog, Fluffy.'

She looked at Fluffy. 'Is he good to eat?'

Fluffy stepped back to hide behind Thomas. 'No!' I snapped. 'No eating dogs!'

Matilda shrugged and finished disappearing through the wall.

'That was creepy,' I whispered under my breath and Fluffy barked in agreement. 'Who would eat a dog?' I looked at Leif. 'She couldn't read – you saw that, right? So she couldn't have written that message.'

He shook his head. 'You look at that body and tell me she's not responsible. He's not far now. Come on. Then you can eat your words and choke on them,' he muttered under his breath.

Yikes. Nice fella.

We followed.

Chapter 28

All in all, I estimated that we walked about a quarter of a mile into the mine away from the lift. I resisted the urge to continually look behind me but claustrophobia was building and the feeling of the earth around me was oppressive.

Leif finally stopped. 'There.' He pointed ahead.

I could see a shape and flicked on my headlamp to examine it. This headless body, unlike the other two, had been mutilated; at first glance, it looked like it had been raked deeply with claws.

Gunnar had shown me different claw marks as part of my training so I could tell a bear shifter's claws from a werewolf's, and there was something off about these. The incisions were too neat, too precise; I'd have bet good money they'd been made with knives.

I walked around looking for tracks or drag marks. It was obvious the dwarf hadn't been killed here because there was no blood soaking the ground and there should have been a lot of it. Neither was blood visible on the clothing, despite the deep scratches. The wounds had been made post-mortem.

'See? The hag killed him with her claws,' Leif said, his jaw set to stubborn.

I shook my head. 'This dwarf wasn't killed here. If it were the hag, why would she move him?'

'To intimidate us.'

I almost said, 'She doesn't need to intimidate you, you're terrified of her already,' but I held my tongue. I ducked down to check the deceased's boots. Sure enough, the same dark soil from the tailings pile was there. I stood up. 'Leif, tell everyone who goes to the tailings pile to take a buddy. No one should be out there without a partner or two.'

'It won't stop the hag,' he said sullenly.

'It might not, but it may deter the murderer or at least give us a witness. Please, just do it.'

'Fine.' He crossed his arms over his chest. He was done listening.

Sidnee took photos as I examined the corpse. I even used the blacklight but there was no splatter. And the boots didn't lie; I was looking at another trip to the tailings pile.

I had Fluffy sniff the body then collected what evidence I could, which was limited to a dirt sample from the victim's boots. There was no extra hair this time. 'Have we identified the victim?' I asked Leif as I worked.

'His name was Evgard Appleton.'

'I'm sorry for your loss,' I told him. He nodded but his face remained hard and unmoving. 'What did Evgard do?' I asked.

'He mined, but most of the time he was in an office. He was the local head of the union, the Alaska Miners' Association.'

'A union?' I looked at Thomas. I had no idea how unions worked when you lived in a hidden paranormal town, but people seemed to have ways to connect with the outside world while keeping us secret. Thomas's expression said he'd explain later.

'Yeah, we have a union. We aren't animals,' Leif bit out.

'I didn't mean to imply…' I trailed off. Thomas had been right: tensions were high and everything I was doing was making Leif angrier. I needed to do my job and vamoose. 'Did Evgard have any kind of relationship with Alfgar or Helmud?'

'Besides working in the same mine? Not that I know of. I'd have to talk with another AMA officer to see if there were any complaints or claims relevant to them.'

'If you could send me the names of the union reps, I'd be grateful,' I said firmly. Leif grunted. 'As soon as you can, please,' I added. He glared at me, pursed his lips but nodded.

'You all done Sidnee?' I asked.

She nodded. 'I don't think there's any more we can do here, unless we can take the body?'

'No,' Leif said firmly.

'Then we're finished.' I turned to Fluffy. 'Can you get a scent, see if we can follow it?'

He smelled the body and moved away, pausing to look back to make sure we were plunging into the tunnels after him. I really didn't want to.

Thomas frowned. 'Leif, stay with the body. Baldred said someone was coming for it shortly.' Leif nodded stonily.

We followed Fluffy until he stopped abruptly and whined. He'd lost the scent. 'Where does this route lead?' I asked Thomas.

'It's a little-known route to the tailings,' he replied.

The lighting was now sparse. 'All right, I don't fancy delving in deeper. Can you lead us back to the main route and out of here?'

'Of course, follow me.' Thomas escorted us out.

As we walked back to the car park, I was so relieved to see the sky even though it was bright sunlight.

Adrenaline spiked through me as we approached the SUV. There were glass shards on the ground around it and the back window was broken. Shadow! Panicking, I dashed to the car. Shadow could be hurt – or worse! It didn't bear thinking about.

As I arrived, panting, I realised that the glass had been pushed *outwards*, not inwards. A new panic gripped me and I flipped open the back door. Shadow's cage was nothing more than plastic goo melted into the rubber mat. My lynx had done something like this before at the academy when his shadow had lifted off him and melted his cute little Nomo vest.

Now he'd done it again.

Shadow was gone.

Chapter 29

I looked desperately as Thomas, who was a few steps behind me. 'What's wrong?' he panted.

'Shadow's gone.'

'Taken?'

'No, he escaped, and he's...' I didn't know how to finish. He was a cat through and through, but he was something else as well – something *other*. I didn't know what he'd been thinking or if he'd just been tired of being cooped up. I turned to Fluffy. 'Can you find him, boy?'

He looked at me, whined then started searching. Puffing a little, Sidnee caught up. 'What's up?'

'Shadow's missing – it looks like he took himself off for a walk,' I explained, worry like a weight in my guts.

'That little stinker.' She pulled a face but I could see she was worried too.

Fluffy left the car park and crossed the road that led to the tailings area. He was trotting past a place where most of the brush and trees had been cleared when he suddenly stopped. When I caught up, he was looking around and sniffing the ground so I waited until he lifted his nose again then followed his line of sight.

Shadow was in a tree: he must have leapt into it from the spot where Fluffy had lost his scent.

My heart gave a firm beat as my panic eased. Shadow was fine, not catnapped or dead, just an idiot lynx with a longing for the wild. That thought gave me a pang: maybe he wasn't getting enough outside time, enough freedom. I needed to do better.

I looked up at him and put my hands on my hips. 'What are you doing up there?' I demanded.

He looked down at me and gave one of his barking mrows, then stared into the distance again. 'What are you looking at?' I asked him.

Sidnee and Thomas joined me. Thomas looked amused at the crazy cat lady talking to her half-grown lynx in a tree. I nodded at Sidnee. 'She talks to him, too.'

She grinned impishly. 'Sure, but I don't actually expect him to reply!'

I rolled my eyes. 'I'm going up. You guys stay down here and laugh it up.'

I'd never climbed a tree, not even as a child, but it didn't look too difficult; there were plenty of branches and I was a vampire with extra strength and speed. I started to pull myself up. Shadow looked agitated, but he was definitely looking at something and my gut said I needed to see what.

I kept going. About halfway, my jeans caught on a sharp branch and the fabric made a distinct ripping noise. Whoops... I was now showing my friends a good chunk of luminous white butt cheek. When Sidnee giggled, I ripped off the branch and threw it down at her. Thomas deflected it effortlessly.

'My hero.' She batted her eyelids at him. Ugh.

I pulled at the loose fabric, but there was no way it would be covering me up again anytime soon. The jeans were toast. I glared at Shadow. 'You'd better have a damned good reason why you're up there. These were expensive!'

The cat was at least twenty feet up the tree, which didn't *sound* like much, but I made the mistake of looking down. I didn't have any particular fear of heights, and I was sure I'd survive if I fell, but it took a moment for me to reorient myself.

I kept going, cursing as I went, until I was near enough to Shadow to look in the same direction as he was doing. At the end of the road, before it curved and headed off to the tailings pile, there was a truck and a tractor. The truck was full of what looked like tailings and around it was a group of armed men in camouflage.

I squinted, but my eyes weren't lying. Armed men dressed like soldiers. No one had mentioned a protection detail, so my first thought was ... MIB.

Oh fuck.

I turned and scrambled down as Shadow ran down the tree and jumped free. His descent was effortless and elegant, a real contrast to my panting and exposed arse.

I didn't dare yell at my companions because I didn't want the armed men to hear us. We'd been planning to go to the tailings and if Shadow hadn't escaped, we'd have driven right into them. And there was a lot of them. They would have easily overpowered the three of us.

Once I was back on solid earth, Shadow leaned into my legs so hard that I wobbled. 'Good boy,' I praised him, stroking him firmly. 'You're a very good boy.'

'There are armed men up ahead,' I whispered to Thomas. 'Did the mine hire protection?'

He shook his head then reached into his coat and withdrew a serious-looking handgun. 'Go back to the vehicles. I'll check it out.'

I glared at him. 'I think you'll find that *we* are Nomo officers. *You* go back to *your* vehicle.'

Thomas looked amused as he shook his head and melted into the trees next to us. After three seconds, I could neither see nor hear him. Someday, I wanted that kind of skill. I turned to Sidnee. 'Umm, what just happened?'

She grinned and fanned herself. 'Damn, that's hot. He's so sexy.'

'He's just completely ignored my instruction.'

'True, but I'm kind of happy for him to take point on this one. He knows what he's doing. We're Thelma and Louise.'

'We are not! We're totally more Cagney and Lacey.'

Sidnee snickered. 'You might be Cagney, but I'm definitely Thelma.'

'We need to work on your self-esteem,' I muttered. 'I can't let Thomas do our job. I'm going to get the SUV and drive up there.'

'Okay, I'm going with you.'

I didn't argue; she had as much right to kick butt as I did – and she was starting to look worried now that Thomas had disappeared. 'Fine.'

We hurried back to the car park with Fluffy and Shadow following dutifully, piled into the SUV and roared out of the mine car park. I headed out to the road and turned left. Initially I'd thought I was scared, but now I realised that I was angry, deeply angry at everything the MIB and the black ops group were doing to my friends, my town and me.

I floored the accelerator and clumps of mud flew up behind me.

Thomas stepped out of the woods beside the tree that Shadow and I had climbed. I slammed on the brakes, but the combination of the sleet and mud sent the car careening.

'Shit!'

Chapter 30

I wrestled the vehicle back under control, narrowly missing Thomas who looked as cool as ever. He gestured for me to roll down my window. 'They're gone,' he said darkly.

I blinked. 'What do you mean, gone? I saw them not five minutes ago!'

He shrugged, his stoic mask back in place. 'They just disappeared.'

'Are portals a thing?' I asked, 'Like, could that really happen?'

Thomas shrugged. 'I've never seen one but that doesn't mean they don't exist. Plenty of people haven't seen the beast beyond the barrier but we know it's real.'

'Terrifyingly so.' Sidnee shuddered.

'What about all that machinery?' I asked.

'It's parked up blocking the road, but no one was inside either vehicle.'

'That's weird. I'm going up there.'

Rather than argue, Thomas climbed in the SUV.

Shadow was standing on the console between us, looking through the windshield. He mrow'd at us as if he was agreeing that we needed to go forward. What did my cat know that I didn't?

We stopped beside the deserted truck and tractor and climbed out. The tractor was to the left, but the truck was covering the majority of the road. Shadow squirmed again. I wasn't sure about releasing the lynx but he was too quick for me to stop him. He raced over to the tractor and disappeared beneath it; it was one of those big monsters with a huge scoop in front.

'Shadow!' I hollered, but he didn't stop. I muttered a few choice words and followed.

Thomas was looking around and I lost track of him as Fluffy and I went after our occasionally loathsome lynx. I crouched under the tractor's raised scoop then ducked between its front tires. I had to crouch low but at least I didn't have to crawl in the mud. My torn jeans were a lost cause, but I still didn't want to be soaked through.

There was a hatch beneath the machine that looked like a metal lid you'd see on a sewer in a street. It had been hidden by brush that had been recently cleared away. So portals were a no-go, but hidden tunnels were a go. 'Thomas!' I called.

He and Sidnee came over and we all stared at the hatch. 'They must have gone down there,' Sidnee said. 'That's how they got away so quickly.

'Did you know this was here?' I asked Thomas.

'No – and it shouldn't be. There is no sewer access around here. I have no idea what it's for or how long it's been here.'

'Those guys have access to the mines from here, and the dead dwarves had mud on their boots from here. Who's willing to bet these men are involved?'

'I won't take that bet,' Thomas said.

'Me neither,' echoed Sidnee.

I checked the tractor over, but didn't see any keys to start it with. It was less problematic than the truck covering the road anyway.

I hopped out of the truck. 'Okay, I'm calling Gunnar. Something stranger than murder is going on here and we need to work it out, like, yesterday.'

Shadow rubbed against my legs and put a foot on the lid. I rubbed his head. 'Yes, you're a good boy. I see the hatch. We wouldn't have found it without you.' He purred. My cat was going to be the death of me.

Gunnar was yawning when he answered his phone. 'Bunny, what's going on?'

'We have another dead dwarf at the mine. Even stranger, we just saw a group of armed men disappear into a hatch under a tractor near the tailings pile.'

'Armed? Describe them.'

'Five men in camouflage with rifles – they were dressed like the ones we dispatched in Sitka.' I paused. 'Gunnar, I swear to you they're MIB.'

He swore violently. 'Do *not* go down that hatch! We don't know what's down there and I won't risk any of you.'

I was already considering charging right in; if we left it too long, the men could be anywhere in the sprawling mine. Fluffy was here, we could track them with their scent …

'I mean it!' Gunnar barked, interrupting my plotting. 'Grab a CCTV camera from the back of the SUV and set it up out of sight. We need more intel before you go off half-cocked.' He knew me so well.

I hesitated and Thomas looked at me sternly: he knew me, too. I huffed. 'Fine. I'll place the camera, but then we're heading to the tailings. That'll be the murder site.' I hung up before Gunnar could protest further.

I relayed his instructions then went to get the camera. We placed it at a spot that gave us a clear view of the hatch and made sure it was concealed. As long as the tractor stayed put, we were golden. As back up, I placed a second camera in the trees to watch the tractor.

Once done, we checked out the truck that was blocking the road to see if we could move it. We could go around it but earth nearby looked soft and I didn't want to get stuck. It was another mile to the tailings pile. I didn't particularly want to walk with armed men around, but I had to see if I could find the murder site.

Thomas had taken the passenger side of the truck. 'Keys!' he announced.

I shook my head in disbelief: the keys were on the dash. This was just plain weird. The dwarves wouldn't leave heavy, expensive equipment lying around with the keys in it; they had buildings where they parked this stuff when it wasn't being used. The armed men must have stolen the vehicles to hide whatever they were up to underneath them ... but surely they realised the equipment would be missed?

I swallowed hard as a thought occurred to me: unless they had someone working with them in the mine, someone who would cover for the missing equipment?

Thomas moved the truck so we could manoeuvre around it and we headed up the road to find the site of a murder.

Chapter 31

The brief daylight had already waned, but it wasn't so late that everyone would have gone home from work; even so, the tailings area was completely deserted. It might have been because the road was blocked but that didn't feel right because we'd managed to move the truck. Anyone who'd been down the road could have moved it, too.

Where were the workers who had to go back down the road to leave? I rubbed my hands up and down my arms to smooth the goosebumps that were threatening to erupt.

Thomas was on high alert. Before I knew it he'd also moved off, presumably in search of the armed men. Sidnee and I looked at each other then focused on our task. 'Fluffy,' I called. 'Can you find the dead dwarf's blood?'

He gave me a look that for all the world said, 'Duh.'

I'd left Shadow in the SUV, but with the window broken and his crate melted he could come and go as he pleased. Despite that, he'd seemed happy to curl up and sleep which I found oddly reassuring. I was learning to trust his instincts, and his instincts right now said it was safe for him to snooze. A little of the tension left me. We were okay – for now.

Fluffy started searching methodically. Since we didn't have dog-level noses – although I was pretty sure I'd smell blood if I got close enough – Sidnee and I looked around. The dwarf had bled out so there had to be a lot of blood somewhere. Humans had approximately five litres of the stuff; though shorter, dwarves were pretty stout and I guessed they'd have close to four litres.

I signalled Sidnee that I'd work one side of the tailings pile and she nodded and moved to the opposite side. We worked for about fifteen minutes before Fluffy's bark caught our attention and we both hurried over to him. He was standing over a patch of ground, but his body language was uncertain.

'Do you smell blood?' I asked him.

He whined. I guessed that meant no. 'Do you smell Evgard Appleton?'

He barked. He could smell the dwarf. I looked at Sidnee. 'Where's all the blood?'

Sidnee shrugged. 'Dunno. Down the hatch?'

I choked back a nervous laugh. 'Funny.'

'We don't *know* he died here,' she pointed out. 'That's just supposition. Evgard had tailings' dirt in his boots but that doesn't mean he was killed here, just that he was walking around here before he died.'

'True.'

'They could have murdered him anywhere.'

I grimaced – that was what worried me. Without the head or a forensic examination of the body, we had little evidence to point to what had happened. I didn't even know if the victim was dead before the marks were made on him. I hadn't noticed any bruising to indicate he'd been slashed before he died, but I hadn't been able to look at the body too closely. And who had the head? *If* the dwarf *had* died here ... the only one who would meticulously take the blood too was a dwarf.

'Do you think the dwarves are involved in this?' I asked Sidnee.

'What?' Sidnee was genuinely taken aback. 'They think it's the hag.'

'Do they? Or are they just acting like they do?' My phone rang, interrupting us: Connor. I swiped to answer. 'Hi, you okay?'

'We've got an issue.' His tone was grim.

'I don't like the sound of that.'

'You're not going to like it one bit,' he warned me.

I braced myself. 'Hit me.'

'Apparently there was an offer on the mine this fall.'

'An offer? Someone tried to buy it? Was it up for sale?'

'No, it wasn't for sale and apparently none of the other owners were informed. Liv and Calliope knew nothing about it. You'll need to check with Thomas.'

'He's on site with me – I'll ask him.'

'According to Goren Flankson, the dwarf I interviewed, the dwarven council handled it on their own.'

'Surely they couldn't accept an offer without a majority agreement?' I asked.

'The council has a controlling interest in the mine, though they have to inform the other owners and have a vote followed by their written agreement to the sale.'

'So the dwarves turned down the offer?'

'They did.' He paused. 'It gets worse. One of the people they met who was representing the anonymous buyer was a local water shifter.'

My stomach lurched. 'Do we know who it was?'

'We do. Chris Jubatus.'

My mind racing, I froze for several moments until I realised I was staring at the phone. I choked out, 'Chris Jubatus? Selkie, and Sidnee's drug-dealing bastard of an ex-boyfriend?'

Oh shit. Cogs started turning. Chris had tried to buy the mine. He had no money of his own; we'd frozen his assets when he'd rolled out of town so I knew exactly how much he had. He wasn't trying to buy it for himself, and he wasn't representing Calliope because she already had a share in the mine. No, he'd been trying to buy the mine under the radar for the MIB ... and now we had armed men crawling around it and several deaths. It couldn't be a coincidence.

Sidnee had stopped moving when I'd spat out her ex's name and she was staring at me, wide-eyed.

'The one and the same,' Connor confirmed.

'This changes everything,' I said tightly. 'I was thinking some dwarves had been responsible for the deaths to try and frame the hag, but now I think the MIB is trying to scare away the dwarves. They didn't have any luck buying it, so now they're trying to get it through any means necessary.'

I bit my thumb. 'Maybe Helmud saw something – he wasn't supposed to be in that part of the mine.' His was the one body we actually had. 'We should get toxicology to check for fisheye.'

'Henderson was human,' Connor pointed out.

'Exactly. We have no idea what fisheye does to humans. What if it's as deadly to them as to us? There has to be a reason why the MIB have been so selective in using it, otherwise, they'd have sprayed it across all known supernat towns.'

'You might be right,' Connor said grimly.

'I need to speak to Gunnar. That interview with Goren, have you got notes on it?'

'Better.' He sounded pleased. 'All of the interviews have been recorded. I'll email a link to you both.'

'Thanks. Connor ... be careful.'

He sounded resigned when he said, 'I'm not the one stomping on their heads right now. You be careful, Bunny.' He hung up.

I turned to Sidnee, who was looking wan, then called, 'Thomas! Sidnee needs you!' I wasn't sure exactly where he was, but moments later he ran out of the woods. He took one look at Sidnee and bundled her into his arms. 'Hey baby, what's wrong?'

She burst into tears. He held her close, rubbed her back and sent me a questioning look over her shoulder. 'We think the armed men are MIB,' I explained.

Thomas's face didn't change; he'd already suspected that.

'Last year, Chris Jubatus tried to facilitate another buyer to buy your mine,' I went on.

Thomas's jaw tightened. 'First I've heard of it,' he said darkly.

'The dwarven council decided to keep the offer to themselves but they rejected it anyway. Since they have the controlling interest, it wouldn't have mattered if *you* had wanted to sell.'

'We could have shared our portion of the mine,' he pointed out.

'Did you want to?' I asked curiously.

'No. I like having multiple income streams.'

'How much is your share?'

'Liv, Calliope and I each have ten percent. The dwarves hold the remaining seventy percent.'

'But the dwarves didn't sell,' I pointed out.

Thomas nodded grimly. 'So the MIB decided to start a campaign, frame the hag and make the dwarves *want* to leave the mine.'

'Exactly.'

'What if he's here?' Sidnee said quietly into Thomas's shoulder.

'Chris?' I asked gently.

She nodded, her head still averted. 'I'm over him, I swear, but I don't want to see him. I don't want to...' She trailed off. 'Fuck him. Just fuck him.'

Thomas stroked her back. 'You can stay with me, at least until we're sure he's not in town.'

Sidnee drew back to look at him. 'Are you sure? I can be real messy.'

He gave a lopsided grin. 'Good thing I'm tidy, then, isn't it?'

She smiled and stood on her tiptoes to kiss him.

I moved away to ring Gunnar. 'You better not have gone down that hole!' he said when he answered. So much had happened that it took me a moment to realise what he was talking about.

I laughed. 'No, sir, I didn't. And I'm damned glad about that.' I filled him in on everything we knew – and everything we suspected.

'I'd already ordered toxicology on Helmud Henderson,' Gunnar said. 'I'll call again later and ask for them to test specifically for fisheye. Get your ass back to the office. We need a plan of attack.'

'Yes, boss. En route.' I hung up.

Sidnee was calmer. Thomas still had his arm around her delicate waist. 'Did you see anything when you looked around?' I asked him.

He shook his head. 'I couldn't find anyone.'

'How many people should be working here at this time of the night?'

He checked his watch. 'There should be at least four people. They might be getting ready to close down for the night, but it shouldn't be deserted. Not like this.'

'Who supervises this area?'

He scrolled through his phone and finally gave me a name. 'Sven Ogelvie.' He pressed the call button and I heard the ringing tone at the other end before the call flipped to voicemail. At the beep, Thomas said, 'It's Patkotak, call me back.' He tucked the phone into his jacket pocket. 'He should be at work. Let's hope he was on the phone or in the john and calls back soon.'

As we turned to walk back to our vehicles, I saw Shadow leap from the broken window – and then a huge explosion knocked us all to the ground.

I pushed myself slowly to my feet. Sidnee was also standing up, but Thomas wasn't moving. I rushed over but Sidnee beat me to him. She threw herself down next to him, her hands clutching and unclutching.

I leaned down to check his pulse. It thrummed strongly against my fingers. 'He's okay!' I said. Or at least I think I did, because the blast had knocked out my hearing. Immediately I realised that, my ears made a clicking sound and I moved my jaw to rebalance the pressure. Noise was restored in a rush that made even the slightest sound seem like a roar.

Finally Thomas's eyelids fluttered open. He groaned, then rolled to his side and tried to sit up. Sidnee grabbed his arm to help him. 'What the fuck?' he mumbled.

Yeah: what the actual fuck? 'I don't know,' I admitted. 'Something went boom.' I looked around and saw a huge cloud of dust and smoke in the distance. A chill ran down my spine. My voice, when it came out, was a harsh whisper. 'My God, I think there was an explosion at the mine.'

Thomas swore and rolled to his feet. 'We've got to get over there,' he said grimly. 'Can you call the fire department?'

I pulled out my phone and dialled. '666. What is your emergency?' the perky female voice asked, as if people dialling 666 were inquiring about party supplies. It was the number of the dedicated emergency line for supernats; sometimes supernat emergencies weren't compatible with calling 911. Okay, most of the time.

'We need response at the Chrome Mine in Portlock,' I said briskly. 'There's been an explosion.'

'Who am I speaking to?'

'This is Officer Barrington with the Nomo's office. We need immediate emergency response.' I paused. 'Send everyone.'

The voice on the other end stuttered a bit. 'Yes, of course. On their way.'

I hung up and called Gunnar. 'We felt it,' he said grimly. 'The whole town heard the boom.'

'We're going to need all the emergency personnel here as soon as possible," I said.

'From the sirens, they're already on their way – and so am I. Are you and Sidnee all alright?'

'Yeah, we're fine. The blast knocked us down but we're not injured.'

Other than swiping at his ears, Fluffy seemed to be okay. Shadow was nowhere to be seen. Dammit: I should have kept an eye on him! The moment he woke up, I should have known something was going down – that lynx really did have a sixth sense. I hoped that he was hiding because cats were sensitive to noise and vibration and Shadow was more so than most.

'We gotta go!' Thomas called. 'Move!' He already had the engine running. Much as I hated the idea of leaving Shadow wherever the fuck he was, I also knew that my feline fur baby could definitely look after himself.

The windows of the SUV had been blown out but Thomas had wiped the glass off the seats. 'We're going to the mine, Shadow!' I yelled before we set off. I doubted he'd understand because he wasn't a shifter like Fluffy, but it was worth a try. I was worried but lives were at risk and we had to see if and how we could help; I'd come back for my cat before I went home.

Thomas drove like a man possessed; I didn't blame him, though I did clutch onto the door handle. As we tore down the road, I texted Connor that I was okay but there had been an explosion at the mine.

The car park was littered with debris and the whole entrance to the mine was gone, leaving a gaping hole in the hillside. My jaw dropped. The debris was still smouldering and producing noxious smoke. I coughed as it hit the back of my throat.

There were dwarves and humans everywhere, most of them moving and moaning; supernats tended to be harder to kill, which was one plus. Sidnee, Thomas and I jumped out of the SUV, spread out and ran to help those nearest to us.

I ran over to one of the moving bodies, a dwarf. I checked him over: his hair was singed; he had cuts and scrapes and probably a broken wrist. I helped him up and moved him to a clear area.

'Less serious injuries here,' I barked to Sidnee and Thomas. They nodded and moved another two of the walking wounded to sit with my dwarf. All three were obviously in pain and shock, but they weren't in mortal danger. Sidnee grabbed supplies from the SUV and gave them each some painkillers and a thermal blanket.

I went to the next dwarf, triaged and moved him to the less serious area. A vampire, blood pouring out of him, was moving towards one of the dead dwarves intent on getting some fresh blood. 'No!' I said hastily. 'They can't go to the afterlife unless their whole self is burned, including their blood. Here, bite me.'

The vampire hesitated for a second and then took the wrist I offered him. His fangs bit into my wrist and I cried out in pain. I guess this dude hadn't learned the neat hypnosis trick that Connor could do. I gritted my teeth. He wouldn't need much blood to kick start his healing, so it would be over soon. You can cope with anything for fifteen seconds, right? Except maybe decapitation.

With a panicked shout, Connor was suddenly there. He ripped the vampire off me, reared back and punched him in the head. 'Connor! No! I offered!'

He turned on me, chest rising and falling rapidly. 'Fuck! Vampires don't feed off vampires, Bunny!'

I blinked. 'Because it's rude?'

'Because they can't stop! He would have sucked you dry!' His panic was evident, his eyes blown wide.

I licked suddenly dry lips. 'He'll be okay, though?' I looked at the unconscious vamp who was already visibly healing.

'I should kill him,' Connor said tightly.

'No!'

'Your blood,' he hissed to me. 'You're a *hybrid* Bunny, remember?'

'Okay, so?'

'So there's a reason why the council is scared of hybrids. Beyond the fact that you can feed on auras, if a vampire feeds off your blood they'll be in thrall to you. Totally and utterly. He'll do whatever you want forever – he's your slave, Bunny!'

He shook his head. 'And if he lives we'll have to hide him, hide his blind obedience to you.' His expression was grim and he took a step towards the fallen vampire. 'Better he dies.'

'No!' I snapped. 'I didn't save him to have you kill him! Look around you – there's been enough death tonight.' I held onto his arm and looked pleadingly into his eyes. 'Please, Connor, we'll deal with this together. But don't kill him.'

Connor blew out a long breath as he looked at me. 'You'll be the death of *me*,' he muttered, but he turned and shook the vampire until he awoke. 'Go to my old cabin and remain there until we come for you.'

The vampire ignored Connor and looked glassy eyed at me. 'Mistress,' he said happily.

Oh boy. I swallowed hard then repeated Connor's order. 'Go to Connor's cabin and remain there until we come for you.'

The vampire floated to his feet and was gone in a second. 'Shit,' Connor said. 'Shit.' Visibly upset, he scrubbed a hand through his curly dark hair.

'What?' I asked.

'That's Parker.'

'So?'

He grimaced. 'He's been one of my biggest rivals since I arrived in Portlock, and now we'll have to bring him into the heart of our group if we're going to hide this. I'm not sure the other vampires will buy such a sudden change of heart.'

'We'll work it out,' I said stubbornly.

I'd never seen Connor look uncertain before and it was unnerving to see it now. 'Yeah,' he agreed hollowly. 'We'll work it out.'

'How did you arrive so quickly?' I asked.

'I was at Kamluck,' he said. 'I ran.'

I blinked. 'That's some run you've got there.'

He gave me a crooked smile that warmed every inch of me. 'I will always run to you, Doe.'

Sirens blaring, the ambulances arrived and interrupted our moment. The firemen followed moments later. Connor and I split up to help the emergency teams, and I pointed out the more seriously wounded dwarves to the paramedics.

We worked for hours. The injuries worsened the closer we got to the mine until there were only dead bodies and scattered limbs. At one point my phone buzzed in my pocket – I'd missed a call from Helmud's dad. Hard to worry about that amongst all that surrounded us.

Gunnar finally found me as I was staring into the caved-in mine. I hoped Matilda was okay; I knew elementals were tough, but even the toughest being would die if they were blown to smithereens.

My boss looked as rough as I felt; he was covered in blood and mud and his eyes were weary. We'd all go on seeing this scene for some time to come. He put his arm around me. 'Let's go home, Bunny. We're done.'

I didn't move. I couldn't. I was numb.

Gunnar continued, 'I've sent Sidnee home with Thomas. You need to go too.'

I shook my head slowly. 'Gunnar, there are a lot of hurt people but there should be more.'

He frowned. 'What do you mean?'

'I've seen maybe thirty people out here, including the bodies, but there should have been at least a hundred miners coming on and off shift. Where are the rest? Vaporised?' I paused and realised I hadn't seen the one dwarf I needed to ask. 'Have you seen Leif?'

Gunnar frowned. 'No, but I didn't work the whole field.'

I nodded. I should have looked for Leif, investigated the hatch under the tractor, found Shadow, but just then I didn't have the energy – or the heart. We'd already worked through the night and dawn was coming again. I was dead on my feet. Dead-er.

I met Gunnar's eyes. 'The men that went down the hatch had something to do with this, and someone at the mine must be helping them. That's why the casualties have been minimised. We need to get back to the hatch and check the cameras we put up.'

'We will, but not now. Our people are exhausted – you're exhausted, Sidnee is wiped out and I'm finished, too.' He looked at the mine. 'We'll make mistakes, mistakes we can't afford. Something is going on here and we need all our wits about us. I've tagged April and she's heading in to the office – she'll call if there's an emergency. Now, go home and rest, and we'll make a plan tomorrow. That's an order.'

I wouldn't let it go. 'Gunnar, if it is the same people – those MIB assholes – they had a *submarine*. We need to check the water,' I said stubbornly. I was swaying where I stood. Man, I really wanted to go home and snuggle with

Connor and my pets, then sleep for a one hundred years.

'Shadow...' I sighed.

Gunnar tugged his rough beard. 'What about him?'

'He ran off when the mine exploded. I need to find him.'

'Tomorrow, Bunny,' he said gently. 'One night in the wild won't harm him – far from it. He'll be in his element. Go home, that's an order.'

I shook my head again, but the movement almost knocked me off my feet. Fluffy whined, and as I looked up a vision walked towards me through the smoke and debris: Connor, with Shadow on his heels. My mate was dirty, his shirt was torn – and he was perfect. A half-sob caught in my throat and I ran to him.

He caught me and I clung to him. 'Let's go, Doe. We've done all we can. Now it's time to take care of you.'

I shuddered. 'It was so bad.' I looked around and let myself really see the scale of the disaster. This might be the worst thing that had happened to the town since the barrier went up. 'Where did you find Shadow?'

'More like he found me,' Connor said wryly. 'I was helping load someone into the ambulance and he just appeared.'

I pulled back and gave Shadow a scritch behind his ear. 'Thank God you're okay.' I bundled the huge lynx into my arms to give him a squeeze, and for once he didn't try to jump away. I turned to Gunnar. 'Okay, I'm ready to go home.'

'Good. Ring me when you're up.' He fixed Connor with a hard stare. 'Look after her.'

'Yes, sir,' Connor said, with no trace of irreverence. We watched the big man trudge off; his shoulders bowed as if he had the weight of the world on his shoulders.

Connor turned to me and his eyes softened. 'You look undead on your feet, my love.'

I smiled. 'Yup.' I leaned back in. 'I want your magnificent shower, tea – and you.'

'Your wish is my command,' he murmured. 'Let's go.'

Chapter 33

I woke out of the fog of sleep to the sound of my phone ringing. Connor reached over me when I didn't move, looked at the screen and said, 'You have to take it, it's work.'

I groaned and took the phone. I should have been stiff and sore, but Connor had made me drink two cups of blood before bed and I felt fine, if a little on the tired side. I still hadn't worked off the jetlag feeling from weeks of living a daylight schedule at the academy.

'Officer Barrington,' I answered. If I hadn't still been woozy, I'd have realized it was either Sidnee or Gunnar.

'Bunny, it's April.'

Or April. I sat up. 'What's up?' I yawned.

'Just had a weird call from two separate fishermen.'

My brain cleared in an instant; I knew what she was going to say next. She continued, 'They're reporting a submarine in Chrome Bay.'

My heart gave a hard thump. I knew Port Chatham Bay but not Chrome Bay; its name gave me the chills because it had to be the stretch of water closest to the mine. The mine that was now rubble. The presence of the sub made me certain the MIB were here and they were playing their A game.

'Thanks, April. Can you get the fishermen to keep an eye on it and let us know if it moves out?'

'Sure thing.'

'Great, thanks. Are Sidnee or Gunnar in yet?'

'Not yet. Everyone was exhausted. Sidnee said she'd be in an hour late.'

'Okay, thank you. I'll be in soon.'

'See you later.' She hung up.

I collapsed back onto the pillow. The submarine wasn't urgent; if anything, it merely confirmed what we already thought, that the black ops MIB team were here. Where they went, their sub was sure to follow, like Mary's underwater Little Lamb. We didn't have the firepower or manpower to tackle a freaking submarine, so for now I'd take the most sensible course of action: ignore it. The fishermen would keep an eye on it and report if it moved out. That was all we could do for the moment.

Connor sighed. With his vampiric hearing, he'd heard April's side of the phone call too. 'You were right. It's the MIB.'

I sighed, too. 'Yup. Sometimes I hate being right.'

As an answer, he pulled me in tight and I melted against him. Things were just starting to heat up when a ten-kilo cat landed in the middle of us. 'Oof,' Connor grunted.

I slid him a glance. 'Did you happen to get up and feed him, perchance?'

'Nope.'

'Ugh.'

To add to it, Fluffy heard our voices, came in, sat next to Connor's side of the bed and whined pointedly.

Shadow was trying to sneak under the covers between us. I sighed and lifted up the blankets. His fur tickling my legs, he crawled down to my feet then turned around and came back up. 'What are you doing?' I asked him, but his raspy purr was the only response as he lay down sideways in between us, forcing us apart. I, of course, got Shadow's arse in my face.

Connor laughed. 'He likes me more,' he teased.

'He's angry with me for not leaping up instantly to feed him,' I groused. I flipped the covers off and slipped my feet into my furry slippers. Shadow was now lying on Connor's chest demanding cheek rubs and ear scratches.

Fluffy jumped up and took my warm spot. I scowled at him. 'Traitor.' His tail tapped in response, making me grin.

I left the bedroom and went into Connor's kitchen to raid his cupboards. My heart warmed as I opened the cabinets and fridge: I loved that he always had cat and dog food these days.

I put Shadow's special ground meat into a bowl and warmed it. When the microwave beeped, he came flying out of the bedroom. Next I filled Fluffy's bowls and set them down; unlike Shadow, he didn't instantly appear when he heard me.

Part of me wanted to go back to bed – preferably with Connor – but work was already tugging at me. We needed to tackle this MIB splinter group pronto. Even so, I took the time to heat some blood for me and Connor, then turned on the kettle that had mysteriously appeared in the house one day. Carrying the mug of blood into the bedroom, I paused to take in the sight of Connor talking quietly to Fluffy like he was a human. I couldn't have loved that man more.

He caught sight of me, gooey eyes and all, and smiled. 'Hey.'

'Hey. I brought you some blood.'

'So I can smell. Thank you.' He took the mug gratefully and drank it down with relish. 'You go ahead and jump in the shower. I'll make breakfast.'

I sent him my best seductive smile. 'I'd rather not eat and have you join me.'

His eyes darkened. 'Temptress,' he complained. He shook his head. 'You need fuel. I'm predicting another long day.'

I sighed. 'Mr Sensible. I expect you're right. Later?' I asked hopefully. 'Raincheck?'

'Raincheck. Now go, before I change my mind.' He slumped back onto the bed looking a bit grumpy. 'Sometimes chivalry is a pain in my ass.'

I laughed. 'I'm going.'

After my shower, as I was hastily plaiting my hair, delicious scents wafted up from the kitchen. Bacon! Connor had definitely made me bacon! In fact, Connor had made a full English breakfast. 'No black pudding,' he said apologetically. 'So I substituted with Jimmy Dean's.'

'Is that close?' I asked.

'It's just cheap sausage, but tasty.'

'Thank you. I appreciate you making me a slice of home.' I didn't realise how hungry I was until the first bite touched my lips, then I tucked in to it like a starving bear.

Connor sat down to eat with me; it was nice and homey, and something we hadn't done enough of. His house was still decorated for the holiday season with the tree up and multicoloured lights. My own house seemed sterile in comparison. It scared me how much Connor's house felt like home but I pushed the fear down; I was done with letting that particular emotion rule me.

I finished eating and checked the time. 'I've got to go. I told April I'd be there soon.'

Connor nodded. 'I'm going to the councillors' office. You'll be calling us by the end of the day,' he predicted.

He was probably right. Things were about to get messy.

Messier.

Chapter 34

The office was full when I walked in. Sidnee was there, looking clear-eyed and determined, and Gunnar was there looking grim. April appeared tired but determined; she had a huge can of energy drink on her desk, so clearly, she intended to power through another shift.

Sigrid was there, too, dressed in a homespun skirt and her ever-practical boots but with a new addition of tough, flinty eyes. It looked like she was stepping into the breach with us, too. 'At least go and have a sleep in the back,' she said to April. 'I'll man the phones until you wake up.'

'Go,' Gunnar ordered. 'There's a bunk in the back for that purpose.'

'I won't need much sleep,' April promised. 'Shifters can go without when we need to.' She yawned widely then shuffled off.

Sigrid made us all drinks and we clutched them as we perched on plastic chairs in a circle. No one wanted to break the companionable silence because we all knew what was coming next would be grim. This was more than murder: this had been a deliberate mass killing. The thought shook me. So far the MIB group had clung to the shadows, tried to abduct us and subdue us with drugs, but now it seemed the gloves were off.

Gunnar broke the silence. 'It's not like I can contact the government and ask for the MIB's assistance. This splinter group *is* MIB, and they may even be acting with government approval – though Thomas and my other MIB contact assure me that won't be the case. Even so, I can't risk contacting the wrong person. If we're going to take these fuckers down, we don't want government witnesses.'

'Hoorah,' Sidnee said, but without any of her usual levity.

'I'm certain this group is hidden and unsanctioned, but they'd still find a way to block any order the governor gives.' He tugged on his beard.

'What about I go out and look around Chrome Bay?' Sidnee asked.

'Absolutely not!' Sigrid snapped, before blushing lightly and glancing apologetically at her husband. Clearly her presence had been allowed at the office on the basis that she didn't countermand his orders.

Gunnar shot her an amused look that had a distinct 'told you so' edge to it; nevertheless, he agreed with her. 'No, Sidnee, I'm not sending you out there alone. They'd kill you or capture you. I'd feel better sending Calliope – if she'd go.' He frowned 'Then again, she's volatile and she isn't law enforcement.'

He leaned back and the loud squeak of the chair sounded ominous. Abruptly, he brought his fist down on the table. 'Damn it! We aren't sitting here like proverbial ducks. We're not ducks!'

'Yeah!' Sidnee said enthusiastically. 'We're like birds of prey! Bald eagles!'

Gunnar swiped a self-conscious hand over his head. 'Speak for yourself,' he muttered. 'I have a full head of hair.'

'Golden eagles?' I suggested helpfully.

'Do we have to be birds?' Sigrid asked. 'I'm not much of an ornithologist.'

Gunnar huffed. 'The point is, we're not *ducks.*'

'I quite like ducks,' I murmured, making Sidnee giggle. Once she started, she couldn't stop and the helpless laughter released the tension we were all carrying. Even Gunnar guffawed.

As we finally calmed down, his expression turned grim. 'It's time to be proactive, but I won't pretend it won't be dangerous. I propose we go to that hatch in the ground that you found then we go down the rabbit hole to see what we can find. I won't order you to come with me.'

Sidnee folded her arms and glared. 'Try and stop me.'

'Ditto,' I agreed.

Gunnar smiled. 'I'm so proud of you both, you know that, right?'

Sigrid sniffed a little. 'We both are.'

'Group hug?' I suggested.

Sigrid pushed me and snickered. 'Nothing says professional officers of the law like a group hug before we go hunting.'

I grinned. 'I bet the MIB hug it out all the time.'

Gunnar sighed. 'Can we focus? I'm calling a council meeting.'

My eyebrows shot up. 'Shouldn't we explore first?'

He answered by standing up. 'Yes, it'll take the councillors a while to gather. We'll call it, go explore then report back. But first we're going to the gun safe and loading up.'

Sidnee and I smiled at each other. She held out her hand for a fist bump, and of course I couldn't leave her hanging. Gunnar ignored our antics. 'Vest up, ladies. The shit is going to hit the fan in the worst possible way.' He was such an optimist.

We pulled on vests and loaded the SUV with shotguns and rifles. We all had service pistols, and Gunnar and Sidnee had matching magical bulletproof vests the same as mine. Even Fluffy was decked out in his.

Gunnar had called for an emergency council meeting at 3am, giving us a good six hours to check the situation below the hatch before we reported back; better to ask for forgiveness than permission just in case the councillors didn't agree with our course of action.

Connor called me as we were getting in the SUV. 'I'm coming too,' he said, without preamble.

I looked at Gunnar. 'Connor wants to come.' He nodded tersely. 'We're on our way now,' I confirmed.

'Do you have your vest?' Connor asked.

'We've all got them.'

'I'm going to call Thomas.'

'You don't want to wait for the council meeting?'

'Fuck the council. We only have three Nomo officers – we can't afford to lose one. Thomas and I will be backup.'

'Do *you* have a vest?' I demanded.

'I don't need one.' He'd been shot in Sitka but, unlike me, he hadn't nearly bled out; he'd drunk from someone and healed instantly. When I'd been shot, I'd nearly died and it had taken a lot of blood for me to heal.

'Connor...' I started. Even though he was more bullet safe than me, it had nearly killed me to see him get shot.

He gave a short laugh. 'Don't worry, I have a vest.'

I let out a relieved breath. 'Good.' We hung up. 'Connor's bringing Thomas.'

Gunnar gave a grunt of acknowledgement, but Sidnee looked worried. 'I wish Thomas didn't risk himself so much. He's only human,' she muttered mostly to herself.

I met her eyes. 'He is also incredibly deadly and totally capable,' I pointed out.

She nodded, but I could see she was still worrying for him. I suspected I looked the same at the thought of Connor joining us.

Sigrid stayed at the office to man the fort while April slept, and the rest of us set off. We were quiet on the journey to the mine. We drove past the wreckage and debris, dodging wood and twisted steel in the road and chunks of rock and pavement. The worst damage wasn't so visible from the road.

Finally we drove around the mine and the car park to the road that twisted up to the tailings pile.

The tractor was still on the roadside, but the huge truck was gone. I had a very bad feeling about that. Had the MIB left the vicinity? Brought in more people? Had mining personnel come and taken it? If so, who?

The miners had far greater concerns; it had been hard watching the dwarves scour the rubble, not for survivors but for parts of their loved ones, desperately trying to reconstruct the bodies of the lost so that they could move on to the afterlife. Whoever had done this was cold and callous beyond belief. And I couldn't quite shake the idea that someone within the mine had been in on it.

Gunnar parked partially off the road in front of the tractor to keep the approach passable. 'I'll take the cameras.' I volunteered. The feed from them that was supposed to stream to our phones hadn't done so; we were either too far out, had bad coverage or the cameras had been destroyed. They were still hidden in position so I hurriedly grabbed them; perhaps they hadn't been found or the men were still inside the hole.

I brought them to the back of the SUV so we could watch the footage while Gunnar and Sidnee armed up. Both cameras showed the same thing: several more men going down the hatch and one armed man driving the truck towards the tailings' pile.

'We've no idea how many there are down there.' I muttered. We'd seen the original five go down, then the seven on the camera, but we had no idea how many had gone down *before* we'd set the cameras. The MIB could have a whole underground network.

'Did you check for *their* cameras?' Gunnar asked suddenly.

I blinked. 'Umm, I looked around, but no not really.'

Sidnee looked up. 'Has anyone checked for drones?'

Gunnar looked at her sharply. 'Why? What have you seen?'

'Nothing, but it's night time and sophisticated drones have night vision, infrared, thermal, ENVG-B and probably stuff they don't announce.'

I looked at her with an open mouth. 'Umm, have you been holding out on us?'

She smiled. 'It interested me at the academy so I looked into it in my free time. Some of that stuff is wild!'

'What's ENVG-B?' Gunnar asked.

'Enhanced Night Vision Goggle-Binocular. It can see everything at any time – it uses thermal imaging too to give an outline of what's around you. It's not as good as daylight visibility but as close as you can get.' She shrugged. 'It seemed sensible to look into what technologies they might want to use against us.'

'Smart,' I said admiringly. 'We haven't had any calls about rogue drones yet, so maybe they're just using boots on the ground or they're trying to keep their presence unnoticed.' Too bad for them that the local fisherman had seen them.

Just then Connor's truck pulled in behind the SUV and he and Thomas climbed out. We filled them in on the camera footage whilst they got themselves suited and booted for war.

When everyone was ready, we approached the hatch. The sewer-type lid didn't have a handle and, unlike most sewer lids, it didn't have a hole for a key. 'How do we get in?' I frowned as I looked at the useless tyre iron in my hand. 'I guess it opens from the inside, so they must be watching it – or they've set up a communication system so whoever is inside can open the door.'

Connor looked at it and smiled. 'Hand me that crowbar.'

I didn't see anywhere to get the tool under the lid to apply force, but he looked determined as he stared at the cast-iron lid. 'Iron is strong, tough and can hold a lot of weight – but it can be pierced with a high tensile rod and great force.'

He lifted the crowbar over his head with the sharp wedge-shaped end facing downward then, muscles bunching in his arms and back, he drove it down into the lid. There was a loud, screeching bang as the crowbar sank into the metal. Connor bent it downward so he could use it to hook the lid and pull it up.

Only it didn't come up: the screech of metal increased, but the hatch lid stayed put. He cursed. 'It's locked alright. This rod isn't strong enough to break the mechanism.'

'If anyone is close to the hatch, they heard all that,' Thomas said grimly.

We all stared down at the hatch for a few moments, momentarily stumped.

'I was kind of hoping they'd hear the noise, come and investigate and open it for us,' Connor admitted.

We waited. No one came. I tapped my lip thoughtfully. 'Their tunnel has to access the mine somehow. What if it comes out near the site of the first murder? There has to be a reason why they killed Helmud – maybe he saw one of them.'

'Where are you going with this, Bunny?' Gunnar asked.

'If we can't get in here, maybe we should check the other end.'

He looked in the direction of the mine. 'Well, some dumbass blew up the mine so we can't get in there.'

I smiled. 'You're forgetting one thing.'

'What?'

'The hag.'

Chapter 35

'No, absolutely not,' Gunnar said, folding his arms.

'Why not? She's been willing to talk to me so far,' I argued.

'She's dangerous and way too unpredictable.'

I looked at Connor for support, but from the set of his jaw he agreed with Gunnar. 'It's the only way we'll find out what's going on down there,' I said.

Gunnar shook his head. I looked at Sidnee and she raised her eyebrows; she'd totally back me up. I returned my gaze to Gunnar. 'Okay, let's try this – and I'm not asking for permission, boss. This shit is beyond dangerous and we need Matilda's help. I'm going to try to talk to her. I just want you to know what I'm doing and back me up. Please,' I entreated, undoing some of my hard work.

'I'm going with you,' Connor said.

When Gunnar looked at us both and sighed, I knew I'd won.

I still had to tackle Connor. 'Listen, love, I want you with me but the truth is that the hag and I have a kind of rapport and I don't want to push it. It's fragile. Your presence could actually put me in more danger. Besides, she's an elemental so none of us could stop her, hurt her or kill her. It won't matter if you're with me or not.'

Thomas smiled. 'I don't think you're reassuring anyone.'

Connor frowned at me. 'Bunny—,' he started.

I held up a hand. 'I'm doing it. And I'm doing it alone.'

He looked at me, reading my body language and no doubt assessing whether or not he could talk me out of it. I planted my feet akimbo and folded my arms as I met his ice-blue gaze with my green one, and I saw the moment when he resigned himself to the inevitable. He scrubbed a hand through his hair. 'When?'

'Well, there's no time like the present is there?'

It sounded like Connor growled deep in his throat but he didn't object. Truthfully, I wasn't that thrilled at the idea of a little chat with the hag because she made me nervous, but it was our best way forward. If she helped us, we'd find the MIB far faster than stumbling around endless miles of mine. *If* she was willing to help. It felt like a big if.

There were grumbles all round but in the end Gunnar went off to seek out something for our hag's sweet tooth.

The rest of us drove to the mine to see if we could locate a likely spot from which to call her.

It looked like the cleanup operation had started. The bodies were gone, the debris had been shoved to the side by a large loader that was still parked up, and there was a path from the mine to the car park.

It would take some careful climbing to get into what was left of the entrance itself. Basically it was a hole in the hill, not unlike a cave, and I wondered if that was what it had been originally. Maybe that was at the root of the dispute between Matilda and the dwarves: she'd been there first then they'd come by and stolen her nice comfy cave.

Thomas waved to get my attention then pointed at something partway up the hill. 'See that?'

I wasn't sure what I was looking at. 'Nope.'

'Follow me.'

Curious now, I followed him with Connor and Sidnee on our heels. We climbed the mud and debris of the destroyed hill until Thomas stopped about a quarter of the way up to the right of the gaping hole where the mine entrance had been. He pointed. 'See the way the hill is formed here?'

We looked at each other; the consensus was no. Thomas ignored us. 'There used to be another opening here. It's been filled in and nature has reclaimed it.'

That caught my interest. 'You think that this would be a good place to call Matilda?'

'I do. I also think it might be a good spot to look for the other end of that tunnel.'

He was right: it *was* a good place from which to call Matilda. We didn't want to climb to the entrance because it might not be stable and, according to the reports we'd had, the lift was damaged so we couldn't go down to the chamber where I'd met the hag before. This was our best shot at success.

We heard Gunnar pull up and Connor went to meet him. I studied the hill while Thomas continued to explore. 'What did you bring?' I asked my boss as he approached, bakery box in hand.

'They were out of doughnuts so I bought a mix of what was left – some cookies, some mini-pies and one maple bar.'

I sighed. Doughnuts would have been better because we knew she liked those. I would be so pissed off if she killed me for bringing the wrong sweet treat. 'Go on, give me the box and you all retreat to the vehicles.'

Thomas, Sidnee and Gunnar moved away, the latter giving me an inscrutable gaze. Connor grabbed me and kissed me with all his might. 'Careful of the treats!' I squeaked when he finally released my lips.

'Fuck the treats. Stay safe Bunny. Promise me.'

'I'll be back,' I promised lightly, kissing him again, and all too aware that I might be lying.

When they all were safe, I took a deep breath, clutched the pink bakery box tightly and called, 'Matilda, Matilda, Matilda.'

I waited. Then I waited some more. I gave it five minutes, then I called again. Crickets. I waited ten more impatient minutes. I guessed we'd been wrong about this being a good place to try – the idea had been a total bust.

I was turning to leave when I heard a scratching noise behind me. I whirled around just in time to catch sight of metal claws protruding from the mud.

Fuck. There she was.

Chapter 36

I waited until Matilda was fully visible. She hadn't blasted the mud out of the way like last time but dived through it like it was water and she was an Olympic swimmer.

She met my eyes then held up her hands in front of her like paws and started to hop like a rabbit. Everyone's a comedian. She was mid-hop when her eyes focused on the box in my hands. As she stopped hopping and lunged for it, I hastily pushed it forward before her talons could catch my skin. She ripped off the top and started gobbling down the treats like she hadn't eaten for a year.

I sat on a nearby rock and waited. Watching her silver teeth flash was disturbing, so I focused instead on watching the cookies and cakes disappear from the box. When she'd finished she handed me the empty box, which I thought was interesting. She knew from last time that it wasn't good to eat and she knew that I'd dispose of it for her.

I folded it up while Matilda settled next to me on the rock, sprawling against it like it was a comfy sofa. I wasn't sure how to start, mainly because I didn't know how well she understood English.

My mum might have been on my shit list, but she'd always insisted that everything went better if you were polite and I agreed with her. So, open with politeness. 'How are you, Matilda?'

She looked at me blankly, either not understanding the question or the concept behind it. Had nobody ever asked her how she was before? I cleared my throat and tried again. 'I was worried. Were you safe when the mine blew up?'

She squinted then looked at the place where the outer structure of the mine was missing. 'Big noise,' she nodded, her willow-like hair swaying as she moved. 'Mountain wobble and shake!'

'Yes. That was the explosion.'

She cocked her head. 'Explosion bad,' she grunted.

'I agree. It was very bad. Many people died and others were badly hurt. And the mine was damaged.'

She nodded. We sat in silence for a moment while I cast around for a way to segue into the purpose of my visit. In the interests of brevity, I decided to go for broke. 'Matilda, have you seen strange men in the mountain? Men not from here hanging around the mine?'

She squinted at me again as she tried to understand. I clarified, 'We saw men with guns go into an underground tunnel that probably comes out in the mine. Do you know about them?'

Her expression darkened. 'They mean. No bring sugar snack.'

My heart gave a loud thump. Yes, she knew about them. 'Yes, very mean. Very bad men.'

She gave a clear harrumph. 'They no let Matilda go to secret place. Not their say where Matilda go!'

The surprise clearly showed on my face, because she lifted one of her large hands and touched one of my eyebrows with a metal claw. I froze. 'Hair over eyes, jump like rabbit.' She laughed. 'You two rabbit!'

'They're called eyebrows,' I explained and wiggled them for her. She laughed harder. She didn't have eyebrows, so facial hair must have looked alien to her, much like her metal claws did to me.

With another wheeze she got herself under control, though she still looked amused. At least she wasn't trying to rip my throat out, which was a vast improvement on my worst-case scenario. When she'd finally calmed down, I asked 'Matilda, why can't you go to the secret place?'

She glowered. 'Bad magic. No like. Burns.'

Bad magic? I frowned. What could burn a creature made out of pure earth magic? Did the MIB have a ward around their installation? 'How does it burn you?' I asked.

'Bad magic! You no listen.'

I backpedalled. 'I did listen, I just can't imagine magic strong enough to hurt you.'

She gave me a measured look as she probably tried to figure out if I were lying. Finally she nodded. 'Matilda very strong magic. This magic not as strong as Matilda, just *bad*.' She made an odd gesture with her claws, a pinching motions above her head. Maybe the magic around the secret place felt like static, or pins and needles – or worse.

I let that go and moved on. 'Do the mean men come into the mine itself?'

'They in mine.' I could tell she didn't understand the question.

'Do you know who killed the dwarves, Matilda?' She looked at me blankly. 'Did you take the dwarves' heads?'

Matilda exploded in sudden movement that nearly made me piss my pants. I stayed very, very still as she jumped up and down and threw her arms about in fury. Rocks and dirt flew in all directions. 'Stolen!' She howled. She pulled her hair and her ears turned red. 'Bad men take. Steal from Matilda!'

'Matilda, what did they steal from you?' I was pretty sure I knew the answer, but I had to be certain.

'They go to cave and take my prizes.'

I remembered the heads lining her cave. How had the MIB even gotten into it? And why would they steal the skulls? My brain sluggishly connected the dots: the skulls on the pikes had been old: the MIB had stolen them from Matilda. 'They took your skulls?'

'Yes!' she wailed.

'Where did the skulls come from?'

'They are mine!'

'I *know* they're yours – you showed them to me. But where did you get them?'

'*My* people.'

'They were hag skulls?' That made no sense: hags were supposedly made of pure earth magic, not something that would leave behind a skeleton.

Her frustration was evident. 'No.' She searched for a word. 'Husband, husband family, friends. My *people*.'

'You were married?' My voice was incredulous so I hastily added, 'Are there male hags?'

She settled back down enough to laugh again. 'Bunny silly. No, hags always female.' She puffed her chest out with pride. 'Husband was vampire.'

Now *that*, I could relate to. 'Nice,' I said, holding my hand up for a high-five. She stared at it and I let it drop awkwardly.

'Yes,' she agreed, still staring at my hand which was now folded on my lap. 'He good husband. He kill many for me.'

Well, I guessed we all defined what made a spouse 'good' in different ways. I offered a weak smile.

Matilda had had a vampire husband? How did that even happen? Her appearance wasn't even humanoid – did the vampire have a thing about metal teeth? And the academy had taught me that a hag's appearance could vary from humanoid to downright alien. Could Matilda change her appearance at will?

I thought back to her den and her 'family'. There'd been hundreds of skulls in that cave; some were probably dwarves – the ones she appeared to have stolen – but the rest were her friends and family? How long ago had her husband died? And what had killed him?

'I'm very sorry for your loss, Matilda. I didn't know your husband had died.' Or that she'd even had one.

She sat back down on the stone, her short legs swinging. 'Long ago,' she said but her expression was wistful.

'Why keep the skulls?' I asked.

She looked at me like I was stupid. 'They family.'

My heart ached for her; she must be so lonely now. 'Have you always lived in Portlock?' I asked curiously.

She shrugged. 'I live many places. Family came with me.'

'How long ago?'

'Long, long time.'

'If you don't mind me asking, how did your husband die?'

She looked away and I grimaced. I hadn't meant to upset her. 'The Sdonalyasna kill him,' she said finally. 'Before many people come.'

I'd never heard that word, but my heart beat hard once. Was she talking about the beast beyond? Did she know what it was?

'What is the Sdonalyasna?' I said, trying to pronounce the word carefully but probably failing.

She gave me an odd look. 'You know! Everyone know. Can't come in now.' She cackled again.

My God, she knew what the beast beyond the barrier was! Or, at the very least, she'd given it a name. Maybe I could use that to find more information – and more importantly, it might give me a hint as to what Shadow was. And maybe, just maybe, I might learn how to defeat it because there was a prophecy that apparently had my name on it.

The words were etched into my memory: *When the flame-born guardian descends to the night, the veiled city's mysteries will unfold. Thrice shall the cursed wolf's mournful howl sound, heralding the coming of the shadow beast. Love shall be her beacon and with its power, the city might endure the destruction that comes.'* Thanks for that, Mum.

Sdonalyasna. The word sounded like it could be native, but I realized that finding the language and the specific native group it came from might be incredibly hard.

I supposed I could start with Thomas; he'd said he was Inupiaq, from somewhere up north like Danny from the academy. But the beast beyond the barrier was definitely a southern Alaskan creature.

I didn't know what group Stan was from, but since he'd been raised mostly by Gunnar and Sigrid, I doubted he'd retained much of his native culture. There were representatives of several native groups from this part of the state in Portlock: Anissa and Edgy were Alutiiq or Sugpiak, which was the group of natives that had lived in Portlock when the attacks first happened. Maybe it was an Alutiiq word; I'd ask them if Thomas didn't know.

There were also Haida and Tlingit tribal members in town, as well as some Athabascan, Dena'ina, Tsimshian and Eyak, but I didn't have friends in any of those groups.

I grimaced; it might be a word none of them knew. My best bet was Matilda, and she wasn't the easiest to understand.

I was both excited and frustrated. Matilda had come from somewhere with a vampire husband, dragging the skulls from his family and their friends, and had ended up in Portlock when it was fairly uninhabited. During the scare that had resulted in the barrier being built, the beast had killed her husband. At least that was how I was putting her story together.

Matilda interrupted my musings. 'Rabbit girl, you stop mean men?' she asked hopefully. 'Bring more sugar snack. Matilda want back secret place.'

'Where is secret place?' I asked her.

She pointed down at the hill. 'In.' She tapped her chest pointedly. '*My* place. I want back.'

'Could you show me and my friends where to go so we can stop the mean men?'

She squinted at me. 'Bring sugar snack?'

'Yes, I'll bring you more treats'

'Matilda show you.'

'And my friends too?' I gestured to the others by the vehicles. They were watching us, looking tense. I made an effort to appear relaxed.

She grunted. 'And friends,' she agreed grudgingly.

'Thank you. We'll come back tomorrow. Okay?'

'Matilda listen for call.' As she melted into the ground, she pointed to where an eyebrow should have been on her face and laughed to herself. Surely her vampire husband had eyebrows? Maybe he'd waggled them at her to make her laugh. I was surprised how much that made my heart ache and I swore I'd waggle them every time I saw her.

I waved to Thomas, Gunnar and Sidnee to show them I was done, then returned to them. 'What did she say?' Sidnee burst out before anyone else could.

'She knows where they are in the mine – it's her "secret place". It sounds like they have a ward or some kind of field around the spot, so Matilda can't get in. She wants *us* to get in and stop them.' I paused. 'And we need to bring her more doughnuts. We have the council meeting soon, so I suggested we come back tomorrow. I'll put in an order at the bakery.'

Gunnar looked around; everything was still and dark. 'There's nothing we can do here now. Might as well head back, get the council meeting over and done with, then we all have a party to go to, right, Sidnee?'

Her answering smile was faint. 'I'm not sure...' she started. 'So many died. A party seems ... crass.'

Gunnar shook his head firmly. 'It's what we need. Besides, if we're under surveillance from the MIB, it'll be the perfect smokescreen. They'll see us partying and think we've written off the explosion as an accident. They'll think they're in the clear, and when their guard is down, we'll attack.' He smiled broadly, but there was nothing friendly about his expression.

Sidnee nodded. 'Okay, if you're sure. I'll send out a message to say that the party is still on.' She chewed her lip. 'Can you drop me at the hotel on the way to the council meeting? I don't need to be there for that, do I?'

Gunnar shook his head. 'Neither of you do. I'll go and report back. I know how much you love to get ready for these things.'

On the surface his comment appeared sexist, but the truth was he knew us too well. We *did* love to get ready. Out here in the wilds of Alaska, it was rare to have an occasion to dress up, so we went all out when we did. My excitement was building; you could take the girl out of the London clubbing scene, but you couldn't take the London clubbing scene out of the girl.

Gunnar, Connor and Thomas got into one vehicle, Sidnee and I took the other and we all headed back to town, destination party central. I couldn't wait. It was, quite literally, time to let my hair down.

Because if we faced the MIB tomorrow, it might well be the last party I'd ever enjoy.

Chapter 37

Sidnee dropped me off so I could start to get ready. I hadn't had time to order a new dress, but I had one that I'd been saving for a special occasion. It was dark-green silk and it made my eyes pop. It was high necked but bare shouldered and ended mid-thigh; the fabric clung in all the right places, making my lanky form look a little curvier than usual, and the wrap-around skirt that tied in front and gave the illusion of an hourglass figure. I paired it with silver strappy sandals and a matching silver bag.

Okay, it wasn't the best winter wear but Connor was picking me up for the short drive, so I just had to make it to the car and into the hotel. Frankly, I could do that naked if I needed to, not that streaking was on my to-do list. If it ever had been on there, Alaska's freezing temperatures would have pushed it *way* down.

I fed my pets and turned on the TV for them: a nature show about big cats. They were curled up on the couch together when Connor knocked. 'Fluffy, you could shift and come to the party with me,' I said for the third time, but he just sighed and pointedly put his head down on his paws.

I'd found a supernatural counsellor in town and Reggie's first appointment was in a week. It couldn't come soon enough; I was failing him and it was all my fault that he was stuck like this. My bloody mum and her idiocy. That damned prophecy.

I eyed my German Shepherd with such guilt that he barked at me. I gave him a lopsided smile. 'Yeah, yeah.'

There was another firm knock at the door and I gave each pet a scruffle on the head. 'I gotta go. See you guys later.'

When I opened the front door, Connor was standing there in a sleek black suit with a sapphire-blue shirt beneath it. The colour made his eyes a shade darker than normal, as deep blue as the sea. His curls were sort of tamed, meaning he hadn't run his hand through them yet. I decided I preferred them wild and I almost mussed them up myself, but it was obvious he'd taken time over his appearance so I didn't. Besides, I was sure I'd do something to make him run his hands through his hair later. Exasperating him was a gift.

He had brought his Mustang because the roads were clear of snow, and I spotted John and Margrave in the truck idling at the kerb behind it. Both men were suited and booted, but it was clear they were attending the party as bodyguards.

I walked carefully down the steps, gratefully slid my silk-clad bottom onto the heated leather seats and gave a happy little moan of pleasure. If I ever bought a car, I was definitely having heated seats.

Connor's eyes never left me and the fire in them warmed me further. 'If you keep looking at me like that we won't make it to the party,' I said with a grin.

'Is that a promise?'

I tapped him lightly on the arm. 'No! We can't be late, we're supporting Sidnee. Now focus on getting us there.'

He gave me one more scorching look then pressed the button to start the engine. 'I'd much rather take you up on that than go out.'

'Same – but we'd never get out of bed without other commitments.'

He laughed. 'True.'

The motor caught with a roar and we headed to the hotel. 'How did the council meeting go?' I asked.

Connor grimaced. 'About the usual. It quickly devolved into arguing.'

'Anything decided?'

'Unofficially we have permission to storm the mines, but if it goes wrong the council will rescind that permission. They're worried that the dwarves will see it as an act of hostility.'

'Obviously we don't want to piss off the dwarves, but would it be so terrible if we did?'

'The mine is one of the most profitable businesses in town.'

'Fishing, mining, logging.' I counted them off on my fingers.

'Exactly – and mining brings in the most coin and creates a tonne of jobs. It's not just mining itself, but administrative and logistical and transportational ones too. It's a huge operation. If the dwarves went elsewhere...' He trailed off.

'It would be bad for Portlock?'

'Very bad,' he agreed. 'Keeping the mine stable is the whole reason Calliope, Thomas and Liv bought into it.'

'And the profit doesn't hurt,' I said cynically. 'So we have an unofficial green light to storm the place tomorrow?'

'Yep.'

'Who are they sending?'

He sighed. 'Just us. The same team as today.'

I grimaced. We had supernatural strength on our side but five of us against *at least* twelve MIB didn't feel great. Hopefully the narrow tunnels would restrict who could come at us, but now we knew it was the MIB black ops group, we had to take real care not to be exposed to fisheye. 'We'll need gloves and breathing apparatus,' I pointed out.

'I'm on it.' Connor reached over and squeezed my thigh. 'Now forget about all that and relax. Let's enjoy today – who knows what tomorrow will bring?'

I knew. Tomorrow was going to bring a clusterfuck of epic proportions, though weirdly I was kind of looking forward to it. Excitement and nerves were churning in my gut; I vowed I would channel them into my dance moves and shimmy them off.

As Connor parked behind the hotel, I suddenly remembered another night and another dance when Juan had been guarding Connor. 'I'm sorry about Juan,' I offered. 'You must miss him.'

'I do,' he admitted. 'He was my best and only friend for a very long time.'

I swallowed hard, my eyes suddenly damp. 'Well, now you have me,' I said firmly. 'You have lots of friends. You have Gunnar and Sigrid, and Sidnee and Thomas.' I paused. 'Maybe even Stan.'

He winced at the last name but then gave me a warm smile. 'You've brought so much into my life, Doe. I'm grateful for it.'

'Even with all the complications I bring?' I was thinking of Parker, the vampire I'd accidentally ensnared with my offer of blood. Guilt pricked at me again; it had a habit of doing that lately.

'Absolutely,' he replied without missing a beat. He raised my hand to his lips and brushed them against the back of it. Inwardly, I swooned.

I sighed happily. 'I love you, Connor. You know that, right?'

'I know it,' he agreed. 'And I love you with everything I am.' We kissed in the darkness, the romance of the moment hampered only by his two guards lingering in the shadows.

We walked into the party a little mussed and a few minutes late. I swiped on some fresh lipstick and neatened my hair. Sidnee had decorated the whole place in blue-and-white fairy lights, with a disco ball in the centre of the ceiling. Streamers in blue and silver hung everywhere, changing the room from bland and commercial to sparkly and festive.

There was a bar and a temporary dance floor in the centre, and the staff were setting up a lavish buffet.

Unlike at my 'welcome to Portlock party', I didn't head directly for the tequila. Instead Connor hooked my arm through his and we played the vampire leader and his mate by talking to everyone we knew – or more accurately, all the movers and shakers that Connor knew. I made careful note of new names and faces and the ones he treated with real respect or deference.

When the buffet was finally ready, we filled our plates and sat at a table. Sidnee and Thomas were talking to Stan who was arm in arm with Anissa. I waggled my eyebrows at Sidnee and she grinned back.

She was wearing a floor-length red dress that looked like it was painted on her perfect figure, with a slit to the top of her thigh and a deep neckline. When she turned to look at something Stan pointed at, I saw that the back of her dress was bare and plunged down to the curve of her ass. Thomas was a man possessed, his gaze barely straying from his lover.

Behind his back, I winked at her and fanned myself. 'You look hot,' I mouthed.

She beamed. 'You too!' she mouthed back.

'Hi, Stan,' I said warmly. 'Hi, Anissa, it's great to see you.'

I saw some of the tension slide from Stan's shoulders; had he been worried that I would react badly to his date? You do you, man; love *is*, and that's all.

The six of us sat at the same table. 'Any space for an old washed-up couple?' Gunnar asked as he and Sigrid walked over.

'Speak for yourself!' Sigrid swatted him, making us laugh.

'Of course,' Connor said easily and we all shifted up while Stan grabbed a couple more chairs.

'You look beautiful, Sig,' I said, and she really did. Her blue dress complemented her skin perfectly and she'd taken the time to pile elaborate plaits on top of her head. She glowed with an inner radiance as she beamed and thanked me. 'Thank you, Bunny dear.'

'Where's April?' I asked.

'She's sleeping,' Gunnar confirmed. 'She's going to run house tomorrow for us while we're out.'

Sig's smile faltered.

'Right. Who's on call then?' I asked.

'Yours truly,' Gunnar grunted, tapping the phone on his hip.

'Better you than me!'

'Got some bad news,' Gunnar said quietly. 'We got the letter from Alfgar's locker back from forensics. No fingerprints.'

'Damn.' I sighed.

'No business talk!' Sigrid admonished him. 'Unless you get a work call,' she amended.

Connor had brought champagne for everyone and he poured me a glass. I was planning on sipping mine slowly but I must have blinked because suddenly the glass was empty. Whoops! Connor poured me another without comment but I saw Stan grin. 'Bunny's going to dance on the table later,' he predicted.

I glared. 'I am *not!*' I definitely wasn't going to, now that he'd said that! 'You're going to eat your words.'

Stan smirked. 'We'll see.'

I sipped at my new glass of fizz, relishing the bubbly burn as it hit my mostly empty stomach. I'd had a mug of blood earlier but it hadn't touched the sides, so I dived into my food with gusto. I did love good food and wine, and it was a real pleasure to have a change from my normal diet of frozen dinners and tea. I spotted Anissa snaffling the dinner with similar enthusiasm and saluted her. She was a girl after my own heart.

By the end of the meal, I was feeling smug. I hadn't drunk my date under the table and I was still seated, not singing and dancing on the tables. I gave myself a mental pat on the back.

But I shouldn't have because the night was still young.

Chapter 38

At some point in the evening, Sidnee had talked me into colourful cocktails instead of wine, and after a few spins on the dance floor with Connor I found myself taking the mic from the band's singer and singing a torchy rendition of 'Fever'. Connor's eyes burned in his shadowed face.

After that Sidnee and I danced together to a fun Taylor Swift tune. Halfway through Thomas cut in, leaving me dancing alone. I gestured for Connor to join me but he just leaned forward, elbows on his knees, and watched. I forgot everything and danced for him alone, slow and sultry, my hands roving over my body.

At some point, Sidnee had taken Thomas back to the table and was sitting on his lap making out. I downed another cocktail in one to try to soothe my dry throat but it didn't, so I drank another. My head was swimming and my inhibitions were long gone.

An upbeat song came on and I started dancing faster. After that, I grabbed a couple of tequila shots – and that was the last I remembered of the party. I *may* not have been making good choices.

I woke up with a pounding head and a sour stomach. When I pried my eyes open, Connor was standing over me with a mug of warm blood. I wrinkled my nose. 'If I drink that I'm probably going to vom.'

He smirked. 'If you don't, you're *definitely* going to vom,' he advised. He held the mug closer to me. 'Bottoms up!'

Ugh. As I sat up, I realised I was in Connor's bed. I clutched my head and groaned, then reached out and took the mug. I slammed back the blood – I didn't even raise my other arm to plug my nose. I thrust the mug back to him. He waited a minute then asked, 'Better now?'

I actually was. The pounding in my head was already receding. It was a wonder Connor didn't get drunk more often, given that we had a hangover remedy ready at any time.

I gave him a flat look. 'You know I am.' I groaned. 'I'm a bad fur mummy. Shadow and Fluffy!' I was worried about them, though I knew that if ever they were in a tight spot Fluffy could become Reggie and deal with it. Leaving them overnight wasn't quite the same as abandoning a real dog and cat – that was what I told myself, anyway.

'I've already been over to check on them,' Connor soothed. 'They're fine. I'd have brought them back here, but they seemed happy and we have to leave for the mine soon. They decided to stay home.'

'Maybe we should take Fluffy?'

'You want him deep inside the earth at the mercy of an unstable hag and a group of unknown combatants behind a ward?'

'When you say it like that...' I grumbled. Still, I was used to Fluffy's presence at my heel and I felt a bit off-kilter without him. When he finally got around to embracing his human self, it would be one hell of an adjustment for me, too; even so, I still wanted that for him.

'We have to pick up the doughnuts in an hour, so you better get your pretty ass in the shower,' Connor warned me.

'An hour?' An hour sounded luxurious – I usually got ready for work in half that. 'I'll shower now if you join me.' I looked up at him through my lashes, trying to be sexy. I guess it worked because he kicked off his shoes and started peeling off his clothes.

I giggled and ran into the bathroom – only to see the horror of my reflection in the mirror. My hair was a rat's nest and I had smeared mascara and lipstick all over my face; I looked like a clown after three consecutive performances in a sauna, or a creepy one that lived in the sewers and lured small children to their deaths. I gave a small scream, which made Connor laugh aloud.

'Why didn't you tell me I looked like the walking dead?' I spat out.

He laughed again. 'I hate to be the one to break it to you, Toots, but you *are* the walking dead.'

Good point, well made.

I turned on the jets then jumped in too fast and was hit by ice-cold water. I shrieked and danced in place until it warmed up then hurriedly scrubbed my face. Connor waited until the water was hot then climbed in behind me and snaked his arm around my waist. Since my face was covered in soap and my eyes were tightly closed, I squeaked at the contact.

I turned in his arms to face him. 'I'm not allowed to party anymore,' I said seriously. 'Make a note. No more parties for Bunny.'

He looked amused. 'We both know you're not going to stick to that.'

We did. 'What happened after I danced for you?'

His body tensed. 'You don't want to know, trust me.'

I buried my face in his torso and groaned. 'I have to know. Hit me.'

'Well, you started on shots after the cocktails and there might have been a repeat of the table-dancing incident.' He paused. 'I stopped you when you started to undress.'

'Oh God, did I flash anyone?' He went quiet. 'I did, didn't I?'

'They only saw a flash of your bra before I got to you.'

I threw back my head and groaned. 'Fuck! I'll never be able to show my face in town again!'

'No, I think that's Sidnee.'

I looked up at him startled. 'What?'

He ran his hands over my waist and the curve of my hips to draw me closer. 'Well, she took the mic after you abandoned it and started professing her love for Thomas. It got a bit ... heated.' He leaned down to kiss me, trying to start the shower loving I'd promised him.

'What does that mean?' I demanded, pushing him away slightly.

'Let's just say Thomas scooped her up and took her away to his house.'

I groaned for her. 'She'll be so mad at herself.'

'I don't know – she and Thomas finally seemed to be on the same page.'

'Well, that's something.'

I put Sidnee out of my mind as I sank into his kiss. The heat in my core rose as our lips parted and our tongues met. I was scorching hot even when he pressed my back up against the cold marble of the shower wall.

I loved waking up at Connor's house, even when I was more hungover than a shirt on a washing line.

Chapter 39

I wished Fluffy could be with us but Connor was right: it was too much of an unknown and we didn't need his nose for this. It was better he was safe at home, keeping a watch on Shadow who had made it his mission to scare me half to death at least once a day. I didn't need to worry about my animals for now – and April had promised to take care of them if something happened to me and Connor. You had to think of these things when you were heading into a gun battle.

I dressed in jeans, a sweatshirt and my Xtra-Tuf boots. With the mud and cold rain, I needed the ugly things, and anyway they were comfortable even if they were a sin against all things fashion.

I added my rain jacket to my ensemble before Connor and I headed out to get the doughnuts and meet our motley crew. This time I'd been smart enough to order doughnuts for us as well; I hated smelling them when they were fresh and not eating one. Besides, it might be our last meal. I reached into the box on my lap and pulled out a large, glazed one that was still warm to the touch.

We piled into the SUV; it was a tight fit, but hey, you should always carpool when you can. Even if it's a ride to your possible death.

'Want one?' I asked the others with my mouth full. I'd started to eat before I remembered to offer. My mum would have been mortified.

Connor held out his hand, and I gave him a doughnut. He'd been smart enough to make me a thermos of tea and I took a sip. Heaven.

I was trying to keep my mind off dragging my friends with me into danger. Even though Matilda seemed willing enough to help, she was still an unknown – and we had no idea what was going on with the 'mean men' under the mountain.

Gunnar cleared his throat. 'I got the toxicology on Helmud this morning.'

I sat up. 'And?'

'Fisheye,' he said grimly.

Sidnee whistled. 'Damn.'

I shook my head in disbelief. 'He really did stumble on them. I'd bet a paycheck it was simply a case of wrong time, wrong place.' The cogs in my brain were whirring. 'And

Alfgar,' I murmured. 'Maybe the MIB were trying to cover their tracks, trying to pin it on Matilda.'

'They know the dwarves are scared of her,' Sidnee agreed. 'When Alfgar's death didn't get the result they wanted, they tried a little more obviously with Evgard.'

'I think they're trying to run the dwarves out of the mine,' I mused. 'When their attempted purchase fell through, maybe they decided another method was in order.'

'And this time the method was murder and intimidation,' Sidnee said.

I frowned. 'But *why?* Chromite isn't that expensive. Surely they can buy it easily enough.'

Gunnar tapped his hands on the wheel. 'Maybe it's a component of the drugs they've been creating – fisheye or somnum, maybe.'

I couldn't help noticing we were using a lot of maybes but my gut told me we were on the right path.

Thomas shook his head. 'If they think they can run the dwarves out of the mine, they're wrong.'

'The explosion was a real escalation,' I said. 'I bet they're on a timescale and somehow, we're fucking with it.'

Sidnee grinned. 'I'm always happy to fuck with the MIB's schedule.'

We pulled into the car park. More debris had been cleared and some workers were getting ready to leave for the night. We climbed out of the SUV, girded our loins – or chests – with our vests, picked up our backpacks and weapons and headed up the hill to our rendezvous spot with Matilda. I led the way.

When we were in the spot where I'd talked to Matilda the previous day, I made sure everyone was ready and that the bakery box was visible in my outstretched hand. I called out clearly, 'Matilda, Matilda, Matilda.'

Instead of making me wait, this time she appeared quickly, coming up through the ground like she was on a lift. She reached out her hands and I thrust the box into her impatient claws.

Matilda shoved doughnuts into her mouth at warp speed and it didn't take long for her to devour a full dozen. Yikes, that girl needed to learn to savour her food. When she was done, she licked the last of the icing from her fingers and metal nails with a surprisingly pointy tongue. It looked a bit serpentine and I suppressed a shudder. She thrust the empty box back at me and I folded it flat and shoved it under a rock for retrieval later.

'Rabbit bring good sugar snack,' she declared.

I squelched a glare at the use of the moniker 'Rabbit'. I didn't think she was *trying* to insult me – she did that without any effort. 'I'm glad you enjoyed the doughnuts,' I managed, glad that Stan wasn't there to hear her refer to me like that.

'We go secret place,' she declared. At least she was direct and on a mission.

'Thank you, Matilda. I appreciate you helping us.'

She looked at me for a moment with her black eyes then turned. The mountain opened to her, revealing a tunnel tall enough for Gunnar to walk through without stooping. She walked into it and we followed.

Like my previous trip into the earth with Matilda, the tunnel looked like it had always been there, yet it was forming instantly as she moved. It was fascinating – but again I was disorientated, not knowing in which direction we were going in other than downwards.

The weight of the mountain started to bear down on me as my newly discovered claustrophobia kicked in. I didn't realise I was gasping for air until Connor's hand pressed into my lower back. His breath warmed my neck as he whispered, 'It'll be okay, Doe. Just breathe.'

I nodded and tried to concentrate on breathing normally. As a vampire-witch hybrid, I *needed* to breathe whereas Connor did not. It was one thing I'd missed out on by not being a full vampire.

Matilda stopped suddenly. 'Bad magic,' she grunted, pointing ahead.

All I could see was an earth wall in front of me. 'Matilda, how do we get past this spot to where the mean men are?'

She shook her head then squinted at the end of the tunnel we were facing. The mud fell away to reveal a cement bunker. She backed up until we were almost touching. 'Mean men!' she hissed.

I walked up to where she had sensed the 'bad magic' to see if I could feel it. As I reached out a hand, I felt the prickly barrier. I took a step back. 'Yep,' I said aloud. 'That's definitely warded.'

Gunnar squeezed past us; when he felt the barrier, he jerked back his hand. 'Yep,' he agreed. 'It doesn't feel that strong, though, nothing like the barrier around town. It feels prickly.' He closed his eyes in concentration. 'I'm pretty sure I can break through it, but whoever created it will probably sense me. They must have a decent magic user with them – warding isn't an easy skill.'

'Why would a weak ward affect Matilda?' I asked.

'Bad,' Matilda emphasised, shuddering. I heard a clattering and realised her hands were shaking, her metal nails clanging against themselves. Shit, this really *was* affecting her. Other than feeling prickly; it didn't feel wrong or 'bad' to me and I was baffled by her reaction.

'Didn't you tell me that Liv said the only way to kill an earth elemental like Matilda was with an air elemental?' Gunnar asked.

'Yeah, so?'

'Could the ward have been put up by an air witch?'

It made a sort of sense. Witches were weaker versions of elementals, so although an air witch probably couldn't harm Matilda, they could make her very uncomfortable. The ward hadn't stopped the hag from using her powers beyond it and she'd cleared the dirt away from the bunker, but she didn't want to pass through it.

'Huh,' I said. 'That's actually a pretty great theory.'

Thomas interrupted our musings. 'Gunnar, before you take down this ward, we need to make sure we can get inside of the bunker. Can anyone find an entrance?'

We stared through the invisible ward at a cement wall. I saw no points of ingress. Being able to see in the depths of the ocean, Sidnee had the best eyes in the dark. Luckily, we all had water bottles to help her, so in an instant her eyes flashed black. She moved forward and stared. 'There's an indentation on the right that could be a door.'

That was better than nothing. We had no idea if we could get through it, but having seen Gunnar open locks and seal the barrier temporarily, I knew some of what he could do with his magic. 'Gunnar, can you open the cement door using your trick?' I waggled my fingers at him in an effort to denote his magic.

'I'm not sure,' he answered honestly. 'There isn't a handle.'

Thomas spoke up. 'I say we have Gunnar take down the ward and Matilda can take down the wall. It'll be faster and we'll have the element of surprise.' He turned to Matilda. 'Could you do that?'

Matilda's eyes lit up in the weak light of our flashlights. She clicked her metal nails together and gave one of her cackles. 'Matilda can do!'

Gunnar returned to the edge of the ward. 'Everyone stand back just in case this has some blowback.' We backed away cautiously, even Matilda.

He rubbed his hands together, concentrated, then lifted them to face the ward. He mumbled something in what I thought was Norwegian and a white light blasted from his palms. The ward glowed for a moment before a blast of wind hit us. Gunnar staggered back a few steps, his long hair and beard blown back.

Matilda laughed with delight. The second the ward fell, a large section of the cement wall melted away too.

There was no messing with the hag.

Chapter 40

We could see into the bunker. The area that had disintegrated in the face of Matilda's magic was a bunkroom with about twenty beds. Luckily it was empty. We lifted our weapons and stepped inside.

The door leading out of the room was metal. Whatever this place had been designed for, it was solid and hidden; I bet it would be pretty damn impenetrable without magic and the presence of the wards told us that they weren't averse to using it if it suited them. Bloody hypocrites!

Thomas opened the door a crack then opened it wider and craned his neck to see both ends of whatever lay behind the door. Finally he opened it wide and waved us on. Once I got a good view, I saw we were at one end of the facility. There was only one way we could go, to the right where Sidnee thought there had been a door.

Gunnar motioned for Thomas to step behind him. I thought for a moment there would be an argument, but after a beat Thomas complied.

I could hear machinery ahead but I couldn't place what it was. Gunnar stalked down the corridor past several closed doors with zero signage. He and I stood on each side of the first door that had a high-tech scanner next to it. I tried the knob. Locked. I gestured for Gunnar to do his thing and the door opened at his touch; magic apparently outdid tech.

He opened the door a crack, then wider, shotgun at the ready. 'Clear,' he whispered.

I glanced inside. This one looked like a storage room; there were shelves of canned and boxed food, cleaning supplies and extra blankets. Matilda took a look then went inside to explore. I was sure that whatever she normally ate was pretty boring because she tore open several boxes and tried the contents of them all. 'Come on, Matilda,' I hissed. 'Now isn't the time for a snack!'

'Always time for snack.' She continued focusing on the food and I shrugged helplessly. We couldn't wait for her to finish her mini-banquet because the longer we were there, the higher the chance of discovery was.

We had no choice but to press forward and anyway, she'd completed her side of the bargain and got us to the secret place. What we did from here on was up to us – so we left her behind.

At the next door Gunnar repeated his actions before flinging open the door to reveal a cell with a woman inside. Filthy, gaunt and dressed in dirty rags, she looked up at us with haunted eyes. She had a collar around her neck with a strip of red light around it. Her face showed her utter despair.

'Hey, I'm Bunny. Who are you?' I asked gently while Gunnar backed up so as not to intimidate her. She shrugged but didn't answer. 'Are you the air witch that did the ward?' I asked.

Her eyes flew open wide. 'Yes!'

'I thought so.' I smiled. 'You feel the same. We're supernats. We'll get you out of here.'

She shook her head miserably. 'If you do anything, this collar will blow my head off.'

I looked at it. 'Can I come closer to examine it?' I asked. She nodded and I padded forward. Lifting her lank, greasy hair, I saw that the collar was thick, presumably because of the explosives, and it had a thumbprint lock. It was a nasty piece of work.

'We'll figure out a way,' I promised rashly. 'I'll close the door for now so we don't give away our presence, but we're going to clear out this place and come back for you. Any idea of their numbers?'

'Sorry, no. I only see the same asshole.' She sighed wearily and leaned her head back against the wall.

'Okay, thanks. What's your name?'

'Emma.'

'We'll be back, Emma,' I said as we backed out and shut the door behind us. Once on the other side of it, I closed my eyes. 'Those fucking bastards,' I whispered.

'Discard your rage,' Gunnar instructed crisply. 'It has no place here and it'll get you killed. Be angry later.'

I nodded stiffly and we moved forward to check the next three doors. Either there weren't many people here full time or they were all concentrated in one area, because we found nothing but equipment and humming machines. We didn't stay long enough to identify what they were doing; we could circle back later when the area was clear and we'd rescued the poor witch.

We hit the jackpot in the fourth room. Gunnar peered inside before lifting his finger to his lips to indicate silence. We lined up behind him, weapons ready, then he stepped inside, his shotgun raised.

I joined him and Connor followed. We'd stepped into some kind of control room. One wall was covered with computer screens linked to video feeds from the mine and tailings area. The cameras must have been tiny and very well hidden.

Three men were monitoring the screens and four more were sitting at tables assembling devices. Surprised, they looked up when we entered. They were dressed in camo fatigues and each man had a handgun at their hip. They all reached for them.

Seven guns swung towards us. Gunnar shot one man and the noise blasted our ears. Connor was already behind another with his knife, swiping it across the man's throat.

I felt something slam into my vest that hurt like a motherfucker, but it woke me up and I fired, striking my opponent in the head. He went down instantly. Thomas took out three more in rapid succession, and Connor shot the last one.

When it ended we were standing in a bloodbath, but thinking of Emma locked in that room with explosives around her neck made it hard to feel sorry.

We couldn't stop there, though; we had to clear the rest of the building. If we didn't get out of the room fast, we'd be as pinned down as the group we'd just removed had been.

Thomas was ex-MIB – and probably ex-military – so he had the most experience of this type of thing. He charged down the hall and cleared the next room, which was empty, then moved forward, paused outside the last door and held up a hand to stop us. He pressed his ear against the door then mouthed, 'In here,' – just as the door slammed open and armed men poured out, firing as they came.

Thomas dropped to his knees and started firing back.

Gunnar, Thomas and I were the only ones with clear shots; the corridor was too narrow for Sidnee to join in and we had no idea where Matilda was, unless she was still enjoying the food in the storage area. However, the enemy had the same problem of being in a confined space and our return fire stopped them getting organized.

Thomas was precise and deadly, and his every shot brought down another combatant. Since Gunnar was using a shotgun, he had similar luck. I just kept firing to keep the enemy from having time to aim. I took several shots to my vest and one to my arm; Gunnar grunted as he took fire as well.

We had no cover. Eventually one of the MIB would get in a lucky shot that didn't hit our vests, so we did something that went against all my instincts: we charged.

We needed to stop the enemy from aiming at us, so I drew up the anger that had roared through me at their treatment of Emma, their bombing of the mine and the three murders. With that rage as the catalyst, I raised my other hand and threw a huge, rolling fireball.

Our opponents were disoriented and they turned to run back into the room they'd flooded out of. I counted thirteen dead before we followed. I tried not to notice how many I had burned. Only three were still alive.

Being the most invulnerable, Connor rushed in and took down the last two. The third cowered in a corner, his gun gone, and Connor used him like a blood donor to heal his wounds. He told me to drink to heal my arm and I grimaced; the only time I'd felt bloodlust was when I'd been poisoned with fisheye and then I had nearly drained one of the MIB's creepy generals dry.

But my arm hurt and I could feel blood pouring down it. I didn't know how many more of them there were and I couldn't be incapacitated. I couldn't be a liability to my team, not when it might mean the difference between all of us living or dying.

I knelt down next to my mate. For once my lazy fangs responded appropriately and I drank until my arm stopped aching. When I'd had enough, Connor finished off the soldier by twisting his neck. I grimaced.

Knowing that these fuckers were going to kill us and do evil things to our town, I could let the killing go. I thought of the abused witch, rigged to die in the other room, and I thought about Juan Torres who'd died because fisheye simply touched his skin. All my regrets and guilt about killing went away. These monsters had it coming.

Sidnee was freaked out, though. In her human form she was mild and sweet, and killing disturbed her no matter how evil the bastards were who died. She checked Thomas over for wounds. Like all of us, some rounds had hit his vest and he had a bullet graze on his neck. That one could have ended him. I shuddered. Of all of us, he was the most vulnerable.

Gunnar had a wound to his thigh but the bullet had passed through the outer layer of flesh and the bleeding was minimal.

As we found a first-aid kit and quickly bandaged the wounded, Matilda wandered down the corridor. She poked a few of her 'mean men' and beamed at me when she realized that her secret place was back. She was happy – though her chrome teeth were always a shock – but then she really freaked me out. She flicked one of her long claws at the bodies and they turned to dirt before us – blood, bodies, everything was gone. The power she wielded was *immense*.

She cackled and gave a little dance. 'Gone gone. Mean men gone,' she sang. 'Rabbit girl Matilda friend.'

I gave her a weak smile.

Chapter 41

With the enemy soldiers rousted, we took the time to explore the underground bunker. We started back in the computer room that we'd cleared first. Gunnar went to the tables to try to determine what the men had been building while Connor sat down at the computer to search for intel.

Sidnee and I hurriedly checked the bodies for identification or anything that would help us find out who these people were and what their agenda was before Matilda decided to cleanse this room in her dramatic fashion.

The men were wearing access badges on their uniforms, but apart from those, all their names and insignias that were usually on a military uniform were missing. They must have checked them in to keep themselves anonymous.

The badges had the words 'Knight Stalker'. I shivered. Using the word knight had very lordly connotations. Who did these people think they were? In England a knight *served* their sovereign; were these black-ops personnel using it that way to suggest that they were serving a government overlord? Or were they implying that they were superior to us lowly supernats and were on a righteous crusade? Either way, at least we had a name for our shadowy splinter group. Not that it really mattered what they called themselves; I was happy to call them arseholes.

We didn't find anything else before Matilda gleefully vaporised them. She didn't seem to want to keep *their* skulls. Friends and family only.

Thomas was searching the rest of the room and Sidnee joined him, opening file cabinets and drawers and looking for anything that would tell us what they were doing and why they wanted the mine.

'I'm going to help the air witch, Emma,' I announced. 'Matilda, will you come with me?'

She shrugged and turned to follow. When we reached Emma's cell, I knocked on the door then opened it. Emma looked up as we entered and her eyes widened at the sight of Matilda. A hag: she probably hadn't met one before.

'This is my friend Matilda,' I said hastily. 'She's a hag but she's very nice.' Especially if you brought her doughnuts.

Matilda waved a clawed hand in a way that probably wasn't as reassuring as she intended. I pointed to the collar around Emma's neck. 'That collar is deadly. Emma can't leave the room with it on. Can you make it go away, like you did with the mean men's bodies?'

Matilda squinted at it then leaned in to sniff it before moving back. She flicked a metallic nail and the collar turned to dirt and crumbled to dust. The air witch reached up and felt her neck, then promptly burst into tears. Clearly panicked, Matilda looked at me wide eyed.

'Happy tears,' I explained. 'Emma is glad to be free. You haven't upset her.'

Emma nodded. 'Happy tears. Thank you, Matilda, thank you so much! I thought I was going to die here.'

Matilda patted Emma's arm awkwardly; the tentative nature of the touch and her screwed-up face made it look like she thought the witch had some sort of infectious disease.

Emma wiped the tears from her cheeks. 'They don't deserve any more of my tears. They've wrung enough of them from me.'

'I think those tears were for yourself,' I said softly. 'We all need to cry now and again and there's no shame in it. It's a release, and I'd hazard a guess that you really needed it.'

Emma took a shuddering breath. 'Yes, you're right.'

'Where are you from, Emma?' I asked. She could be from Portlock but I'd never seen her before.

'My full name is Emma Timit. I'm from Anchorage and I work with the Alaska Minerals Commission. *They...*' she sneered with true hatred, 'came looking for information about a mine that had been abandoned for seventy-five years. When I'd given them the papers they requested, they kidnapped me! Somehow they'd found out I was a powerful air witch and they knew they could use me.' Her voice trembled but her jaw was set firm. 'What's the date?' she asked.

'It's New Year's Day,' I said.

'God, I've been here for more than four months. Do you have a phone I can borrow? Helmud will be beside himself.'

I swallowed hard. Helmud. It couldn't be! 'Helmud Henderson?' I asked.

Her gaze sharpened; she'd heard the dread in my tone. 'Yes. My fiancé. You know him?'

Oh fuck sticks. 'Was he a mine inspector?'

She nodded then froze. 'Was?' she whispered.

Double fuck. 'I'm so sorry. Helmud died. He was killed by the same organisation that kidnapped you.'

Emma collapsed onto the floor with a strangled sob. 'Helmud! Oh my God, Helmud!'

To my surprise, Matilda pulled her into a hug. I guessed the hag knew about grief.

'I'm sorry,' I said uselessly. 'I'm so sorry.' And I was. I'd bet any money that Helmud hadn't come to Chrome by chance. He'd come a day early to look for his lost fiancée; somehow he'd known she was close by, buried in the ground in a concrete bunker he couldn't locate. And I was also willing to bet that one of the Knight Stalkers had found him too close to the bunker for comfort.

I didn't say any of that aloud – Emma didn't need to pile any misguided guilt on her heart-wrenching grief – but at least now Helmud's death made more sense to me. It hadn't been an accident or because he'd accidentally strayed into the wrong corridor; he'd been targeted because the Knight Stalkers knew he was sniffing around.

Of the deaths, Helmud's had always stood out. The others had been dwarves and their deaths had been used to frame the hag, to scare the dwarves into leaving the mine that the Knight Stalkers wanted for themselves. Helmud's death hadn't had the same scare factor – and he'd retained his head. Now I knew why: it was because his death hadn't been planned.

They'd dosed him with a hefty dose of fisheye. We hadn't been sure what the drug would do to a human, but now we knew it was as deadly to them as to us. No wonder it hadn't been widely deployed.

Despite the tragic circumstances, excitement poured through me. We were making real progress. Soon we'd be the ones going after the Knight Stalkers and then we could see how they liked it.

Chapter 42

There was a lot of chatter in the communications room when Emma and I walked in. 'What's going on?' I asked.

'Thomas found some documents!' Sidnee was bouncing on the balls of her feet with excitement. 'Look!' She passed me a manilla folder. I opened it and took out the first sheet, an old news article; the paper was old and yellowed, and it felt fragile and flimsy.

The paper's headline was *Reef Mine Closes Permanently*. I checked the date and the byline: 1945, written by a man named Ross Rose. I scanned the short article quickly: it spoke about how the need for iron and chromite had pretty much ceased at the end of the war and that was the reason the mine was being closed.

I did a quick internet search. Apparently there had been two mines in this area, and both had used Chrome Bay to ship out the chromite and iron. The Reef Mine was situated about five hundred feet off Chrome Point on a small island that was connected to the mainland at low tide by a reef; I assumed that was where the name had come from. I put down my phone and turned back to the folder.

The next sheet was a contract that showed the Reef Mine had been purchased a couple of years ago by an organisation called Orion Ltd. I was betting that was a shell corporation for our Knight Stalkers. After that, there were a bunch of mining reports that I didn't understand. 'Thomas?' I called, 'I don't speak mine. What do these reports mean?'

Emma stepped forward and picked them up. 'They mean the mine was a total dud,' she murmured.

'What?'

'No chromite left,' she clarified.

'But the newspaper article says it was closed because of a lack of demand after the war.'

Emma tapped the papers. 'I imagine that's what the owners of the Reef Mine wanted people to believe. They didn't want to admit the vein had been exhausted – they wanted some idiot to buy it off them.' She smiled grimly and look around the bunker. 'These are the idiots.'

I rubbed my lip. 'So they bought Reef, realised it was finished, then tried to buy Chrome?'

'And when that didn't work they tried intimidation instead,' Connor said grimly. 'I got something too.' He passed me another document.

It was a lengthy mission statement. There were a number of reasons for wanting the mine, the main one being that the Knight Stalkers needed chromite as an ingredient in their drug experiments and their supply was running out. They'd bought the Reef Mine not knowing it had been mined out. Apparently chromite in other areas didn't have the same properties as the chromite here, where it had that extra *magical* element that was essential in their drug manufacture. They postulated that it might be something to do with the barrier.

The second reason they wanted the mine was to use part of it as a drug factory. Thirdly, it offered easy access to Portlock and its residents; there was a plan in place to kidnap residents to experiment on once the manufacturing operation was back in full swing.

Finally, the mine had its own port where the super-secret submarine could bring in personnel and take out the drugs under cover of darkness. I smiled. The idiots had failed to consider that this was a fishing port and they'd been spotted right away by our fisherman. The report ended with an amusing note that they fully believed that they could keep all they were doing secret.

Surprise, you fuckers!

I put down the papers and gave the others a summary of what I'd read and my conclusions. 'This is a satellite office,'

I said grimly. This wasn't the victory we'd thought it was. We'd basically cleared out the Knight Stalkers' supplies closet; the real location was the Reef Mine – and a mine that size could hold hundreds of soldiers.

Gunnar scratched his beard, a sign he was thinking. 'Satellite office or not, they're going to investigate when they can't raise anyone here. Before we do anything else, we have to make sure that no one can access this bunker again.'

'We'll find the tunnel that leads to the metal lid we found. We need to close that down, too,' Thomas said.

'I'll come with you!' Sidnee volunteered.

I looked at Matilda. 'I know this is your secret place but we need to make sure the mean men can't come back.'

She folded her arms and looked at me. 'No mean men.'

'I know. We don't want them to come back either, but they want *this* mine as well as the other one.'

'No,' she said firmly. 'This Matilda's. Other mine not as tasty.' She frowned and clicked her metal nails.

I was starting to learn her tells. The nail clicking was when her mood was elevated in some way – not angry, not stressed, just getting there. I honestly didn't want to see her *truly* angry; she might call me a friend but she was scary as hell.

'Can we use your secret place for a short time longer?' I asked.

'You won't eat sugar snack?'

I smiled. 'No, it's all yours! Plus, I'll bring you more doughnuts.'

She gave me a huge metallic grin. 'Matilda share secret place.'

'Thank you, Matilda. I'm glad I'm your friend.' And I was, as long as she stayed away from my skull.

It wasn't long until Sidnee and Thomas returned. 'We might need help sealing the entrance because it looks like it can be opened by remote. Short of bombing it, there isn't an easy way,' Thomas confirmed. 'And if the town hears any more explosions, we'll cause mass hysteria.'

I looked at Matilda and grinned. 'I have an idea.'

Chapter 43

Matilda was a powerful earth elemental and as such she had power over metal, since it was an earth element. The entrance to the bunker was solid iron so it would be easy for her to manipulate.

I convinced her to follow Thomas, Sidnee and me through the man-made tunnel and we wound our way back to the bunker entrance under the tractor. When we arrived, we looked up at the iron lid. From this direction, you only needed to twist a wheel to free it by retracting the eight bars that locked it into the concrete surrounding it. No way could Connor have lifted it even if he'd been Superman.

There were electronics surrounding the exit point indicating some kind of remote access from above. I understood the issue immediately: if we didn't seal it forever, the Knight Stalkers would be back and we'd have to do it all over again. That wasn't a Groundhog Day I'd be keen to repeat. Getting shot hurts, even if it doesn't kill.

'Matilda, could you make it so that the hatch will never open again? That way we can keep the mean men from coming back.'

Clicking her nails, she studied it; she was obviously agitated. 'Matilda make whole tunnel go away,' she growled.

That would work for me, but I hoped she'd wait until we were back in the bunker. 'Okay, we'll go back,' I said hastily. 'When we're safe in the main bunker, you can make the tunnel and access shaft go away.'

We hauled ass because none of us were sure how much time Matilda would give us. Behind us, her cackle rang in the air, then suddenly the pressure increased as the tunnel collapsed.

Matilda was standing behind us. 'Is done,' she said happily. 'Mean men gone from Matilda secret place forever.'

'We are so happy for you,' I murmured.

Sidnee and Thomas nodded. We all wanted to remain on Matilda's good side.

'Will you open the way here for us sometime if we need to look at their computers again?' I asked.

A calculating look slid across the hag's face. 'Bring sugar snack?'

'Yes,' I said smothering my annoyance. I resisted the urge to tell her that sugar may be tasty but it wasn't good to consume it in vast quantities; little and often was the way forward. Still, giving dietary advice to a head-stealing hag probably wasn't a great idea.

'Matilda open again,' she promised.

'Thank you.' I smiled. 'I appreciate that.'

We collected as much data as we could then, exhausted, we all headed out of the tunnel that Matilda had made for us when we'd first come in, collapsing it as we went. Without some serious digging equipment no one was ever getting into the bunker again unless Matilda helped them. I smiled at the thought. *Take that Knight Stalkers!*

Matilda halted at the tunnel's exit. 'Will find you,' she grunted to me. 'Find more mean men.'

I blinked. 'Sure. See you tomorrow?'

She grunted as she watched us leave.

Outside, Emma took a long breath of fresh cold air and stared up at the sky. 'I never thought I'd feel the wind on my face or see the moon or stars again,' she said softly. 'Helmud loved the stars.' She turned to me. 'Can I see him?'

I turned to Gunnar and raised an eyebrow. He nodded. 'He's in the morgue,' he told her. 'I'll take you tomorrow after you've had a chance to clean up, eat and sleep.'

'I ... I don't know anywhere in town.'

'You can stay with me and my wife Sigrid tonight. She's a hearth witch – she'll make sure you're calm enough to sleep and keep you from nightmares.'

Emma smiled bitterly. 'I'll need her help. Thank you. Has Helmud's dad been notified of his passing?'

Gunnar nodded. 'I did it myself.'

'I'd like to speak to him.'

'I can arrange that too,' he promised.

She nodded, but I could see the exhaustion in her face. Connor and I helped her into the Nomo SUV. 'I'll run back,' Connor murmured to me. 'With Emma, the SUV is full so I'll take a detour to my cabin in the woods.'

I blinked. In all the madness, I'd barely thought about Parker and my monumental screw up. I grimaced. 'Okay. Ring me when you're home?'

He nodded, gave me a fast kiss and then a longer one. We both needed it. He turned and was gone. I really needed to up my cardio game because Connor was so much faster than me. Maybe it was an age thing.

Gunnar started the engine. 'I'll drop you home first, Bunny, then Thomas and Sidnee. After that we'll swing by the office and pick up Sigrid.'

'Have you let her know you're okay?' I asked. 'She'll be tearing her hair out.'

'I've sent a message to her and the council.'

Sidnee and Thomas were whispering together in the back seat. Sidnee piped up, 'You can just drop me at Thomas's, boss.'

Gunnar nodded but he was eyeing Thomas in the rearview mirror; he wasn't quite in full father-figure intimidation mode but close. 'You got it.'

He pulled up to my house and I hopped out. 'I hope you get some rest, Emma. Sigrid's food is divine.'

Her stomach rumbled audibly. 'I'm looking forward to it,' she said with a weak smile.

'I bet! Take care. I'm sure I'll see you tomorrow.'

'Yeah. Thanks, Bunny – for everything.'

'You're welcome.' As always, Gunnar waited until I'd unlocked my front door and was safely inside before he motored off.

Fluffy slid off the couch and gave a big stretch then hastily came over to nuzzle me and let me know how happy he was that I was back. In contrast, Shadow raced to his empty bowl and yowled so loudly I thought my eardrums would burst.

I wagged my finger at him. 'You are not starving. It was a long day but I'm still fifteen minutes early for your next meal.' He rubbed hard against my legs, almost knocking them out from under me. I leaned down and scratched behind his ears. 'You're a rascal.'

While Fluffy waited patiently for his supper, I hurriedly filled Shadow's dish. The only thing I paused for was to turn on the kettle which, after the day I'd had, was essential.

Once they were fed, I changed their water and made myself a cup of tea. I was also hungry but I needed a pause, time to unwind. My mind kept drifting to poor Emma; to be freed and to lose her fiancé in the same day was enough to break anyone. And I kept thinking about Parker.

I showered to kill some time. Connor had said he'd call me when he was home and, fast as he was, I needed to exercise some patience. If only I could remember how.

Once I'd washed away the shitty day and the dried blood under the pounding hot water, I felt a little happier. I dried my hair and slid into my pyjamas. I honestly tried hard to stay my hand, but suddenly my phone was in it. Deciding it was a sign, I called Connor.

He yawned into the phone as he picked up. 'Doe, I just got in. I thought you'd already be sawing logs.'

I chuckled. 'No, that's your job.'

'It's too close to daylight for lumberjack jokes.' He yawned again.

'You started it. How was Parker?'

'Okay,' he said cautiously. 'I gave him some blood. Last thing we need is for him to go into a bloodlust.'

'Absolutely. Did he say anything?'

'Not really,' he admitted carefully. 'He asked after you.' I winced. Connor sighed. 'This whole thing is eating at you.'

'How do you do that?' I demanded.

'Do what?'

'Know what I'm thinking.'

'Because I know *you*. You have a huge gooey heart that still beats in your chest. You will always worry about others.'

I was silent. I'd never thought of myself as particularly kind hearted; I'd grown up selfish and that was how I saw myself. Finally I whispered, 'Thanks for seeing that in me.'

His tone was low and soft. 'I see everything in you. You are the good, the better, the best part of me. Now go rest. You need that, too.'

'I will. Goodnight, Connor. I love you.'

'I love you too, Bunny.'

With my mind quieter, I threw a frozen dinner in the microwave, dutifully downed a warm cup of blood and ate. Then, full and sleepy, I collapsed into my bed with my furry companions by my side.

Chapter 44

On my way into work, I decided to stop at the diner to get some coffee. The coffee in the hardware store was delicious but today I needed the full-strength, melt-your-teeth coffee that the diner offered.

As I strode into the Garden of Eat'n, I smiled when I saw two familiar faces having brunch together: Hayleigh and Ray. Hayleigh looked relaxed; the austere bun was gone and her mousy-brown hair was tumbling over her shoulders. Her outfit was far more flattering and it was clear that Ray thought so too because he was gazing at her with open adoration. I was glad that the bear-shifter and his estranged wife were working it out. I hoped this time he wouldn't be so dumb as to offer his wife an ultimatum about her reading habits.

I gave them a finger wave but didn't interrupt. They beamed at me in return, looking so happy it made my heart smile. I'd done good work there, for all that it had felt like a nuisance case at the time.

When I got to the office, Emma was there with Gunnar and Sigrid. She smiled up at me. 'Hey, Bunny.'

'Hi Emma, how did you sleep?'

'Better than I expected,' she said honestly. 'And you weren't kidding about Sigrid's food!'

'I know, right? I've eaten at plenty of Michelin-starred restaurants and they're not a patch on Sigrid.'

Sigrid blushed. 'Oh hush!' she objected, but I could see that she was pleased. She pulled me into a hug. 'Okay, sweetheart?' she asked quietly. 'Gunnar said you were shot.'

'Just a little – a graze on my arm,' I assured her.

She looked amused. 'I'm not sure you can be shot "just a little".'

I grinned. 'Nothing a little blood didn't fix.'

'Thank goodness for that.' She eyed me critically. 'Did you get enough rest?'

'I'm fine,' I promised, quietly pleased by her motherly fussing. 'Thank you.'

Gunnar was holding a pad and clearly making notes on a statement for Emma. 'Sorry to interrupt,' I said.

'No worries. We're just wrapping up.'

'Cool.' I turned to the air witch. 'Can I ask you a question?'

'Sure.'

'Did you ever hear your captors talking about someone helping them in the mine?'

She frowned. 'There was one call but I can't remember the name.' She paused. 'Something that made me think Chipmunk.'

I blinked. 'Chipmunk?'

'You know the TV show? Alvin, Simon, Theodore?' She hummed a TV theme tune.

I didn't know any Alvins, Simons or Theodores – besides that total wanker, Theodore Thorsen, from the Academy. 'Theodore Thorsen?' I offered.

She shook her head, 'No, that wasn't it.'

I hazarded a guess. 'Alfgar?'

'No. Sorry.'

Abruptly I thought of the elder, Baldred, and his son, Delvin. Delvin, who hadn't wanted us to raise Alfgar's body. Delvin, who had red hair, like the strand we'd found on Alfgar. Delvin, whose father was an elder and who would definitely have access to keys and anything else the black-ops group wanted. Delvin. Yeah, that made a whole lot of sense.

'Delvin?' I asked the air witch.

Emma clicked her fingers. 'Yes!' she said excitedly. 'That's it! Sounds like Alvin! That's who that bastard was talking to!' She grimaced. 'It made me sing the chipmunk theme tune for three days straight. It's funny what connections your brain makes.'

Gunnar looked grim. 'I'll call Baldred, get them both in. I'll make it look like some more routine questions on Evgard and Alfgar.'

I steepled my fingers. 'Do we have time for that. If we're raiding Reef Mine today...'

'I'm still waiting to hear from one of my contacts at the MIB.'

I blinked. 'Gunnar, is it wise to use them?'

'I trust Henderson completely,' Gunnar said gruffly. 'The same as I do you. He'll handpick a team he trusts, too. It'll be small but we still need their help because we're going to be outmanned and outgunned. So while we're waiting for them, let's nail Delvin.'

I grinned. 'In that case ... let's do it.' April passed me a freshly brewed cup of tea, the perfect chaser to my gut-burning coffee. I could have kissed her. 'Thanks!'

She tapped Gunnar's notes. 'You all done with these?' He nodded. 'I'll type them up before I go for the day.' She stifled a yawn.

'You know that you're the best thing since sliced bread?' I told her.

She grinned. 'I do, but it's nice to hear it all the same.' She winked and took the notes back to her desk. 'All done,' she announced a mere ten minutes later before printing Emma's statement out for Gunnar to check over. Happy with it, he passed it to Emma to sign.

'You even got in the Delvin thing,' Emma said to April, clearly impressed. 'Now that's a good secretary. You don't want to come and work for the Alaska Minerals Commission, do you? I can always use a good secretary. You can work remotely.'

'Hey!' Gunnar objected. 'No poaching the staff!'

Emma laughed. 'If they're happy, they won't be poachable.'

'I love it here,' April said. 'It's crazy but I love the job, so thank you but no. I'm a Nomo girl all the way.'

'Damn right you are,' Gunnar said gruffly. 'You're valued here.'

April's face split with another yawn. 'Well, it was worth staying late if only for all of the compliments. I wanted to stay for Sidnee, but I'm going to have to go. You all be safe.'

'We will,' I promised.

'And give 'em hell.'

I nodded darkly. 'We will,' I repeated.

April left, and Gunnar called Edgy to come and collect Emma. When he hung up he told her, 'Edgy is a little rough around the edges but he'll see you safe to

Anchorage. I know you're anxious to see your family and Helmud's.'

'Thank you.' Emma hugged Sigrid and then Gunnar. 'Thank you all for the kindness you've shown me. I appreciate it more than I can say.'

'You have my number,' Sigrid said. 'Stay in touch, let us know how you're getting on.'

'I will.'

Edgy's beat-up truck drew up outside and Emma looked at it dubiously. If she was nervous about the vehicle, wait until she saw the plane. He jumped out of the truck and her mouth dropped a little at the sight of the one-armed man. 'His plane has been modified,' I said hastily before he walked in.

'One arm or not, Edgy Kum'agyak is the best pilot around,' Gunnar vouched.

Emma pasted a smile on her face. 'Great.'

None of us bought it.

As he walked in, Edgy shot me a finger-gun gesture. 'Fanged Flopsy Bunny-o, good to see you.' The hint of an Australian accent always took me by surprise since he looked native Alaskan, but he'd spent a lot of years Down Under and the Aussie accent still clung to his voice.

Emma stared at me. 'Okay, now I *have* to ask. How come you're called Bunny?'

Inspired by Edgy, I riffed, 'I lost a leg once and spent six months hopping everywhere until it grew again.'

The pilot chuckled. 'Bold one, mate! Not many people can regrow a limb.' He patted the air under the stump. 'More's the pity.'

I grimaced. Okay, maybe that particular story had been in bad taste. 'Sorry, Edgy.'

'No worries. I tell everyone I lost my limb to a shark. These bullshit stories help us keep our air of mystery.' He winked. 'The ladies love a man of mystery.'

'I'll take your word for it,' I told him.

'Let's rock and roll, Emma, and get you home. I've checked the weather and it should be plain sailing. Flying. You get me?'

'I get you,' she replied.

Sidnee arrived with Thomas following close behind. 'Hey, it's a party!'

'Not quite,' Gunnar grunted. 'No shots. No dancing on the tables.' He looked sternly at the both of us and we studied our shoes. Yep, we'd done that.

'Bye, Sidnee, Thomas,' Emma said. 'Thanks for the rescue.'

'Anytime,' Sidnee said cheerfully.

Emma winced. 'I'd rather not repeat it. Let's keep it as a one-time deal.'

'Seems fair.' Sidnee gave her a gentle hug.

Emma left with the pilot and we all watched as they drove off.

'So,' Sidnee said. 'What's new?'

I leaned in. 'You've got some catching up to do.'

Chapter 45

Once Sidnee and Thomas were all caught up, we decided to divide and conquer. Gunnar had heard from his MIB contact and was going to meet him. Sidnee and Thomas would go rattle the council's cages and pressure them to join us in our dubious mission. We didn't have any soldiers to take with us into the Reef Mine – besides the ones on loan from Gunnar's contact – but every single one of the council members was deadly in their own right. Volatile as fuck, but deadly. It would even things up a little if we had Stan, Liv, Calliope and Mafu with us.

And me? I was going to capture myself a murderer.

Baldred looked weary, more stooped over his cane than I recalled from our previous encounter, and even then he'd been doing an impression of Old Father Time albeit his hair was still largely brown rather than silver.

I showed him and Delvin into the interview room, casually switched on the recording equipment and read them both their rights. Baldred's eyes bored into mine and his expression was resigned; I realised that he knew of, or at least suspected, his son's involvement.

'Thanks for coming, gentlemen,' I started. 'We've got a few loose ends to tie up.' I smiled at Delvin. 'Firstly, I wondered if you'd be good enough to donate some hair for forensic comparison to the hair found on Alfgar.'

'How dare you!' Delvin blustered. He made as if to stand up. 'This interview is over!'

'Sit!' Baldred said, his quavering voice replaced with a cracking whip. Delvin sat. 'You are going to answer this nice young lady's questions,' he ordered.

'Officer Barrington,' I said primly. I hadn't gone through weeks of hard work at the academy to be called a nice young lady; I was an officer and damned proud to be one.

'Of course,' Baldred said. 'Officer Barrington's questions. Go ahead, officer.'

'Thank you.' I smiled at the Elder. Since the cat was well and truly out of the bag that this was not a light chat, I went in heavy. 'I have a witness statement that confirms you colluded with the Knight Stalkers to remove the dwarves from the Chrome Mine.'

Delvin flinched when I spoke the name of the splinter group. Next to him, Baldred slowly buried his head in his hands. His son glared at him. 'Don't you dare act ashamed of me! I am the dwarves' future! I have borne your ineptitude for too long.'

'His ineptitude?' I said, remembering my interview with Faran Ashton. 'In letting Alfgar marry for love?'

'It was a disgrace!' Delvin pounded a fist on the table. 'A dwarf from our family, marrying a human? An absurdity!'

'Is that why you cut off his head? Was he so foul in your eyes he didn't deserve an afterlife?'

He sneered at me. 'I didn't touch a hair on his head.'

'Maybe not, but you were there, weren't you? That's why you objected so strenuously to Liv raising him – you were worried Alfgar had caught sight of you. You marked him out for killing, and you were there when his head was removed. You're refusing the DNA sample because you know your hair will match the one we found on him.'

I searched Delvin's face; his jaw was set and I knew he would refuse. I had to up the ante. 'We can compel you, you know? Get a council order for the hair sample to be taken by force.'

He licked his lips. 'I didn't touch him,' he reiterated. 'You can't do anything to me! *I* didn't harm him.'

I leaned forward with a pleasant smile and lowered my voice conspiratorially. 'There's this charge, conspiracy to murder.' I winked. 'We use it when people plan a murder, even if their hands aren't actually dirty. Like it or not, you killed your cousin. Someone else might have blood on their hands but you gave the nod, didn't you? You chose which dwarf to kill. We have a witness statement and we have DNA evidence.' Kind of. 'You're going away for this, Delvin, so you might as well tell the truth and give the poor families closure.'

He pinched his lips shut.

'What did Evgard do to you?' I asked. 'Why was he on your shit list?'

Baldred sighed. When he raised his head, his eyes were wearier than anything I'd ever seen. 'Delvin was always jealous of Evgard. When Evgard secured the position as head of the Miners Association, a position of great power, I saw his anger. His jealousy.'

'Shut up!' Delvin roared. 'Shut up old man!'

'When Evgard was the second to die, I suspected,' his father went on unhappily. 'So I ordered Leif to follow Delvin.'

Delvin stilled. 'What?' he hissed. 'You ordered Leif to follow your own son?'

Baldred ignored him. 'Leif has photos of him and some human soldiers putting heads on spikes and driving them into the ground.'

Delvin twisted and raised a fist as if to strike his father, but I leapt up and had him pinned to the table, his arm pushed behind him. Vampire speed had its uses in an emergency. 'I'd like to see those photographs,' I said to Baldred.

He nodded. 'Of course. I was going to bring Delvin before the dwarven council, but perhaps it is better that the Portlock council handle his sentencing.'

'Father!' Delvin screamed at him. 'Don't you dare abandon me to the council.'

'It is you that has abandoned me,' Baldred said sadly.

'Delvin Simonson, you are under arrest for conspiring to murder Alfgar Simonson and Evgard Appleton.' I smiled. 'And the assault of Baldred Simonson.'

'I didn't touch my father!' he protested.

'No, that would have been assault *and* battery. Assault is fear of an attack, whether physical harm follows or not.' I cuffed his hands behind him. 'Let's go.'

'Where are you taking him?' Baldred asked.

'Our cells.'

Baldred slumped, looking more despairing than ever. I felt bad for the guy, but that wouldn't stop me delivering justice.

I frogmarched Delvin to the cell, dumped him inside and slammed the metal door shut. The wards engaged and, just like that, Delvin forfeited his freedom.

Chapter 46

Baldred left, promising to get Leif to come in and give me a witness statement about what he'd seen; he also confirmed that he'd forward the incriminating photographs to the Nomo's office.

I checked my phone and saw a message from Sidnee. All the councillors were on board so we'd have a full house for our raid on the Reef Mine.

'Sorry, Sig,' I said. 'We have an occupied cell now. Do you mind hanging here and watching the monitors?'

She gave an easy smile. 'No problem.'

'I'll send April a text message so she knows we need 24/7 coverage.'

She smiled. 'Bunny, we've got this. You worry about your raid.'

'Okay. But I should complete the paperwork for Delvin's arrest,' I said anxiously.

She made a shooing motion. 'I can do it then I'll send it over to the council's office. Go on, Bunny. And Bunny?'

'Yes?'

'Stay safe, sweetheart.'

'I will.' I gave her a firm hug goodbye. 'You'll look after Fluffy and Shadow?' I asked quietly. 'If I—'

'Don't say it!' Her eyes were watery. 'Of course I will. Go on now, darling. I don't want you to see me cry.'

I jerked a nod because my own eyes were hot, then grabbed my vest and a bag of weapons and headed out to meet the others at the council chambers.

We had the strongest supernats and humans in Portlock. We had a water dragon, an immortal necromancer, a demi-god, a vampire prince, a walking human armoury and a polar-bear shifter, plus their seconds all had special skills. We also had – I hoped – a top-notch MIB team with modern weapons. It had to be enough.

The minimal intel wasn't ideal, but we didn't have much choice other than to attack immediately. We needed to strike before the Knight Stalkers realised what had happened at their bunker, if they hadn't already. Part of me was hoping that they'd already evacuated the mine and scarpered.

There was a cold ball of dread knotting in my stomach. I was a police officer, not a soldier. I was good with drunk and disorderly shifters, theft or murder – but war? War wasn't my thing. Still, it was what the Knight Stalkers had brought to us and I was no shrinking violet.

When I walked into the council chambers, not everyone was there; Liv and Stan were missing. Gunnar was near the stage with a man in camo who must have been the leader of the MIB team. I looked around for the rest, but there was only him; Gunnar had said he was heading a twelve-man team so I hope they hadn't backed out. I had a moment of anxiety before I realised the others were probably with the boats, weapons and equipment. It wasn't wise to leave that stuff unprotected.

Stan strode in with Mads Actos, both of them dressed in pull-off clothing for easy shifting. They didn't really need weapons because they *were* weapons: a polar bear and a Kodiak brown bear had to be among the top predators in North America. I definitely wouldn't want to face them.

Stan's jocular humour was missing and his expression was dark and severe. I wished like hell he would make a Bunny joke but he didn't; he was all business.

Calliope and Soapy had their tridents, and I assumed Calliope had her pearlescent shell. Maybe I'd finally find out what it did, but it was more than likely she'd lose her temper, shift and just start eating the enemy.

Liv was the last to arrive – pulling a goat behind her. He seemed docile and trained to walk on a halter, and I assumed he was drugged because he wasn't going to live out the night. I wondered what a necromancer could do with the death of a single goat. Liv had freed the banshee spirits and healed the barrier with one, so my hopes were high.

She was wearing one of her colourful kaftan dresses, belted at the waist. Around her throat was a heavy gold choker with her scarab in the centre like a cameo. I shuddered. That beetle always gave me the creeps, plus who wore a dress to a gun battle? Liv, that's who.

The mayor looked implacable. He was wearing traditional Polynesian garb and holding a short, thick staff. It didn't seem wise to bring a stick to a gun battle, but I didn't say so. Hopefully it had a whole array of magical power that he could shoot out of it.

We were as ready as we could be. Connor made his way to me and looped an arm around my waist. His presence was reassuring, but the knots in my stomach still didn't unravel. I pressed a soft kiss to his shoulder and he squeezed me in response.

John was standing behind us, but Margrave was absent. As Connor's number two, I guessed he'd stayed at Kamluck to take over the reins if something happened to us. John was wearing a bulletproof vest and enough weapons to give Thomas a run for his money. When I met his eyes, he flashed me a grin; he was excited for the hunt.

Gunnar banged a gavel and we fell silent. He cleared his throat and ran through the current situation so that we were up to date, then he introduced Camo Man. 'This is Henderson. He will be in charge of running this op. He's been briefed on the intel we received from the bunker and on your abilities and strengths. Second in command is Thomas Patkotak. If Henderson goes down, look to Patkotak, then me. Any questions?'

Nobody spoke; I thought that, like me, most of them were unsure how to proceed – but they were all determined.

Gunnar nodded then looked at us one by one. 'Let's show these intruders how Portlockians defend their home. Let's send a message the Knight Stalkers can't fucking miss. Head down to the north harbour. The boats are waiting. Get ready and move out!'

Everyone snapped into action, pulling on warm jackets and rain gear. Those of us with bulletproof vests put those on first.

We were heading into the danger zone and we knew it. Chances were not all of us would return alive, supernat or not.

Chapter 47

The boats were Zodiacs, made of rubber, open to the elements but with fast engines. They each held eight armed combatants.

Henderson briskly arranged us into a mix of MIB and Portlockians for each boat. I was with an MIB soldier, Connor, Liv and John. Our boat was the least crowded because of Liv's goat; no one had been sure how the animal would react during the rough ride. Liv had scoffed at that, saying that she had complete control over the animal.

Once we were loaded and briefed, Henderson gave the signal and we headed for Chrome Point. I leaned into Connor and clasped his hand tightly. Neither of us spoke. John watched us with a bittersweet longing on his face. He was happy for us, but the ache of losing his wife was still with him. I thought about his excitement and hoped he wasn't using this op as suicide by Knight Stalkers. His depression had started to lift now he was working with

Connor, and I hoped he'd give himself a chance to recover even more.

I looked into the dark water then sat up straighter as I saw a flash of gold, a flash I'd seen before. A moment later, I saw it again. 'Connor!' I hissed, pointing to where the water dragon was pointedly keeping pace with the boats. The huge eel-like creature was gargantuan, far larger than it had been before.

He looked over the side and smiled. 'Don't worry, they're guardians.' He dipped his fingers into the water then lifted them up; after he'd done that a few times, the water dragon mimicked him by raising its huge head from the waves.

'Don't shoot!' Connor shouted. 'It's friendly!' The MIB soldiers were tense as fuck, but they held their fire.

The water dragon rose a little further, still keeping pace with us. 'If you'd like to help,' Connor shouted to it, 'there's a submarine in the bay that is threatening Portlock.'

The water dragon opened its mouth and screamed a noise that was almost as painful as a banshee's wail. Then, with a huge flick of its tail, it dived beneath the surface. 'What the hell?' the soldier in our boat said.

'That's our water dragon,' I explained. 'They look after us.'

The soldier looked at Connor. 'You think it can really take down a whole submarine?'

Connor smiled grimly. 'If you don't ask, you'll never know. It's certainly worth a try.'

'It wasn't that big last time I saw it,' I pointed out. 'Are there two of them?'

'No, just the one,' Connor said. 'They change their size when they want to.'

I stared. 'How?'

He grinned. 'Magic, Doe.' Even after months in the paranormal world, magic still surprised me.

It felt like we reached Chrome Point in an instant – and the journey also felt like a year. Still, I was cold and damp from the ride, and happy to get on solid ground again.

We climbed onto land and the soldiers tied off and secured the boats. We fell into the positions as we'd been instructed and set off at a light jog towards the mine entrance. The plan was that the twelve-man MIB team would go in fast and hard and clear out the Knight Stalkers as quickly as possible while we were their back up.

I wasn't sure what to think about that. First off, that gave our MIB soldiers all the power – were we even certain they were on our side? Gunnar thought so, and that should have been enough, but I'd had my fill of the MIB and I didn't trust them. Still, Connor had encountered

Henderson before and had begrudgingly admitted that he trusted the guy on this. With both Connor and Gunnar vouching for Henderson, I worked to set my anxieties aside; they had no place here.

But I wasn't the only one who was worried, because I saw Thomas speaking pointedly to Henderson and the next thing I knew he'd joined the team. Sidnee grabbed my arm hard and I jumped at the sudden contact. 'Did Thomas just insert himself into the cannon fodder team?' she asked, her voice shrill with anxiety.

I nodded. Her grip was starting to hurt. I laid my other hand over hers to let her know what she was doing and to offer the little comfort I could.

Her eyes went mer black. 'No, I won't let him.' She let go of me and lurched forward.

I hastily pulled her back. 'No, Sidnee. You have to let him do what he feels is right if you want a future with him.' I thought of Hayleigh and Jacob. 'You can't dictate to your other half what they do and don't do. It has to be a partnership, a meeting of equals,' I insisted.

'We can't have any sort of future – equal or not – if he's dead!' She tugged against my hand.

'Either way, you would lose him,' I said firmly. 'This is who he is. Let him see that you can handle this – that you know he can handle himself.'

She stopped and her shoulders drooped. 'I need something to do. I can't sit around and wait.'

'Believe me, when we're into it we'll wish we *were* still outside waiting. Besides, we aren't going to sit around. We're surrounding the other entrances to make sure no one escapes.'

Despite my words, Sidnee's eyes were still mer black and I knew she was using the darker side of herself to stop herself plunging into the mine after Thomas.

Connor and I took our positions and kept our guns aimed at our spots while Sidnee partnered with John to do the same. Once everyone was in place, Henderson and his team – including Thomas – headed in.

It was totally silent except for the sound of waves in the distance – but then the pop of suppressed gunfire erupted from inside the mine, together with shouts and screams that were impossible not to hear.

We held our positions as we heard screams and gunfire for the next few minutes. One of our soldiers came stumbling out of the mine; he'd been shot in several places but his vest had saved his life. He gave the signal for us to step up before he collapsed on the ground and the MIB medic started administering aid. We were up.

Henderson had impressed on us that we were the last resort, but now the friends and family I'd found in

Portlock were being called into battle. Things obviously weren't going well. Well, here goes nothing, then.

'Don't use your fire,' Connor murmured to me. 'We can't risk anyone finding out the truth about you. If anyone sees you using fire, I'll have to kill them to protect us.'

I swallowed hard and nodded. I knew he was right: we needed to keep my hybrid status under wraps. When we'd stormed the bunker I'd been with friends who knew I had fire magic, even if they didn't fully appreciate what that meant for me. But today was different; today I was surrounded by council members and MIB soldiers, and though I trusted the council with my life I didn't trust them with my secrets. Evidently, neither did Connor.

I took a deep breath then, as if someone had flipped a switch somewhere, Connor was moving forward and I was on his flank. John and Sidnee were on our six. Stan and Mads had already shifted and were galloping ahead. The bears were moving fast and they'd be inside without us as backup if they didn't slow down. Connor came to the same conclusion and we upped our pace.

Calliope and Soapy had their tridents extended to full length and currents of live electricity skittered over the tips of the tines. Calliope looked at me and gave a half-grin – like John, she was enjoying herself. She held up her pearlescent shell and a twisting opalescent light emanated from it, weaving around her and Soapy. What was it? A shield? I'd have to wait to see.

The one that surprised me the most was the mayor. He was bare chested, in a Polynesian style kilt with only a short thick staff as protection, but as I watched his bare skin morphed into something that looked like tree bark and he grew in size. The staff extended and a billow of fog came over to conceal him. Totally cool.

Gunnar was next to us, his shotgun in one hand and his handgun in the other. He never used magic as a first line of defence, mainly because it took a lot out of him. Or maybe he trusted the old-fashioned combination of lead and gunpowder more.

Liv had found a spot on the hill above the mine. Her hair was free, her afro loose and blowing in the wind, and her colourful kaftan was a focal point. She looked like a goddess of death. Goddess or not, she was utterly nuts because she'd made herself a target. Part of me wanted to yell at her to come down but I knew she'd scoff at me and there was no time for arguing.

Her goat was by her side. With a quick swipe of her athame, the goat's lifeblood started to pool into the copper bowl she was holding. The goat sank to its knees then toppled over as the blood drained and Liv took its very lifeforce into her being. I felt the now-familiar pull of her magic and wondered what she was about to do.

Her laughter accompanied me into the mine, sending an additional skitter of ice down my spine. Something big was happening.

And I wasn't sure if it was a good big or a bad big.

Chapter 48

Connor and I sprinted towards the mine. Stan and Mads were already inside, Calliope and Soapy were close behind them, and Connor and I came next at vampire speed. The mayor followed with Gunnar, and Sidnee and John brought up the rear. John was keeping pace with Sidnee, who was slower; if we survived, I'd make sure to tell him how much I appreciated that. He was keeping my bestie safe.

It was utter chaos inside the mine. There were a lot more than thirty Knight Stalkers and they were prepared for us. It was clear they were deeply embedded and had plenty of supplies and weapons.

'Anyone worried about a cave-in?' I asked, but no one answered. Just me, then. I tried to push my claustrophobia to one side. I'd never known I suffered from it until my first stroll down the Chrome Mine.

Calliope and Soapy, surrounded in their opalescent shell magic, advanced ahead of us until I lost them in the gloom.

We had to go down a long corridor that had tunnels branching everywhere – and we'd only advanced through two sections. The rest were too heavily fortified.

Connor and I moved to the right of the passage with five of our MIB team as the others spread out on the left side. The bodies scattered on the ground showed that our group had done well, but even so we were down three and there were at least a hundred Knight Stalkers. Was it too soon to call a retreat? I was really good with that option.

'We aren't going to make it much further unless we can get behind them,' I overheard Henderson say to Gunnar.

Gunnar nodded. 'I'll get my people on it.'

We had comms and Gunnar was speaking into his, though I didn't know who to. We hadn't brought digging equipment and I doubted we could find another entrance and get behind the Knight Stalkers before they figured out what we were doing. We were at an impasse; an impasse that meant every second someone was closer to being shot or killed.

I needed to do something.

'Matilda, Matilda, Matilda!' I called out desperately. She'd said she'd come with us to the mean men, but I had no idea how long it would take her to cross from the other mine given the expanse of water between them. But she *was* an earth elemental and below all that water there was earth, right?

Calling Matilda's name gave me another idea. 'Yo!' I shouted. 'Aoife!' There was a beat and then the teenage banshee appeared in front of me. 'Care to help?' I asked. 'Can you go deep into this place where all the enemy soldiers are and let out a scream?'

She shot me a mischievous glance. 'I am tired but I can manage one full scream before I'm spent.'

'I'd appreciate it!'

She gave me a thumbs-up and disappeared ahead of us. I plugged my ears, but even so I heard her scream rip through the mine. That had to have done some damage to a good number of the fuckers!

Silence reigned for a moment and then I heard a bear's roar accompanied by the crack of a shot: either Stan or Mads had taken a hit. Thankfully it was followed by more screams – human this time – so it seemed like the wound hadn't been fatal if our guys were still dishing it out.

A wave of Liv's magic passed over me again and the tugging in my guts reminded me she had something up her billowing sleeves. The magic pulsed again hard, and the three of us lurched forward before we had time to plant our feet.

'Down,' Connor barked.

I nodded. We backed up to an area where there was better cover and crouched down. Something big was stirring. 'What the hell was that?' Sidnee whispered to us once we were under cover.

'Necromancy,' I whispered back.

The bodies that lay between the battling parties suddenly lurched and rose jerkily to their feet. It was as freaky as hell, and the shots died away as everyone on both sides of the conflict stared in horror. Once the bodies had gained their feet, they charged towards the enemy. They were fast and deadly: there were no shambling zombies in Liv's world. I wanted to cheer.

The enemy reacted once their initial horror had worn off and started shooting at the newly risen. They peppered the bodies head to foot with bullets but nothing stopped their advance, and once a dead body grabbed a live one they bit into its throat and silenced their screams. Because of Liv's power, once someone fell they rose again.

We charged behind her army of the dead and gained some ground. I had no idea how long her power would last but in that instant I was grateful for her terrifying magic. We made it to the enemy's last stronghold before she burned through her death magic and the necromantic bodies collapsed. I would personally make sure that goat had a beautiful funeral.

I realised that the gunfire had suddenly stopped. It was difficult to see what was happening ahead: it was dark and there were too many combatants. The shots were replaced by shouting, then the floor of the mine rumbled and we tumbled to the ground. Loose dirt filled the air; had the gunfire caused a cave-in?

Finally I stood up, brushing stones and dirt from my hair and clothes; Connor and John were doing the same. We looked at each other, not sure what to do next, but finally we huddled close to the wall and advanced. No enemy fire met us; in fact, there seemed to be no enemies once we'd stepped around the bodies of Liv's dead.

Once we were past them, we saw what had caused the rumbling: the floor of the mine ahead of us had collapsed. As I looked closer, I saw that a huge cement slab had been pulled back to reveal choppy waves. A number of boats were being loaded up – the Knight Stalkers were retreating!

As I peered into the hole, I saw the last of their people climb into one of the boats carrying someone, probably one of their wounded. He turned as though he sensed me watching him and looked up. His blond hair was distinctive, as was the hand with the single middle finger pointed at me. Chris fucking Jubatus!

'Chris!' I shouted, then realised what he was carrying. My stomach lurched as I spotted Thomas's features. Holy shit!

There was a scratching noise and Matilda walked out of the wall. She looked around, frowned at the hole then clicked her fingers and it was gone. She'd filled it with earth. 'Bring it back!' I said hastily. She looked confused. 'The hole!' I cried. 'Bring it back.'

'Earth should not have *holes.*' Matilda said. 'More air then.'

I groaned. 'Matilda! Please! Open it back up!'

She shrugged as if I were crazy but obligingly opened it again. I peered down. The boats had completely disappeared and I hadn't seen in which direction they'd gone. Fuck!

'Do you need hole?' Matilda asked.

Filled with despair, I shook my head. 'No. You can close it now.' Even if we jumped into the sea, we were too far from our own boats to give chase, and the Knight Stalkers' boats had already travelled too far for even Sidnee and Calliope to follow then. I knew that once Sidnee heard that Thomas was gone, she'd swim towards him until she dropped dead with exhaustion if she thought there was a chance of saving him. This was a mess.

My heart ached – but then I brightened. Sidnee could get inside Thomas's house and we could scry his location. He'd been kidnapped, but this was far from over.

'Chris was there,' I told Connor. 'He took Thomas.'

Connor swore darkly. 'We have to finish the job and clear the mine. Maybe we'll find some more intel on another location where they might take Thomas.'

There was no one left in the mine except us; our enemies had even taken the time to destroy their drug lab. All that remained was rubble and junk – and skulls. Lots of skulls.

'My family!' Matilda cried, tears of joy flowing down her cheeks. She picked up one of the skulls and kissed it. 'Husband,' she murmured, cuddling it to her chest. The moment was cute and gross in equal measure.

'That's how the dwarves will feel when you give them *their* skulls back,' I said pointedly,

She shuffled. 'Only took few,' she complained.

'Well, give them back. All of them. And then you can keep the rest.'

She smiled happily and flashed her metal teeth before picking up her husband's skull and pushing it into the earth. One by one, she did the same with the rest. Who knew that the Knight Stalkers had a whole freaking store cupboard of skulls? I guessed they'd stolen them from the hag, hoping to make her angry and violent. They'd been stirring things between the dwarves and Matilda, but it had all come to nothing and that gave me a grim sense of satisfaction. I did so love to foil a plot.

But I was all too aware that, with Thomas taken, this was far from over.

Chapter 49

Once the Reef Mine was secure, I checked anxiously for my fellow Portlockians and found them all alive, although most were wounded. The only one who wasn't there was Thomas; I'd been hoping against hope that I'd seen an illusion and he'd be there on the shore pulling Sidnee into his arms with that tender look he had only for her. But he wasn't.

Sidnee reached the conclusion at the same time as me and her face twisted in fear. 'Has anyone seen Thomas?' she asked loudly.

I bit my lip. 'I'm sorry, Sidnee. I saw Chris – Chris Jubatus—'

'Fuck Chris,' she snarled. 'Where's Thomas?' She'd started to shake.

'Chris … he took Thomas.'

'What?' she breathed.

'He kidnapped him.'

'That *bastard*.' Her eyes flashed back to mer-black. 'I'll kill him myself.' Her hands flew to her top as if she was going to strip off and shift into a mermaid to chase her ex across the whole fucking globe if necessary.

'Sidnee, my love, calm down. You need to think rationally. Once they stop moving, we can scry Thomas.'

'Unless they get him somewhere warded!' she snapped back.

'This is the Knight Stalkers we're talking about. They don't like magic.'

'They used Emma! They used a fucking air ward against Matilda!' She was panting, her eyes wide with panic.

'Thomas is alive,' I said firmly. 'And I swear we will find him. But you can't run off half-cocked. That will get him – and you – killed. We have to be smart, Sidnee honey. You know I'm right.'

Her eyes leached to their usual brown and she started to cry. I pulled her into my arms as Gunnar looked on, obviously heartbroken for her. 'We'll find him,' he vowed gruffly. Sidnee leapt from my arms to his and let herself collapse against him.

Our MIB team was busy setting charges; when we were well away, they blew up the cursed mine so it couldn't be used against us again. Next to me, Matilda snorted at their work. 'No good,' she sniffed. She disappeared into the mine, presumably to collapse the whole thing properly.

Sometimes, her power was more than a little scary. If she'd arrived sooner, the tide of battle would have changed far quicker. Maybe then Thomas wouldn't have been taken and we would have captured that shitbag Chris for ourselves.

Shoulda, woulda, coulda helped no one so I put my thoughts aside, but in my heart I plotted revenge against the selkie for once again breaking my best friend's heart.

We didn't dare leave Sidnee alone. Gunnar and I debated whether she was better with me or with him, but since Sigrid was still at the station we decided my home was the right place for her for now. Connor came in too, and quietly told Fluffy and Shadow what had happened as he sorted them out with fresh food and drink.

Meanwhile I helped a near-catatonic Sidnee into the shower. She was like a large doll who moved when directed but froze after she'd complied. It freaked me out, but she didn't need me to lose my mind right now; one of us needed to keep our shit together.

I tucked her into the spare-room bed once she was clean and warm. I couldn't get her to eat or drink anything, but I'd fight that battle in the morning. I left water and some biscuits next to her bed; it was the best I could do.

I pulled the door almost closed and slunk back to the kitchen where Connor was waiting. He was looking at his phone with what looked like amused triumph. 'What's up?' I asked.

Connor's grin widened. 'Our resident water dragon kicks ass and takes names.'

My eyes widened. 'It didn't?'

'It totally did!' He laughed. 'Apparently it coiled around the submarine and squeezed until the damn thing ruptured. I love it.'

Despite myself, I grinned. 'That water dragon is scary as heck. I'm glad it's on our side.'

'Damn right.'

'A bit like Matilda,' I added.

Connor's smile faded as he looked towards my spare room. 'How is Sidnee?' His eyes were warm with concern.

I shrugged helplessly. 'Not great. She's not responding at all – she's completely shut down. It's hard to watch.'

He pulled me into his arms. 'She's been through a lot. She needs time and sleep. She'll get through this, like all the rest of her trials.'

Throat tight, I nodded. I didn't realize I was crying for her until Connor tenderly wiped the tears from my face. 'She'll be okay,' he murmured. 'And Thomas is going to be okay. That man was born invincible.' His tone was grudgingly admiring.

I appreciated his efforts but we both knew he was lying. Thomas was human, and if I'd been a betting girl I'd have bet that Chris had been lurking around Portlock for a while. Sidnee hadn't been discreet at the party by declaring her love for Thomas for all and sundry to hear, and Chris was the jealous type. There was a reason he'd taken Thomas and it couldn't be anything good.

Poor Sidnee. She needed time to process all of this, but she'd already had so much shit to deal with in her young life. She was stronger than anyone I knew, but there was a fragility that she kept hidden behind her sunny personality. She didn't deserve this. Sometimes life was so damned unfair.

Connor must have sensed my dark thoughts because he brushed the hair back from my face. 'She's strong. She'll pull through this and we'll get Thomas back.'

I nodded. I had no idea how to start, but I had to remember that Thomas was a force to be reckoned with. He'd been in the MIB; although these dark forces had him now, he'd figure out how they worked and use it against them. I half-hoped he'd rescue himself before we had a chance to do so.

Until then, I would take care of Sidnee. She needed me to remind her what a strong, independent and amazing person she was. She had a steel core. She just needed to remember that.

Fluffy leaned against my legs and I bent down to scruffle his ears. I looked around for Shadow, but he was nowhere to be seen. 'Damned cat,' I mumbled and then, because I was unsettled and worried, Connor and I searched the house to make sure my lynx hadn't sneaked out.

The last place I looked was Sidnee's room – I should have started there. Shadow's eyes reflected the light when I opened her door. He was at her head and she had a hand buried in his fur. Soft sobs were coming from her but her eyes were shut; she was asleep, crying in her dreams.

Shadow was the comfort she needed now. He laid his head back down and I heard his raspy purr as he poured out his heart to help heal hers. How had I ever thought, even for a moment, that he might grow up evil? I smiled at him and pulled the door almost closed so he could get in and out as he wanted. I had the best cat.

I pulled Connor back to the kitchen. 'Shadow is helping Sid. I need to give him more credit. He's usually driving me nuts, but this time he's really helping.'

Connor flipped on the kettle and we settled onto the kitchen chairs.

Everything seemed surreal. I'd come back to Portlock from the academy, where I'd foiled an unnamed group that I now knew was the Knight Stalkers. I'd returned to multiple murders – and to foil the Knight Stalkers once again. I wished the fuckers would just get the damned message but it was becoming clear that they wouldn't. The only way to end this, truly end it, was to take the fight to them.

I was done with being reactive; it was time to be proactive. And taking Thomas? That was just the spark that we needed to ignite the powder keg. I took a sip of my tea and looked at Connor. 'If they want war, it's time we gave it to them.'

A slow smile crossed his face. 'Now you're talking, Doe.'

'I'm done talking,' I said honestly. 'Now I'm all about action.'

Connor smirked. 'Yeah? I have some moves of my own.' He winked.

I set my mug down. 'Do you, now? Then show me what you've got, Connor MacKenzie.'

'With pleasure.'

About Heather

Heather is an urban fantasy writer and mum. She was born and raised near Windsor, which gave her the misguided impression that she was close to royalty in some way. She is not, though she once got a letter from Queen Elizabeth II's lady-in-waiting.

Heather went to university in Liverpool, where she took up skydiving and met her future husband. When she's not running around after her children, she's plotting her next book and daydreaming about vampires, dragons and kick-ass heroines.

Heather is a book lover who grew up reading Brian Jacques and Anne McCaffrey. She loves to travel and once spent a month in Thailand. She vows to return.

Want to learn more about Heather? Subscribe to her newsletter for behind-the-scenes scoops, free bonus material and a cheeky peek into her world. Her subscribers will always get the heads up about the best deals on her books.

Subscribe to her Newsletter at her website www.heathergharris.com/subscribe.

Heather's Patreon

Heather has started her very own Patreon page. What is Patreon? It's a subscription service that allows you to support Heather AND read her books way before anyone else! For a small monthly fee you could be reading Heather's next book, on a weekly chapter-by-chapter basis (in its roughest draft form!) in the next week or two. If you hit "Join the community" you can follow Heather along for FREE, though you won't get access to all the good stuff, like early release books, polls, live Q&A's, character art and more! You can even have a video call with Heather or have a character named after you! Heather's current patrons are getting to read a novella called House Bound which isn't available anywhere else, not even to her newsletter subscribers!

If you're too impatient to wait until Heather's next release, then Patreon is made for you.

Heather's Shop and YouTube Channel

Heather now has her very own online shop! There you can buy oodles of glorious merchandise and audiobooks directly from her. Heather's audiobooks will still be on sale elsewhere, of course, but Heather pays her audiobook narrator *and* her cover designer - she makes the entire product - and then Audible pays her 25%. OUCH. Where possible, Heather would love it if you would buy her audiobooks directly from her, and then she can keep an amazing 90% of the money instead. Which she can reinvest in more books, in every form! But Audiobooks aren't all there is in the shop. You can get hoodies, t-shirts, mugs and more! Go and check her store out at: https://shop.heathergharris.com/

And if you don't have spare money to pay for audiobooks, Heather would still love you to experience Alyse Gibb's expert rendition of the books. You can listen to Heather's audiobooks for free on her YouTube Channel: https://www.youtube.com/@HeatherGHarrisAuthor

Stay in Touch

Heather has been working hard on a bunch of cool things, including a new and shiny website which you'll love. Check it out at www.heathergharris.com.

If you want to hear about all Heather's latest releases – subscribe to her newsletter for news, fun and freebies. Subscribe at Heather's website www.heathergharris.com/subscribe.

Contact Info: www.heathergharris.com

Email: HeatherGHarrisAuthor@gmail.com

Social Media

Heather can also be found on a host of social medias including her Facebook Page, her Facebook Reader Group, Goodreads, Bookbub and Instagram.

If you get a chance, please do follow Heather on Amazon!

Reviews

Reviews feed Heather's soul. She'd really appreciate it if you could take a few moments to review her books on Amazon, Bookbub, or Goodreads and say hello.

Other Works by Heather

The *Portlock Paranormal Detective* Series with Jilleen Dolbeare

The Vampire and the Case of her Dastardly Death - Book 0.5 (a prequel story),

The Vampire and the Case of the Wayward Werewolf – Book 1,

The Vampire and the Case of the Secretive Siren – Book 2,

The Vampire and the Case of the Baleful Banshee – Book 3,

The Vampire and the Case of the Cursed Canine – Book 4,

The Vampire and the Case of the Perilous Poltergeist – Book 5,

The Vampire and the Case of the Cozy Christmas – Book 5.5,

The Vampire and the Case of the Hellacious Hag – Book 6; and

The Vampire and the Case of the Malevolent Mermaid – Book 7.

The Other Realm Universe:

The *Other Realm* series

Glimmer of Dragons- Book 0.5 (a prequel story),

Glimmer of The Other- Book 1,

Glimmer of Hope- Book 2,

Glimmer of Christmas – Book 2.5 (a Christmas tale),

Glimmer of Death – Book 3,

Glimmer of Deception – Book 4,

It is recommended that you read *The Other Wolf books 1 to 3* before continuing with:

Challenge of the Court– Book 5,

Betrayal of the Court– Book 6; and

Revival of the Court– Book 7.

The *Other Wolf* Series

Defender of The Pack– Book 0.5 (a prequel story),

Protection of the Pack– Book 1,

Guardians of the Pack– Book 2,

Saviour of The Pack– Book 3,

Awakening of the Pack – Book 4,

Resurgence of the Pack – Book 5; and

Ascension of the Pack – Book 6.

The *Other Witch* Series

Rune of the Witch – Book 0.5 (a prequel story),
Hex of the Witch– Book 1,
Coven of the Witch;– Book 2,
Familiar of the Witch– Book 3; and
Destiny of the Witch – Book 4.

The *Other Detective* Series

Frustrated Justice – Book 0.5 (a prequel story),
Veiled Justice – Book 1,
Mystic Justice – Book 2,
Arcane Justice – Book 3; and
Savage Jutice – Book 4

The *Witchlight Magical Mysteries Series* with Ella Stone

Secrets of the Frostbound Cottage – (a prequel story),
Secrets of the Forgotten Heir – Book 1,
Secrets of the Deadly Nightshades – Book 2; and
Secrets of the Eternal Flame – Book 3.

About the Author - Jilleen

About Jilleen

Jilleen Dolbeare writes urban fantasy and paranormal women's fiction. She loves stories with strong women, adventure, and humor, with a side helping of myth and folklore.

While living in the Arctic, she learned to keep her stakes sharp for the 67 days of night. She talks to the ravens that follow her when she takes long walks with her cats in their stroller, and she's learned how to keep the wolves at bay.

Jilleen lives with her husband and two hungry cats in Alaska where she also discovered her love and admiration of the Alaska Native peoples and their folklore.

Stay in Touch

Jill can be reached through her website https://jilleendolbeareauthor.com/

Jill has also just joined Patreon! What is Patreon? It's a subscription service that allows you to support Jilleen AND read her books way before anyone else! For a small monthly fee you could be reading Jill's next book, on a weekly chapter-by-chapter basis (in its roughest draft form!) in the next week or two.

If you're too impatient to wait until Jilleen's next release, then Patreon is made for you!

Social Media

Jill can be found on a host of social media sites so track her down at https://linktr.ee/gypjet.

Other Works by Jilleen

The *Paranormal Portlock Detective* Series with Heather G Harris

The Vampire and the Case of Her Dastardly Death: Book 0.5 (a prequel story), and

The Vampire and the Case of the Wayward Werewolf: Book 1,

The Vampire and the Case of the Secretive Siren: Book 2,

The Vampire and the Case of the Baleful Banshee: Book 3,

The Vampire and the Case of the Cursed Canine: Book 4

The Vampire and the Case of the Perilous Poltergeist – Book 5,

The Vampire and the Case of the Cozy Christmas – Book 5.5,

The Vampire and the Case of the Hellacious Hag – Book 6; and

The Vampire and the Case of the Malevolent Mermaid – Book 7.

The *Splintered Magic* Series:

Splintercat: Book 0.5 (a prequel story),
Splintered Magic: Book 1,
Splintered Veil: Book 2,
Splintered Fate: Book 3,
Splintered Haven: Book 4,
Splintered Secret: Book 5; and
Splintered Destiny: Book 6.

The *Splintered Realms* Series:

Borrowed Magic: Book 0.5 (a prequel story)
Borrowed Amulet: Book 1; and
Borrowed Chaos: Book 2.

The *Shadow Winged* Chronicles:

Shadow Lair: Book 0.5 (a prequel story),
Shadow Winged: Book 1,
Shadow Wolf: Book 1.5,
Shadow Strife: Book 2 ,
Shadow Witch: Book 2.5; and
Shadow War: Book 3.

Review Request!

Wow! You finished the book. Go you!

Thanks for reading it. We appreciate it! Please, please, please consider leaving an honest review. Love it or hate it, authors can only sell books if they get reviews. If we don't sell books, Jill can't afford cat food. If Jill can't buy cat food, the little bastards will scavenge her sad, broken body. Then there will be no more books. Jill's kitties have sunken cheeks and swollen tummies and can't wait to eat Jill. Please help by leaving that review! (Heather has a dog, so she probably won't be eaten, but she'd really like Jill to live, so... please review).

If you're a reviewer, you have our eternal gratitude.

Printed in Great Britain
by Amazon